BRAD CONVERSE

The Lords

First published by Happy Foot Press 2022

This novel is entirely a work of fiction. The names, characters and incidents portrayed in it are the work of the author's imagination. Any resemblance to actual persons, living or dead, events or localities is entirely coincidental.

First edition

ISBN: 979-8-9866835-0-8

Cover art by Andy Bridge
Editing by Joe Pierson

This book was professionally typeset on Reedsy.
Find out more at reedsy.com

With gratitude to
Betty Converse
Stacy, Chris, Alyssa & Mary Sparks
Pat Rankin
Janie Steiner

In memory of
Ronald Converse
Helen Agnew
Al & Mary Lou Steiner
Danny Parsons
Erna Riordan

Contents

Chapter 1

Keeping events straight becomes difficult the longer time passes. Biases creep in. Dreams become reality. But it seems only right to try to start at the beginning, or at least my beginning. It felt sometimes like everyone in the Territories just had a beginning and an end. The middle blurred into a flurry of mundanity. I knew it even when I was young. How could anyone really feel important in the world of The Lords?

By the time I came around, of course, it was just the way the world was. Given my origins, I was lucky I wasn't stuck in one of the more militant territories. America might be boring, but at least there were still elections and social programs.

All my early government experience, unfortunately, was with the American Child Protective Service, an institution whose mission seemed to be finding new ways of introducing chaos into the world. I was named Simone for the doctor who brought me in and Smith because it was the required designation for unidentified children within the ACPS.

I tried to get information over the years from them, but my abandonment was never followed up on. I even tried finding the doctor who found me, but that led nowhere as well. It seemed as though no matter how many rabbit holes I went down, the only thing I knew was how I got my name.

After the maze of dead ends, though, this was the life I had. Even while I was filing ACPS requests on a weekly basis, I found myself retreating to books. Not having a personal history of my own, I felt drawn to the history of others. Biographies, historical texts, anything that could bring to life these special connections other people shared. Even without a real family tree, I could still feed off the stories of others, escape into their lives.

I was the rare baby who never got adopted or fostered. Then the toddler. Then it just starts to become clear what's going to happen. And living in an orphanage doesn't really foster long-term friendships. You see five or six best friends leave, you get a little guarded. So, the books, their stories, were my socialization, as one-sided as the conversations may have been.

There were exceptions, obviously. Lucille, Grace, Elizabeth. All real people outside the pages of my books. It had been heartbreaking seeing Grace and Lucille go, but by the time Elizabeth was adopted, I barely even bothered waving goodbye. If the growing feeling of resentment as kid after kid left drove me toward solitude, the guilt over not feeling happy for them left me there.

It was a long time after Elizabeth left that I finally opened myself up again. His name was Peter, brought to the home in fifth grade by his aunt. His parents had died, and she couldn't handle his outbursts. Some people are quiet and defeated when they're brought in, but Peter was giving full-throated pleas, promising he'd never cause trouble again. He kept it up the entire trip down the hall of the boys' wing as his aunt walked calmly out the door, never to be seen again.

Surprisingly, angry eleven-year-olds are not among the most popular adoptees at the orphanage, so I assumed he might be around for a while; plus, I liked his spirit. And maybe his green eyes. And that swoosh of black hair that flew in from the left side of his face. Regardless, I suddenly had a friend again.

During those four years, people passed by like phantoms, barely perceptible in the secret world I shared with Peter. I taught him all the tricks of the orphanage: where the staff kept the good snacks, when it was safe to sneak to the lounge and watch TV, and how to get onto the roof. We'd sit back and watch the stars for hours, commenting on shapes and patterns, trying to forget that gravity held us down.

When we finished eighth grade, our chances for adoption had officially become infinitesimal. For the government, of which we were wards, this meant we were destined for apprenticeships. So, in a land of personal freedom, a series of quizzes, essays, and psychological examinations would dictate our careers.

I had known this was coming, but I'd chosen to ignore it. The government had always been my de facto parent, so I'd made peace with the fact that they had their say. Peter, on the other hand, was flipping out. He had finally settled into a routine after losing his parents, and now it was being ripped away from him. Depending on the day, he ranged from vaguely melancholy to outright hostile.

The exams were done over the course of three days and seemed more focused on our temperament than on our interests. Perhaps there was something to it, but I was puzzled when my resulting assignment was delivered. For starters, I had no idea America had a royal biographer. Yes, Lord Nathaniel was our protector. And yes, we did have honorary titles for all The Lords and their offspring, but we were still a democracy.

I also had no idea how to write a biography. I had read plenty of them, but it wasn't something I'd ever attempted to write. This was obviously why it was an apprenticeship, but what if I hated it? Or worse, what if I was terrible at it? Was there a backup plan?

The *royal* part indicated I'd be around Lord Nathaniel, which gave me a little swell of nervous excitement. The only news around the orphanage was gossip about the teachers and what we found in months-old magazines left in the lounge. And no matter the month, one magazine or another always had a profile on Lord Nathaniel. Suddenly, I was going to see for myself whether their fawning was justified.

Peter was happy for me, maybe even a little bit jealous, but he was still terrified for himself, having not yet received his assignment. I hoped they were taking extra time to find a job that would give him a home. That was what he was going to miss. What he was always trying to find again.

Heading back to my room, I thought about how little I had to take with me to the capital. I was the only kid in the history of the orphanage to have her own room, mind you, but the converted janitor's closet wasn't exactly full of luxuries. I got it at the start of seventh grade. I joked that it was because I knew where all the bodies were buried. In fact, with the exception of one teacher and our nurse, I had been at the orphanage the longest.

Looking at the tiny room, the only place that had ever belonged to me, I felt a pang of sadness. The one plus side of perpetually lowered expectations, however, was that the government dormitory I'd soon be living in was probably going to seem like a mansion. Still, I was about to truly start something new for the first time in my life. It was overwhelming in ways I had never experienced before.

Going through the small clothes rack, I pushed past hand-me-down hand-me-downs in colors best described as indifferent. I stopped when I got to a light-blue blouse the staff had gotten me for my most recent birthday. Paired with any of my faded skirts and standard-issue black flats, I was good to go. Five minutes in, and I already had my first-day outfit picked. Of course, that had also dictated the next four outfits, and then I was out of suitable clothes.

Having vastly overestimated the time I'd need to pack, I hunted down Peter on the roof. He had finally gotten his assignment: military. Nothing past that, no branch of service or helpful hint as to where he might be going or what he might be doing. He'd always been a little hard to read, but his eyes were his tell. Wide like a carnival barker when he was lying and scrunched to tiny slits when something had hurt him. This time, though, they just hovered in the middle, giving away nothing.

We sat on the roof that night, knowing that I would be heading out in the morning, his back against the concrete wall that penned us in, my head nestled in his side. Our fates were decided, so for one more night, we fell back into familiarity without skipping a beat.

"You think we'll see each other again?" he asked with an alarming degree of sincerity.

"What do you mean?" I said, looking up into the comfort of his face. "Of course, we'll see each other again. What kind of question is that?"

"I don't even know where I'm going to be," he said.

"But you know where I'll be," I snapped.

"Oh, so it's all on me," he said, flashing his devilish grin.

"Unless you want to start divulging military secrets."

"That could get me in trouble." That grin could jump-start a car.

"I'm sure you'll find a way to make it work."

There was a minute of silence, the night sky alive with stars overhead. The noise from the streets below dying down as the city fell asleep. A perfect minute of quiet in which every bit of loneliness I'd ever known just disappeared, in which I felt connected to everything.

"What happens if I die?" Peter asked, breaking the moment.

"You're not going to die," I replied.

"But if I do?"

"I won't forget you," I said.

"Promise?" he asked, turning his head away.

"I promise," I said.

We sat there long into the night, willing it to last even a minute longer than the one before, knowing dawn brought change.

Chapter 2

I headed to the train station on my own the next morning, rebuffing multiple attempts by Peter to escort me. It was a day of fresh starts, and I was done with goodbyes, over the tears. The ride was short but lengthened by anticipation, giving time for doubt and fear to gain footholds in my mind. This was the biggest thing I'd ever done, and I was doing it entirely on my own. It was time to see what I was actually capable of, whether I could succeed or was destined to fail.

I had been to the capital on a field trip once, but seeing it now, knowing I was going to be living here, made everything real. The Capitol Dome stretched so far into the sky that it looked like a second sun. Held aloft by glistening, swirling diamond supports and reachable by a glass elevator, it was the top tourist attraction in America. The entrance to its ground-level reception area, where I was scheduled to begin orientation, shone with gold, a statue of Lord Nathaniel holding the world aloft rising high above the doorway.

More swirling diamond columns supported the structure, lifting to the ceiling in glistening, curling strands. The ceiling itself was five stories high and decorated with precious gems illustrating the cosmos. The floors glittered with multicolored patterns reflecting off the mosaic in ways that made everything feel like a slow-motion film shot in a swimming pool.

Which was not helping my immediate confusion. It had quickly become clear that I wasn't the only new apprentice arriving that day. A crowd swarmed the lobby, and booths lined the room, letters hanging above them. There was a procedure in place, and while it wasn't complex, it was unexpected. I momentarily panicked.

Luckily, I was quickly accosted by a frenzied woman who looked at my assignment letter and pointed me to a line under a sign that said S. Dazed, I headed in that direction as she spun off to guide the next confused person.

The crowd was massive, which made me wonder just how many apprenticeships the government supplied. It looked like they ran the gamut in terms of age, so that explained part of it. While shifting my weight back and forth in line, I kept wishing Peter was with me. Outwardly, I may have been putting on a strong front, but inside, I was a jumble of nerves.

To block out the crowd, I sank into my head. Thinking back over my tests and submission samples, I tried to determine what pegged me as biographer material. No feedback was supplied, but I assumed they'd liked my writing samples. The entire experience felt surreal. I kept straightening my blouse, my poverty shining like a beacon against the dancing lights.

By the time I made it to the front of the line, my stress level had risen to nauseating. Nevertheless, I handed my assignment letter over and managed a smile, all without vomiting. The expressionless woman on the other side of the desk sorted through a box at her feet, handed me a packet, and grunted out a room number.

Having successfully deciphered the grunt, I soon met my mentor, Stan Lewinkowski, an incredibly underwhelming squat man. He spoke about Lord Nathaniel nonstop from the moment I entered his office. At first, I assumed it was to get me excited about the job, but it quickly became clear this was simply bragging. When he finally switched to explaining what I would be doing, I unconsciously let out an audible sigh of relief.

The Royal Biography was to be the lasting official record of the American Territories under the rule of Lord Nathaniel. Each territory was developing their own historical records along similar guidelines. While initial regulations called for posthumous publication, the unexpected longevity of The Lords had opened up discussions about releasing portions over time.

Stan gave me some samples of his work to look over. I was young, I knew, but I'd read my share of biographies, and that wasn't what Stan was writing. This was a commissioned portrait, obsessively presenting only the best side of the subject. It dazzled and glistened, but there was no substance beneath the sheen.

"No matter what Lord Nathaniel is doing," he explained to me in his teaching voice, "ask yourself, *Why is it good for the American people? How is this showing the Lord's mercy and nobility? How can this help further Lord Nathaniel's legacy?*"

In my head, I couldn't imagine how this was going to work out. I might have been slightly starstruck by the thought of working with Lord Nathaniel, but I wasn't going to pump out propaganda. I decided to do my best to tone down the praise and see what I could get away with.

With some time to finally settle into my modest room near the main building, I found I could barely move. I had made it through the brief orientation, but now I was going to be starting both my first job and an entirely new life on my own.

As it turned out, I was so busy, I barely registered the complete change in my life, the months an aberration of activity on my barren timeline. Stan had me escort him to every press conference and public event, although it often felt like I was just his gopher. Or in the worst circumstances, his wingman, making introductions to women and listening to him try to woo them with stories about work.

My first meeting with Lord Nathaniel made it obvious how easy it would be to just give in and be awed. He was the ultimate celebrity, powerful but effortless in all things. There was something lonely behind his smile, though. He would have us over for dinner to discuss matters relating to the biography, never demanding changes but often asking for expansion on certain topics. It was always the three of us at one end of the long oak table and Prince Sebastian, who was only a year older than me, at the other. Sebastian wasn't unfriendly, but he was most definitely aloof.

Those early months of my new job were marked by constant amazement. Even visiting Lord Nathaniel's home was like walking into a space-age fantasy furnished with items only procurable by someone able to smash a mountain apart with his fists.

I'd be lying if I didn't say it made me want more of it. It made me feel important too, even if only by proximity. I was falling into the clutches of America's signature disease, fame, but I continued to claw my way out every night. Fate may have made me fame-adjacent, but nature had made an observer, not a star.

For his part, Lord Nathaniel was always polite and courteous, but composed, prepared. The hardest part was getting over his age. He looked every bit as young as he had in the history vids I'd seen. He did seem heavier, not in mass but gait. Otherwise, he could have stepped straight off the screen.

Every encounter with Lord Nathaniel was on his terms. For Stan, it didn't matter, so long as he could say he had been invited to meet with the Lord himself. It was the dinners that confounded me more than anything. I had always imagined meals to be a time of bonding, but even when Nathaniel and his son interacted, there was a palpable sadness filling the space between them.

Sebastian was the Lord's only living child, heir apparent to the throne, but weighed down by some invisible burden. He'd often remain silent throughout dinner, trailing the vegetables on his plate through rich, buttery sauces. He would comment when prompted, but otherwise paid little attention to his surroundings. If Sebastian's depression was visible, his father's sadness sat just below the surface, a pool of doubt and regret only discernable from up close.

For Stan, these meals were times of openness and honesty, in which Lord Nathaniel explained his dream for America and his optimism for our future. I described them as awkward. Playing along with the propaganda was frustrating, but who knew what would happen if I poked my nose into the relationship between father and son. If Stan didn't kill me, maybe Lord Nathaniel would. Poking a god seemed like a losing proposition.

Just a year into my assignment, Stan Lewinkowski was hit by a car. He had been leaving a bar where, according to reports, he had spent the evening regaling a group of women with tales of his encounters with Lord Nathaniel. I felt bad for him, but my mourning was brief. As a mentor, he had been a nonentity, and I was used to people disappearing.

When I was called to Lord Nathaniel's residence after the accident, I wasn't surprised that something was happening. I figured that they'd be bringing in a new biographer or just reassigning me to a different apprenticeship. I was surprised that he was telling me himself, though. He had been very kind in our interactions, but it was hard to tell how real that truly was. I can't even imagine my face when he told me I was going to be the new biographer.

"Why?" I asked him, assuming it was a joke. "I'm sixteen. Surely there's someone more qualified."

"You already know the process," he said with a respectful nod, acknowledging the validity of my statements. "I've seen the writing Stan let you do, and I'm pleased with it."

My heart flipped a little bit.

"But you don't want to do that sort of writing, do you?" he asked me. I was hesitant. Was this a trap? Was there a right or wrong answer? "No, sir," I responded.

"Why?"

"A good biography, or any narrative really, shows the flaws, the mistakes, the regrets. It lets people form a connection with the subject, and it helps inform their understanding of the choices that person, in this case, um, *you*, made."

"I agree," he said before I could continue. I was stumped, no words ready for that response.

"Stan was a technically proficient writer, but I've been thinking more and more about how I'll be remembered. His narrative reads like biblical text. I may have ended up in this role, but I started out a normal person. Seems right I should be portrayed as one. You'll have greater access to me, including opportunities for unscheduled chats."

"Stan told me you'd never let him attend anything other than planned events," I said, not sure why I was still talking, which I think amused him.

"He never asked. There will still be some limits, obviously," Nathaniel added with a gentle sternness, "but we can worry about those when we reach them."

Shut up. Shut up. Shut up. Thank him and graciously leave, do it, do it! I thought, right before saying, "Are you sure about this? I mean, I'm really honored, but like I said, I'm sixteen."

"You have a gift, Simone," he said. "Plus, you completed a year of your apprenticeship. It seems to me that makes you the most qualified candidate."

He dismissed me kindly, wishing me a good night. I started to think of how to frame the story of this man, someone whose power was only matched by a half-dozen other individuals on the planet. I had to do exactly what Stan had never done: find the scientist Nathaniel used to be. Of course, never having lived without The Lords, it was hard to imagine a world in which gods didn't walk the Earth.

Chapter 3

When revisiting the history of The Lords, it's sometimes hard to find the truth amid the legend. Sure, there was archival footage, but even those straightforward frames were since embellished with new information and bizarre secrets, some more believable than others. The new history of civilization was the fuel of tabloid journalism.

The earliest reports, those from before the media blitz ensued, are the easiest to believe on their surface. On Christmas Day 1969, the news reported that a comet had crashed on an uninhabited island. Details were scarce, but the world was abuzz. Coming on the heels of the moon landing, people were optimistic but nervous.

Once it was deemed that the impact site didn't pose a health risk, an argument ensued over who had jurisdiction. As most people know from junior high history, before The Lords, there were tons of different territories with different rulers, and lots of those territories had been part of an organization called the United Nations. So, once the dust settled, that organization's Security Council was in charge.

The Security Council quickly brought in some of the world's most brilliant scientists in order to choose seven to send to the site. Each scientist would be allowed to bring a team of consultants and assistants, but to ease mounting political tension, only the seven would have access to the impact site itself.

The permanent members of the Security Council were the big guns:

the US, the UK, the Soviet Union, France, and China. Not surprisingly, scientists representing each of them were selected. Everyone was vying to be the first (or only) one to get information. While politics played their part, each member of the team was at the top of their scientific field.

In retrospect, it's clear why they didn't state what these fields were openly. It made sense to have a chemist, astronomer, and biologist on board. A case can be made for having a physicist and mathematician there as well. Once you've gotten to the linguist and engineer, the comet story begins to deflate a little. In the end, it was an eclectic group that brought together the best minds from the Big Five with a physicist from Nigeria and a biologist from Germany.

Within half a day of being on site, they presented their first finding: The comet wasn't a comet. It was a spacecraft. Looking back on the events, they really dropped the ball in not hiring a PR spokesperson. The scientists stated their assessment bluntly, took no questions, and left the stage quickly, chaos erupting in the briefing room.

And when the press panics, the world panics. Some people thought it was the apocalypse, others the resurrection. With reporters as anxious as everyone else and publishers always looking to increase circulation, major newspapers turned into conspiracy rags.

During this worldwide freak-out, amid all the snowballing fear, there was no news for almost two days. It doesn't sound like long, but it practically set the world ablaze, riots breaking out in cities around the globe as people who felt left in the dark vented their frustrations.

When the scientists finally returned to give their next briefing, they seemed slightly more prepared. Nathaniel Prescott of the United States had been elected their spokesperson. He was nervous, speaking with an unsteady voice, while Viktor Kalashnikov, Russia's beast of a scientist, glared at him from behind. The Cold War was alive and well, it seemed, even at the site of a UFO crash.

"Ladies and gentlemen," Nathaniel haltingly started, "I apologize for the delay in the presentation of our findings. The craft itself is highly sophisticated, but we have completed our initial assessment. For starters, the ship is an unmanned vessel. There's no sign of any pilot or passengers having been in or around the ship. Upon entering the craft, we found what appears to be a message. Professor Cartwright's team from the UK has been working with linguists from the Russian delegation to decipher its meaning.

"Additionally," he continued, "there is a shifting display of symbols within the ship, which we are actively working to decode based on order and frequency. We have also been determining the safest methods to open what we believe to be a number of cargo containers.

"Tests are being conducted on every surface within the capsule, as well as on samples of the air within the capsule gained prior to its full exposure to our atmosphere." He said this with a note of irritation, as though someone had left the door open by accident.

"As a number of scientists have publicly pointed out, the current location of the craft does indeed put it in a prime position for any airborne particles to achieve maximum atmospheric penetration. The teams from China and Nigeria have already developed a shield that will keep any contaminants contained to a sealed area around the ship. This shield has been in place for over a day now, and tests have shown it to be completely effective. We've measured air quality consistently since arriving and have found no sign of any contamination.

"Time is short, and this is the information we have to give you presently. Due to the sensitive nature of, well, everything, no questions will be taken at this time." This, of course, led to the yelling of many questions. Hands reached heavenward, desperately hoping to get one more bit of information.

"No questions!" Victor Kalashnikov yelled into the microphone. The press in the United States of America had labeled him the Iron Bear, a

Soviet powerhouse of mental and physical strength. The fear of every good patriotic American, the Bear was a symbol of achievement to his countrymen. His yell made every person in the room go silent, with the exception of Nathaniel.

"Thank you, Doctor Kalashnikov," he said before returning his attention to the press. "The seven of us will be returning to the site immediately to continue our work. We are in constant contact with our teams, who are working around the clock. We hope to have more information soon."

Nathaniel turned, ignoring the questions that began to spring up again. Victor looked out at the audience, a snarl crossing his face. The questions immediately became quieter.

The news footage and the articles at that point became so full of speculation and devoid of answers that they work better as sociology studies than they do historical documents. People were terrified.

When reports came that the craft had exploded, real panic set in. The teams at the crash site quickly confirmed that the shield had held, and there was a tentative sigh of relief. Then it was revealed that the scientists had been in the shielded zone at the time of the explosion.

Camera footage from just outside the blast zone reached the networks in record time and was shown repeatedly. In it, a net of electricity springs to life just as the ship tears apart. Oddly, the explosion appears coordinated, the ship breaking outward in neat pieces of metal that fit together like a puzzle. As the metal hits the outer edges of the shield, the electric net stretches like a balloon, bulging outward, almost reaching the camera. Then it holds.

Quickly and without warning, thick green geysers shoot upward, forcing the top of the shield into the air, trying to break through. Then the interior fills with a green gas, and finally the entire inside is just a green fog. Seven of the world's greatest minds entombed within the shield that had protected the world.

They were immediately memorialized as heroes. Across the country, people held vigils, some still hopeful, but most in appreciation. Even as the mourners gathered, though, governments were calling for emergency measures to protect against future attacks. The placement of the ship. The precision of the explosion. The dispersal of the gas. It all felt intentional.

Two days later, the alien substance finally cleared, and the shield was lowered. In the center of the area, amid the debris of the wreckage, were the seven scientists. They were unconscious, but miraculously alive.

Medical respondents, their biohazard suits giving them the appearance of spacemen, retrieved the bodies before the entire area was quarantined and destroyed. All items that had ever been part of the ship or in contact with the ship were torched completely. Special equipment was even brought in for some of the metal. The world wasn't taking any chances.

The scientists were unconscious for weeks. Then they woke up. All at once, to the second, according to every report from the time. None of them recalled those final moments. Otherwise, all seven were in perfect health. The Earth had won a clean victory. It was celebrated by people across the world, maybe the last time anything was.

When the Iron Bear returned to Moscow, press came from around the world to watch the national hero shake hands with the leader of his country, cameras trained on what was sure to be a moment worthy of every front page. A celebration of victory. The Bear put his left arm gently on his superior's shoulder, as one would an old, dear friend, and then rammed his right fist through the man's chest as though it was tissue.

Footage from the scene backs up the horror of the witness reports, which described it, essentially, as a bloodbath. Viktor ignored the other dignitaries on the stage, who were crawling over each other to get out of sight, but his dislike of the press led him to his next kill. He leapt into the audience, full of rage, acting on instinct, hungry.

He grabbed fleeing reporters out of the air, tossing them around like paper, breaking bones with the flick of a finger. When he finally stopped and composed himself, he got back on the dais and addressed the few cameramen brave enough to have continued filming. His words were translated as quickly as they could be at the time, but no one who heard the Bear's tone needed help understanding what was going on.

"As of this day," his speech went, "I am the leader of Mother Russia and her territories. Our leaders have created a toothless country unable to provide even for its own people. I will change this, but you must have faith in me. I saved you all once, and now I've been given the power to do so again."

In the days that followed, each country that had sent a representative as part of the seven confirmed that the Bear's abilities weren't unique. All of them were experiencing similar biological enhancements. Luckily, none had been quite so readily violent as Viktor, but people were nervous, many wondering if the scientists were being controlled by whatever sent the spacecraft.

It was certainly an understandable fear. It was one thing to trust these people with science-based problems but an entirely different one to trust them with godlike abilities. The extent of these powers had started to leak. It was a list that would ultimately include invulnerability, flight, eye lasers, and enhanced strength, speed, agility, hearing, sight, smell, and healing. There were other minor powers one Lord or another might have, and each of The Lords seemed to be gifted more in one area than another, but that was the overall rundown of abilities far beyond those of mortal men.

Nathaniel spoke to the United States, vowing to use his abilities only in the service of his homeland. Most other countries were hearing these same speeches, the scientists opting, outwardly at least, to soothe the concerns of their countrymen instead of killing them.

Voices became louder in the press and from the public at large. How could anyone be sure of the world's safety with these people running around? How did they get these powers? Did they know they would get them? Was the spacecraft good or evil? People didn't know what was going on, and from the lack of response, it appeared no one in government did either.

It started to come to a head, protests being shut down by force in a number of countries. In one instance, Heinrich Gruber, Germany's contribution to The Lords, dropped a bus on a crowd of demonstrators. Police fired on the scientist, but he shrugged their bullets off. By the time the military arrived, Gruber had finished killing the local precinct.

With news cameras providing a live feed, the scientist fired beams from his eyes that destroyed everything in their path. And he didn't hold back. Cars exploding, buildings collapsing, people disintegrating. It remains one of the most terrifying, haunting things ever televised. By the time the camera cut out, it was clear evolution had taken a leap—and that nothing could stand in its way.

It was at this point that someone finally thought to look past Gruber's official bio. That's when the world discovered that he had been a Nazi officer. He had almost refused his place on the team, worried his cover would be compromised. While that fear had come true, he no longer viewed it as a problem. In fact, his sudden prominence emboldened many supporters who had been holding their tongues for decades.

The meeting of The Lords that resulted from the Gruber tragedy is a story that relies entirely on faith, since there were no outside observers. What is consistent among all accounts is that six months after the event that made these seven humans into something more, they returned to the scorched area where it began and hashed out a plan that would reshape the world.

In what was suddenly the American Territories, the account of the meeting came almost exclusively from Lord Nathaniel. Real, unfiltered news from other countries had started to slow to a trickle as borders closed.

According to Nathaniel, The Lords held a vote. Really, they held *the* vote: does mankind still rule? While Lord Nathaniel said that he didn't agree with the majority, he was bound to honor the results.

Seven gods. Seven pieces. In the end, he said, he at least knew he could maintain democracy for the people in his territory.

Lord Nathaniel took as much land as he could. The scientists mostly stayed close to home, although the proximity of many of them led to the claiming of distant lands for a few. While the American press expressed confusion and anger, their immediate focus was on what might happen elsewhere in the world. The main concern: while Gruber or Kalashnikov might have been invaluable members of the scientific team, they were just plain scary.

Gruber was particularly odious. Unfortunately, his genius couldn't be disputed. He both created and improved chemical weapons for use on his own people during World War II. And in this brave new world, Gruber was suddenly the Lord of the German Territories, proudly heralding the beginning of the Fourth Reich. Nathaniel and others of The Lords managed to limit Gruber's territory and secured a seventy-two-hour evacuation agreement with him, helping relocate as many *undesirables* as they could before the slaughter began.

The few bits of news that crept out from the Reich over the years indicated that the newly infirm and handicapped were regularly euthanized, ensuring national resources were used for the betterment of the best and brightest. Knowing the horror that could be had made it difficult for the press to beat up on Lord Nathaniel.

He promised to let local, regional, and national governments continue to run as they already had, with one centralized representative government to oversee the welfare of the full Territories. After sorting out some land disputes and existing crime issues, he swore to keep his distance, except when he thought intervention was necessary for the public good. America was to be a model of human freedom in an age of gods.

Looking back, it's easy to see how people got swept up in it. I mean, if this was what's happening, at least you were getting the good end of the stick. And it wouldn't have made a difference had they continued to voice their concerns. The world didn't belong to them anyway.

From there, the clippings and appearances get more and more sanitized. It's easy to piece together where Nathaniel was during different key events, but there's no way to know *who* he was. Stan's predecessors hadn't been quite so fawning, but their accounts were dry, devoid of humanity, unhelpful.

Some of the last useful footage of Nathaniel came from the two times he stopped the Bear from invading America. These were the early years of The Lords, and they seem to paint a less human picture of America's sovereign. There's a defiance in his movements, like he's refuting the notion of limitations, of humanity. Like he's not *a* god, but *the* God.

Chapter 4

Lord Nathaniel was true to his word, sitting down with me for regular one-on-ones, inviting me to secret meetings, and even having me accompany him on a family trip to Russia. Leaving the Territories wasn't something people did. At least not people I knew.

Mind you, I could just barely make out Moscow as we flew in, and the palace staff seemed sworn to silence. I was only allowed on certain portions of the grounds, and only during certain times of the day. I couldn't leave the immediate area at all. My curiosity was foiled at every turn, so I was both thrilled and terrified when an invitation arrived for a meeting with Lord Viktor.

This man had gleefully torn reporters apart at a press conference, and he was asking me to interview him. I hoped his anger had mellowed with age.

When I met Lord Viktor, the first thing I noticed was how wrong the films and reports had gotten it. He was far scarier, towering over me like a giant as he introduced himself, his wide, jagged smile adding a glint of insanity to his already intense features.

I managed to get a grip on myself and started to feel better once we were both seated. As his wide grin shrank, the craziness went with it.

"I hope you are enjoying your stay in my country," he said politely.

"Everyone's been very kind," I responded. "I was hoping to see a bit more of Moscow while I was here, of course."

"Yes, of course," he said, his head bobbing in sympathy, "and I wish this was possible also, but this is standard policy given by my security personnel. It's their safety protocol. Not for me, of course, but for the people. Working in Nathaniel's palace, I'm sure you understand."

"Of course," I said, sensing this wasn't a point to push. "Forgive me, but may I ask why you invited me to meet with you?" I asked sweetly, deploying my most innocent smile. "You're not known for your love of journalists."

He gave a hearty laugh and waved a fleshy *Oh No You Didn't* finger in my direction. He stood, his laugh turning to a light chuckle as he walked to his desk and retrieved two glasses and a bottle of vodka from a freezer disguised as a globe before returning to his seat and pouring us each a healthy amount.

"I know the drinking age is not same in America as in Russia, but when in Rome," he said as he offered me mine.

"Thank you," I said, accepting. I'd had champagne and wine at some events since coming to the capital, but my only previous experience with vodka was when Peter stole a half-full bottle from a staff party at the orphanage. We drank it on the roof while everyone was too busy to notice, taking heavy sips from the cheap plastic neck, choking down the bitter, thick liquid, eventually becoming silly and laughing at everything and nothing. Little kisses. *I dare you* kisses. First kisses. Looking up at the stars, finally feeling weightless.

Viktor made a toast, and I snapped back to the present. I clinked my glass and drank with him, the vodka effortlessly sliding over my tongue and down my throat, cleaner and richer than what I'd sampled at the orphanage. I set the glass down, clear liquid still washing against its sides. I needed to keep my wits about me.

"Do you mind?" I asked as I pulled out my small digital recorder.

"Please. What would you like to know?" he said, eyeing the recorder with pity. The parts of the palace in which I was allowed were

23

kept historically accurate for tourists, but I'd stumbled across a few wayward examples of Russian tech. Pity was the correct response to my recorder.

I suddenly realized that in the brief time since getting the invitation and meeting the Bear, I hadn't actually prepared questions. I had another sip of vodka.

"How would you characterize your relationship with Lord Nathaniel, particularly given some of your past disagreements?" I hoped I wasn't pushing too fast, but I wasn't going to softball my way through this.

"I think," he started, giving me a nerve-wrackingly inscrutable look, "that we have come to respect each other as brothers. I admit to you, as I do to my people, that I had much to learn in my early days, and still today. But then, I was angry at what had happened to my country. I blamed America and focused selfishly on my rage instead of on the development of solutions. I needed to grow up, as you might say. Learn to see things from the other side."

"So, is this trip purely social, or do you two have particular goals?" I asked, feeling empowered given Viktor's candor so far.

"I think we always plan for social and end up debating policy into the night," he said with a light chuckle. It was getting easier to relax in his presence, to forget the man I had seen punch a hole through another man. "In some ways, these visits are as much for the children as for us. It is difficult to grow up so different from others, so we try to give them time with one another, even now that they're not really children anymore."

I realized that I hadn't seen much of Sebastian since we arrived. He had immediately left with Viktor's daughter, Anna. Her brothers, twins dubbed Terror 1 and Terror 2 in the tabloids, trailed after them conspiratorially. I felt pretty sure Sebastian only wanted time with one of Viktor's offspring, and I also felt pretty sure he wasn't going to get it if her brothers had anything to say about it.

"Do you and your family spend time with families from other territories also?"

"We do," Viktor answered, "but there's a special bond between Nathaniel and myself. I respect him in a way you can only respect someone who's beaten you unconscious. Twice."

I gave a quick laugh without even thinking and looked back at Viktor. He had a steel look in his eyes now, radiating fury. His head tilted ever so slightly, one eye squinting just a bit. I suddenly thought I was going to die. Right as the apology began to form on my lips, he suddenly burst out laughing.

"Got you!" he said. "That I learned from Nathaniel."

"I'll have to thank him for that," I said under my breath, which just caused the Bear to roar even louder. I did a quick reality check, realizing how surreal the situation had become, and made myself have another sip of vodka, hoping it might help make sense of everything. It did not.

"May I ask you some questions?" he asked me as he took a gulp from his tumbler.

"I suppose so," I said, unsure what I could possibly know that was worth sharing.

"What is life like in America? For the people?" he asked sincerely. "Like you, I rarely see much of the places I visit. Too many state dinners and public appearances."

"Well, I'm not the best example of a normal life," I replied, "but I think that people feel safe for the most part. Maybe too safe sometimes?" I immediately regretted adding the last part.

The issues of homelessness and hunger had been solved quickly in Nathaniel's government. While some people made more than others and everyone still wanted a bigger piece of the pie, even the poorest could afford to live healthy lives. Things were good, but something was missing.

"And you?" he asked. "Do you feel safe?"

"Sure, I suppose," I started. And then I stopped, wondering if I was committing treason.

"I am only asking how you see things, what your experience is. This isn't about my dealings with Nathaniel. Plus, the only record of this conversation is the one you own," he told me, gesturing at my pitiful recorder. "No one will hear anything from me or my staff." There was something about his tone, about his entire persona since we'd first sat down that made me want to trust him, and being cooped up in the palace had left me yearning to say something, anything.

"Well," I began, "I was an orphan, so my life wasn't typical, but I never felt in danger or wondered if I could survive. The changes Lord Nathaniel made were positive. I think the problem is you."

"Is that so?" he asked in a tone that was either good or very, very bad.

"Not just you," I quickly clarified, exaggeratedly waving my hands and then taking another sip of vodka, "but all of you. The Lords. Your children. Before you, it was a race to the top, but you, your abilities, your seeming immortality, it all set the bar too high to encourage aspiration."

"I can see your point," he said somewhat skeptically, "but would it be better if we hid among you? If we had let our most vulnerable countrymen continue to suffer, would mankind have eventually evolved to fix the issue?"

"Oh, I don't know," I said a little lightly. "That's a dangerous path to follow. It's easy to theorize, but when it comes down to it, you can't change the past. Or can you?"

He started a bit as he realized I actually meant that as a question. "Regrettably, I've thus far been unable to change the past. And trust me, there are many things I would change."

"Like what?"

He gave a small chuckle, then a deep inhale. "I've been a poor father. My children are dear to me, but I'm little more than an obstacle to them. I was an angrier man in their youth. An absent man. That's the man whose offspring I've raised."

"They seemed very devoted to you the few times I've seen you together," I said, trying to hit the fine line between reassuring and pandering.

"I'm sure they love me in their own way," he responded in defeat, "but whatever game they're playing, I've never figured out the rules."

"Well," I choked out after a sip of vodka, "I have to admit that I was kind of scared to meet you. You know, with the whole ..." I then proceeded to mime Lord Viktor punching through a man's chest. *No more vodka, Simone.* I took a sip from my glass. "I mean, you can be a little intimidating. Not right now, but other times."

To my immediate relief, he seemed amused by the oddity of it all. "Again, I take responsibility for the sins of my youth. I just wish they hadn't taken a toll on others."

I began to feel a little dizzy. It had to be the vodka. I wasn't exactly a drinker. I could feel Lord Viktor studying me.

"Are you okay, Simone?" he asked with concern. He had one of his people bring over a glass of water. "Real Russian vodka. Stronger than that cheap American swill."

"I'm fine," I said, the water bringing me back to my senses a bit. "I'm really sorry about that." Then I took another sip of the vodka, which set Lord Viktor into another fit of laughter.

"No need to apologize," he responded after catching his breath. "You're a delight. And Nathaniel showed me your latest chapter. Don't say a word, or," he repeated my chest-punching mime, "but you're a much better writer than my biographer."

"I'm sorry, My Lord?" a man who had stood silently by the door inquired.

"You're just not very good, Pavel," Lord Viktor said kindly, "but I like having you around. You're awkward and strange."

"Thank you, My Lord," Pavel replied, his tone bridging gratitude and sorrow.

"Yikes," I whispered.

"Indeed," Lord Viktor quietly replied. "I forget he's there half the time. But I've kept you long enough. I know how busy your schedule must be."

"No," I said, desperately hoping this wasn't the end, "I'm completely free if you feel like talking more."

"Unfortunately, I've got to get back to work on a secret project." He leaned in and whispered, "Time travel." He pulled back out, punctuating the joke with a wink and a grin.

"Well," I said, taking the last sip of vodka in the glass, much to Lord Viktor's amusement, "keep me posted on your progress. Thank you so much for the invitation."

He chuckled softly as he sipped on his vodka. "It was truly my pleasure, Simone. I hope you were satisfied with our conversation." He gave me a hearty hug before sending me kindly on my way.

Going back to my room, I cursed myself briefly for not asking more or better questions. Would they have led anywhere, though? I had just gotten more candid insight into the Bear's personal life than I could ever have read in a standard interview. He had actually opened up. While that realization calmed one stressor, I suddenly tried to remember how much I'd opened up. I tried to blame the vodka, but I knew I'd been dying to have a real two-sided discussion for days.

When I got back to my room, I immediately played the recording. Listening to the conversation, I found myself smiling at Lord Viktor's little jokes and asides. Even though the effects of the vodka hadn't worn off, I was still embarrassed by the later portions. That, luckily, was the extent of it, though. I hadn't said anything truly disparaging or untrue.

I started to look ahead to what were finally going to be some busy days. The schedule for the wrap-up included exciting rounds of sit-downs with Russian officials. I honestly wasn't sure which side was doing the interviewing.

I spoke to senior staff members of both the mansion and the government, getting verbal press releases from all of them. It was days of the same sanitized information coming from different people's faces. I felt like screaming. And then came the invitation to speak with Anna, Lord Viktor's daughter.

Her security, a man who introduced himself as Aleksei, remained in the room during our discussion. He was clearly there to veer me away from sensitive topics, but I was okay with that, since she could have killed me with a well-aimed sneeze.

I noticed that they were close, Aleksei and Anna. She deferred to him. Lord Viktor's words ran through my head. Aleksei seemed to truly care about Anna. Was it possible he'd provided what her father couldn't? I tried to think of Sebastian's caretakers and minders, but they came and went with a frequency that made learning their names pointless.

Anna was a perfect young lady. She was about the same age as Sebastian, with impeccable skin, hair, and manners. A royal from birth, her legs always crossed perfectly at the ankles, and her smile was reassuring and ever present. She knew all the right words and correct phrasing, and even her gestures screamed *authentic*. I immediately distrusted her.

"Have you enjoyed your stay?" she asked politely, her English tinged with a huskiness that was as sexy as it was intimidating.

"Yes, it's been lovely," my thin voice replied. "I didn't really get out much, of course. What's it like? The social scene, I mean."

I wasn't even sure what I meant.

"I don't get out much," Anna replied, her perfect smile momentarily twitching. "I read, listen to music. The same things I imagine people do in America."

"Yeah," I said, fighting to get this back on track, "I've just been so busy here that I didn't really get a chance to find out what people do for fun, when they go out, I mean. Or are there really popular movies or songs or just anything unique about the culture here?"

She whistled some bars of a song. It didn't sound like something that would play on American radio, and even coming from her well-honed mask of happiness, it was dark and foreboding.

"I'm afraid I don't know that one," I said as nicely as possible.

"It's probably not a big hit. Or maybe it is. I'm sure I wouldn't know. Our father used to play it for us before bed. He would tell us *Ruling is not about popularity. It is about power.*" Her smile had disappeared, and something in her eyes seemed distant.

Aleksei cleared his throat so loudly that I jumped. Anna shook off whatever had come over her.

"I'm sorry," she said, "there's just been so much to do lately that I'm afraid I haven't gotten as much sleep as I normally do."

"Please, don't worry," I replied, attempting to ignore the weird zone-out. "This is my first time on the road with Lord Nathaniel, and I haven't slept very well either."

"Are our beds not good enough for you?" she asked with a smile that seemed to strain the limits of her lips.

"Oh, no, that's certainly not what I meant. I was just saying ..."

"Are you telling me I'm wrong?" Her eyes had raised in defiance.

Aleksei immediately ran over and whispered in Anna's ear. She began to calm instantly.

"I do apologize," she said sweetly, "but I'm afraid I have another appointment I must attend."

She rose to leave, walking away with Aleksei's arm in hers, whistling the somber tune that played her to sleep as a child.

I found myself startled by her lack of connection to humanity, and it made me realize that Sebastian had the same issue. I wondered how the next generation of rulers truly regarded the population. Their parents had lived as humans, but they were born gods.

Aside from the interviews, there were multiple celebrations in honor of Lord Nathaniel, some press conferences, and more than a few run-ins with palace staff as I kept trying to stroll off the grounds, desperate to get even a glimpse of the city, which was hidden from every vantage point I could access.

While the trip had proven interesting, I was so frustrated by the end of it that I was thrilled to be going home. On the plane, Lord Nathaniel handled a few matters with one of his councilmen and then called me over to the seat across from him. Sebastian sat a few rows back with his headphones on, looking sullen, detached.

"How did you like Moscow, Simone?" Lord Nathaniel asked, glancing up from the last few papers he needed to sign.

"Well, I enjoyed the palace," I replied. "I didn't get to see the city, unfortunately."

"I'm sorry about that. I should have warned you before we left. Lord Viktor has some very strict rules."

"He explained it to me," I said.

Nathaniel put the papers aside and caught my eyes. "When did he do that?" he asked without accusation. I still felt like I'd been caught doing something wrong.

"He asked for a last-minute interview a few days ago," I responded, feeling a knot form in my stomach. "I assumed he had okayed it with you. I didn't even think to check."

He waved my concern away. "No, it's fine, I just didn't know he had requested to speak with you. What did you two talk about?"

"Oddly, philosophy mostly," I told him. "Family stuff. A little bit about the relationship between the two of you. I recorded the conversation if you'd like to listen to it."

I was a little relieved when he told me he was sure he would see everything of interest when I submitted the chapter to him. I figured I might leave a few things out. After all, the biographer shouldn't be the subject.

Chapter 5

Lord Nathaniel continued to loosen his guard around me. I hoped I was gaining his trust, but whatever was happening, I welcomed it. I felt as though I finally had purpose.

I was beginning to develop a real portrait of this reluctant god. He was patient with everyone but his son and often questioned his opinions of adversaries and allies. In the end, though, loyalty was his defining trait. He was loyal to family and close advisers, and he seemed to have a sincere loyalty to his territory. He felt obligation deeply, but he let his personal life falter as a result.

He had lived long enough and grown so powerful that he took his invincibility for granted. Sebastian's, however, was another story.

The only times I sensed fear from Lord Nathaniel during those days were when he was in public with Prince Sebastian. He was never out of arm's reach of his son and always hyper aware of their surroundings. Sebastian had inherited great power of his own, but his father didn't seem to acknowledge it.

It was a touchy subject, and by the time I finally worked up the nerve to ask him about it, he surprised me with his response.

"I wondered when you'd get around to something more personal," he said while pouring me some lemonade and himself a scotch. "It's not vodka, which Viktor claims is your favorite."

"Let me explain that," I began.

"It's fine, Simone." He grinned. *"When in Rome* and all that. I trust you. So, let's skip the formalities. You know my history. It's not something I really want to rehash. Kind of hard to pull a *woe is me* when you're in my position, but things haven't been all that great for me since the day I got called up to serve my country."

He sat down, putting my drink on the table before taking a sip from his snifter. "Sebastian is my only living child, but his importance stretches beyond even that bond. If anything were to happen to me, he's the only person The Lords will even consider leaving in charge. Without him, America is over."

"Are you worried about your mortality for a reason?" I asked. Rethinking it quickly, I began to withdraw the question before he waved me down.

"You'll know soon enough," he said with a sigh of resignation. He lifted the leg of his pants, revealing a small wound on his right calf. It was ringed by a pulsating otherworldly red light, keeping time with an inaudible beat. Here and there, small flakes drifted away from the red ring, flickering to black as they fell to the floor, like embers from a campfire.

"I'm dying. I'll be the first of us, but I won't be the last. Whatever's kept me going all these years, it's eating me away cell by cell."

I was stunned into silence, finally breaking it with, "I'm sorry," which I immediately regretted for its inadequacy. "I had no idea."

"No," he said, looking stern, "and it's important no one else does either."

"Of course, Lord Nathaniel," I said sympathetically. "I would never ..."

He cut me off, "Of course not, Simone. I wouldn't have told you if I thought otherwise. There are others in the capital I'm less sure of, unfortunately."

Deciding that was a road I shouldn't follow just yet, I circled back to the start of this conversation. "Is work being done on a cure? Have you started to make transition arrangements?"

He laughed a little, tired but amused. "Yes, to both. The first isn't promising, and proposals for the second are being worked on by a select group of council members. I think we've veered a little off course from our family discussion."

"I'm sorry," I said, suddenly feeling self-conscious.

"No," he quickly responded, "that was entirely my fault. Can't expect to announce your impending doom and then just move on to something else."

"Not really," I said.

"You made quite an impression on Lord Viktor," he said, switching the subject.

"Oh?" I responded, trying not to betray the level of curiosity this provoked.

"He said you were a firebrand." Nathaniel grinned. "But he also said you were one of the few people he's met in ages who actually made him think."

"That's very kind of him," I said deferentially. "I probably crossed a line or two."

"Keep crossing them," he told me. "Sebastian has no concept of what it is to be human or even part of the masses. He's going to need perspective."

"I don't think he'll listen to me," I said sincerely.

"That, my friend, is something only time will tell. We did them a disservice, I think," he continued, "raising them apart from the world we were raised in. Making them feel even more different than they already were. Wu got it right, but the rest of us isolated them."

"I don't think anyone can blame you, all things considered," I said.

"I can't go into all that right now, Simone," he said. "I'm actually getting a little tired. Would you be upset if we postpone the rest of our chat?"

"Of course not, My Lord," I responded. "Do you need anything?"

"Oh, don't start treating me like I'm dying just because I am." He chuckled. "I can still demolish a skyscraper with one fist if I want. I just don't really see the point is all."

"Of course not," I said. "Have a good night's sleep, sir. I look forward to continuing this later. And thank you. For sitting with me, talking with me. It's really been an honor."

"Crap," he sighed, slumping back in his chair. "This is how everyone's going to treat me, isn't it? Go. Shoo. And sleep well, Simone."

As I walked back to my apartment, I thought about a world without The Lords, run by superhuman twentysomethings who had never lived a day as regular people. The chill in the air punctuated the thoughts I'd conjured. Sebastian was odd, but I'd never known him to be cruel. I could only hope the others were the same or better. I thought of Princess Anna, plastic smile, raging eyes.

I could understand why Lord Nathaniel hadn't wanted to go into his history tonight. He wasn't wrong in claiming that life had been unkind to him. He fathered seven children, three girls and four boys. Of those, two of the boys died in childbirth, one girl suffered from a genetic defect that led to her demise, and the other girls were killed as babies, along with their nanny, in a car crash.

Of the surviving boys, Jack was the shining star, handsome, outgoing, and already displaying limited powers at a young age. The press loved him, and he loved the attention. Hardly a day went by without a new picture of the tiny prince. While Nathaniel had proclaimed himself Lord, Jack was the first real royal in the eyes of most Americans.

When a sniper shot Jack through the head before his powers were strong enough to protect him, the nation went into mourning. It was one of the greatest unsolved crimes, and it left Nathaniel with only Sebastian, a cheerful but slight child.

Little was known about Sebastian's mother, which was true for every child of The Lords. There were no living queens, but there were plenty of heirs. The whispered questions lingered in bars and bedrooms: Do all the mothers die? Do they have a choice in becoming pregnant? In staying pregnant?

The only clues were found in one of the earliest tabloid stories of the new era. In those early years, most countries released fluff articles about The Lords, propaganda meant to humanize the gods. Real news was off the table, but gossip about who they were dating, where they were eating, and what they were wearing was ubiquitous. And people ate it up.

Cecilia Stone was at least worthy of the press she received. In pictures and film, her ethereal beauty is striking, wispy features contrasted by bones both sharp and smooth. Familiar but alien in her perfection. The longtime girlfriend of the newly crowned king of the British Territories, her wedding was the television event of the season, and one of the last times American film crews were given full access to another territory.

People around the world watched the event live, dreaming of being plucked from their mundane lives to sit on a throne beside their true love. It was a fairy tale come true. Photos from their honeymoon, first official trips, and even random events were hot commodities, but the couple strategically ignored the commotion, keeping themselves in the news without being ever-present.

The announcement of Lady Cecilia's pregnancy a year later blasted excitement levels through the roof. Every paper in America began including daily updates on the health of mother and child. Gamblers bet on the child's gender. People felt closer to the new monarchy than they had since the ascension of The Lords.

When Cecilia went into labor, televisions worldwide tuned to coverage from outside the hospital. The dream was coming true for so many people, and then things came crashing down. The baby, a boy named Cecil, was healthy, but Cecilia had died during the birth, her story ending perhaps the only way a story like hers could.

Since that time, whatever romantic affairs The Lords engaged in were seemingly off limits, and people forgot the new world ever had a queen.

As for Jack, Lord Nathaniel's favorite son, his assassination happened when Sebastian was still a toddler. It was a huge news story, but at the same time, it was a huge news lockout. Every organization had the same information, and nothing was ever revealed outside of official government statements.

The palace and residence staff members never talked much about it, for obvious reasons, but after a few too many drinks one day after I'd just started my apprenticeship, Stan told me it was as traumatic an atmosphere as he'd ever seen. Not just dark, but truly traumatizing. Sebastian, who had run through the offices every day, was suddenly confined to the residence. There was a rotation of bodyguards posted at the entrances, and no one was allowed to see the boy.

According to Stan, Lord Nathaniel became prone to sudden fits of laughter that would then lead to anger, orders yelled at no one in particular. He would sometimes break down in the hallway between conference rooms, unable to remain composed long enough to cover the distance. His security detail kept him upright and moving, but his sobs echoed through the corridors, saturating every space.

Nathaniel snapped out of it after a few months, and soon Sebastian was given more freedom. Something had changed though. The sprightly kid was gone, replaced by a shy child, terrified of every corner.

It was easy to empathize with Lord Nathaniel, his fears, and the overprotection of his last living heir, but was I sabotaging my own work? Did I really believe that they never found out who shot Jack? It wasn't a topic I wanted to broach with a dying man, and I could think of only a handful of council members who would know, all of whom were smart enough to avoid the royal biographer.

I decided not to head down that path. I wasn't an investigator; I was a biographer. Besides, the true impact of Jack's death was easily seen without detailing the events. Lord Nathaniel wasn't a boisterous person, and I feel certain he wouldn't have chosen the life of a king. For the people of America, it was sometimes hard to remember he even had powers.

A peace between territories had spread throughout the world, The Lords holding true to a noninterference pact they'd made after Lord Viktor's failed invasion attempts. Nathaniel was a figurehead to most people, not someone who made or enforced laws, but someone who represented the country. He didn't fly into action at a moment's notice or, really, at all.

I realized after sitting through a few council meetings, though, that he didn't need to publicly flex his muscles. Every decision the representative government made was based on what one could charitably call *strong advisement* from Lord Nathaniel. It was a realization that chilled me. Having never seen him make what I thought to be the wrong call, I found ways to justify it, but I still saw it for what it was, and I knew that the democracy I'd been promised was a lie.

Chapter 6

As the months passed, Lord Nathaniel's body turned against him even more aggressively. His energy levels were flagging, and the lesions were multiplying, leaving large pits where flesh should have been. Even though his face had been largely spared, makeup was still applied liberally at his increasingly rare public appearances. Excuses were made for early exits. Whatever had given him his powers, it was proving insatiable. Nathaniel had singlehandedly repelled two incursions by the Bear himself, but now he was literally falling apart, luminescent flake by luminescent flake.

When Lord Nathaniel knew his last day was upon him, he called me to his chambers. Alone in the dim room, he looked into my eyes. It was so startling in the instant that I tried to recall how often he'd looked me directly in the eyes, how often anyone had.

I looked for secrets, but all I saw was a man, tired after a life longer than he'd anticipated and scared by the thought of what he left behind.

I think Nathaniel believed that the other six would continue to live up to their pact, but if The Lords were dying, the world was about to pass to a new generation. There was no knowing what that might mean.

A question rose within me. It had been asked for decades, but there had never been a clear answer. "What was released when the spacecraft blew up?" I asked. "Why did it give you powers if it was meant to harm us?"

He glanced away, and I felt a little ashamed for asking a dying man a question he clearly didn't want to answer.

"We knew so little going into the situation," he said. "There were so many unknowns already, and when the backup teams torched the site, they destroyed everything. What had entered our bodies had already adapted, although clearly not very well." He broke into a coughing fit.

"Should I get someone, sir?"

"No, I'm fine," he said, regaining his composure, still looking into the distance, as though he was reliving that fateful day. "We know they were spores. We didn't know what they'd do until after the explosion. We didn't have the time."

"So, you had to assume it was harmful," I said, recognizing the logic.

"Seemed like the right thing to do," he replied weakly. "No way of knowing what would have happened if it hit the atmosphere. I mean, look at me."

"What about the message?" I asked, hoping for something more concrete.

"Never deciphered," he said sharply. "I don't have any new answers for you there, I'm afraid." He started into another fit of coughs and wheezes, which died down after a few moments.

"I imagine you'll be very busy soon," he said to me, returning his gaze to mine. "I've arranged for you to stay on, at least long enough to chronicle my life's epilogue. If Stan were still here, he'd write detailed volumes about the funeral décor, but I don't imagine even my death will weaken your curiosity about my life."

"Stan wasn't really the curious sort," I countered.

I worried his laughter might trigger another coughing fit, but he collected his breath cleanly.

"I'll be sure to talk to him about it if there's somewhere after here," he said.

41

"Do you think there is?" I asked him.

"I'm a scientist. I believe what I can prove. Even with everything I've seen and done, it's difficult to prove the existence of something that relies on faith. Ergo, I'm a little nervous about this dying thing."

I gave a slight chuckle and took his hand, not knowing what to say. He looked into my eyes again, the third time this evening. I had looked for something in his eyes earlier. Now it seemed he was looking for something in mine.

"Remember," he said, radiating urgency, "the truths of a man aren't known until he's gone, not the whole truths at least. Be careful how deep you dig, Simone."

My interest was piqued. "What truths?"

"Just know that things that end unforgivably often begin with the best intentions. I've always liked you, you know. Tenacious as can be, but never a pest."

He looked away then and asked that I send in the prince. I left the room in a daze, not turning back, wanting to remember everything as it was, not from a distance.

Back in the hall, the prince dispatched, I mulled it over in my head. His last words weren't exactly a riddle, but was he warning me of danger or disappointment? I came out of my daze still walking down one of the long halls Sebastian raced through as a child. Lord Nathaniel would be dead by morning, I knew, and the weight of that knowledge rushed over me in sudden wave.

Chapter 7

The next few days, like most following a death, were alive with activity, the irony of which left me unexpectedly saddened. I stuck to the newly dubbed Lord Sebastian like glue. I felt an obligation to try to be a humanizing influence. Whether Sebastian regarded me as a friend, confidante, or nuisance was impossible to discern. He was a true professional at crafting a public persona, polished and unfazed. It wasn't a skill I'd seen him display before.

I missed the easy friendship I had with Lord Nathaniel, but friendships with Lords have limitations best left undiscovered. I wasn't planning on even attempting that with Sebastian. Once I finished with Lord Nathaniel's biography, I would be given a yearly stipend for my service, along with royalties from copies of the multi-volume epic. Having seen so little of the Territories, I had already mapped out my retirement travels. My late teens were looking promising.

Regardless of my trailing him, Lord Sebastian had little time for grief, much less other people. Between funeral plans and preparations for his official coronation, it seemed as though he was always on the move.

I noticed immediately that some of the younger members of the council, just a handful of years older than the new Lord, had taken shifts with Sebastian. One was always on hand to offer advice or shoo away unwanted individuals. As Nathaniel's advisers had always done, these young politicians kept me at arm's length at all times.

It was probably my paranoia, but there were enough glances my way, enough whispers in Sebastian's ear, that I started to get uncomfortable. Trying to keep the feeling in check, I kept my head down and continued to chronicle the events around me. I just hoped I could help keep Sebastian on his father's path before I finished my duties.

On the seventh day following Nathaniel's death and only a day after the public coronation of Sebastian, the chief scientist for the Territories invited the young Lord to a facility spoken of in whispers. A modern legend, the facility was famous for the nearly unattainable level of security clearance needed to even learn its location. Lord Sebastian was informed that protocol required leaving his guards behind.

Sebastian agreed to these terms, which was easy, considering he was the most powerful man in the nation, but he asked that Jason Samson, a lanky member of the council in his mid-twenties, and I be allowed on the tour. When Sebastian refused to budge, he was given his wish, probably only because both Samson and I already had classified clearances that could easily be expanded.

Samson was part of Sebastian's new entourage. He had been given his seat on the council by Lord Nathaniel in an attempt to win over the younger generation. Perpetually bored and vocally self-absorbed, Samson made me fear the future he was supposed to represent.

Why Sebastian asked that I be allowed in the lab was a mystery. I couldn't believe it was something his entourage approved. I decided to have faith in Sebastian's independence. It really didn't matter. There wasn't a chance I was going to miss a guided tour of the most secret of secret labs in the Territories.

When I arrived on the morning of our tour, Samson greeted me cordially. It felt wrong to judge him based only on a feeling, but I'd been trusting my gut my entire life, and it definitely didn't like Samson. Regardless, I cheerfully returned his greeting, excited to see the apex of American science.

The grand facility I'd heard described as an eye-shattering blend of science, magic, and the impossible stood before me. My expectations had kept me from falling asleep for hours, but now I was here.

The narrow, windowless, two-story brick building had no exterior markings except for some crude graffiti. The only entrance, at least on the street side, lacked a handle and included a phone number offering what was apparently a *gud time*. Sebastian pressed his finger to the doorbell, and the handleless panel slid aside so quickly, I jumped. Once we'd all crossed the threshold, the door slid back into place. Samson let out an involuntary whimper. I didn't blame him.

Entering the facility was mind-bending. The hall that stretched from the exterior door to the lab door was impossibly long, in the literal sense. The other door was blocks past where the facility should have ended. Its distance was so surprising that I barely bothered to question how I could even see it clearly.

We made our way slowly down the hall, the walls, floor, and ceiling changing color with every movement of our bodies, every flex of a finger. Grids of light passed by in all directions, exploding into brilliant sparks that created 3-D constellations, twins of each of us, that matched our pace a few steps ahead.

I was so taken in by the light show around me that I nearly failed to notice that the door we were walking toward seemed to be getting farther away. I turned back to gauge the distance we'd gone, only to find the door we entered from directly at my back.

"Lord Sebastian," I said, "look behind us."

"What is it, Simone?" Samson growled before swirling around, his face freezing in surprise at our lack of progress.

"Well," said Sebastian calmly, "I suppose we need to keep walking forward."

"Do you really think that's going to get us anywhere, My Lord?"

Samson asked.

Sebastian seemed to shift a bit, questioning his decision.

"At least we know the way back out," I said.

Samson groaned and pointed an angry finger in my face. "If anything happens to us, I'm holding you responsible." At least the façade of friendliness was gone, and I knew where I stood with him.

"Enough," Lord Sebastian said with restraint. "You're both here because I value your input. Please at least pretend to get along."

As we continued to the sounds of machines gently humming behind walls, floor, and ceiling, I considered what could possibly be worth this much effort to keep hidden. Was it dangerous, valuable, or both?

We continued on the path, even though the door we were walking toward kept shrinking into the distance, growing smaller with each step. After what felt like an eternity, the door snapped out of existence entirely and our 3-D light-selves burst apart. The hallway in front of us was gone, and a glowing red wall blocked our path.

"This is completely ridiculous," Samson fumed. "They can't treat us this way! They certainly can't treat *you* this way!"

Samson twirled around in anger and opened the door through which we'd entered, except the door didn't lead back to where we'd come from. The councilor stopped, stunned speechless. Sebastian and I walked past him through the door, both of us clearly amused.

The laboratory was everything a six-year-old might imagine: large, gleaming machines, flashing lights, and even beakers full of bubbling chemicals. Tables of experiments of every sort littered the main room, which seemingly stretched on forever.

International information exchange had been limited since 1971. While we still traded with the British Territories, little other information flowed to or from our scientific community, or so we had been told.

In this lab, though, science had grown by leaps and bounds, generations beyond anything publicly available. The array of equipment, the look of it, the sound of it—all unlike anything I'd even read about. Everywhere I turned, something amazing and new caught my eye, and then our guide caught up to us.

Doctor Ned Frank was about as bland as his name. He was a genius, though. I'd verified it through research I began as soon as Lord Sebastian mentioned his name. The doctor owned hundreds of patents and had developed game-changing surgical procedures. Information on him went dark very suddenly, and I can only assume it's because he got a very classified new job.

"I apologize for the unorthodox security measures," Doctor Frank said as he walked up to greet Lord Sebastian. "It's part of why we don't allow a lot of visitors. So much work just to get the system set up for you three, I thought we'd have to bring up the subjects from 5A." He started giggling, trailing off with a grimace as he realized the joke was too specific for his audience.

"What was it you wanted to discuss, Doctor Frank?" Sebastian asked, his patience surprising after our delayed entrance.

"It's not very easy to just say, My Lord," Frank began. "I do wish you'd let me go over it with you alone first. I really think it would be for the …"

"The matter's already decided," Sebastian said, calmly cutting off the scientist. Samson nodded his head vigorously in agreement.

"Very well," Doctor Frank reluctantly conceded. "Come with me, please."

We followed him through a seemingly endless maze of corridors, occasionally spotting a scientist or technician busily at work. Frank gave the high-level overview as he led the way.

"Your father established the American Government Laboratory in 1971 to work on programs that were of a sensitive nature. In 1972, he tasked a small, select group of scientists and technicians with discovering what had made The Lords into what they were.

"Since the idiots in charge at the time completely torched the scene, the only real biological samples they had came from Lord Nathaniel himself. Just isolating the structure of the spores that had invaded his system proved difficult, given their rapid mutation."

"Spores?" Samson asked, clearly not having heard this detail before.

"I'm sorry," the doctor said, "I really think we should discuss this ..."

"Already a done deal, Doc," Samson said quickly, clearly as curious as I was about what we were learning.

Doctor Frank glanced at Sebastian, but receiving no alternative direction, he continued.

"From what the scientists could ascertain, the bombs had been filled with spores. It's impossible to even guess the count, but just having seen the tapes, it was clearly massive. When they were released into the shielded area and breathed in by The Lords, the spores attached themselves wherever they could, and since The Lords were trapped in there for so long with so many spores, their bodies were completely invaded.

"Then, the host bodies adjusted, which was the period of unconsciousness right after The Lords were retrieved from the site. During that time, the spores mutated, fitting into the host system as seamlessly as possible. They were smart. They wanted to do as little damage as possible. Their ability to reproduce was prodigious, keeping Nathaniel young and making him stronger every year. Unfortunately, his body wasn't made to handle the energy the spores generate, none of The Lords' bodies were. Certainly not at the dose they'd received."

"Excuse me, Doctor," I said politely, "but why did they all wake up at once? Were the spores communicating?"

"Well," the doctor began, scanning Lord Sebastian's face while awkwardly stretching the word out. This was a man who liked to keep his secrets.

"Yes, Doctor?" Sebastian nonchalantly responded.

In defeat, the doctor caved. "We think so. Information from that period's sketchy, but Lord Nathaniel reported a minor psychic connection with the other six rulers. We studied it to the extent we could, but it's difficult to test if no one picks up on the other side."

"Of course," Lord Sebastian said simply. "Now then?"

"Oh, right. Yeah, those first scientists had to tell the most powerful man in history that his abilities would eventually kill him. I wouldn't have wanted to be part of that. All due respect, My Lord.

"Anyway," the doctor continued, "Lord Nathaniel requested that the research refocus on ways to halt or possibly reverse the damage. It's still the most secret project in the history of the facility. Its name was never written down. No one ever spoke about it. There is, quite literally, no trail that leads to it, paper or otherwise."

He stopped for a reaction, eyeing us with the wonder of a man who thinks he knows how to tell a story.

"You're a little creepy, aren't you?" Samson said.

"Anyway," the doctor continued, shooting a look of death Samson's way, "Regenesis, its name known only to a few people, began small. Once the scientists had done their best to reverse-engineer the bonding process, they had a synthetic spore they could replicate. They began experimentation on rats and other small mammals, but the spores were too powerful. They skipped certain creatures entirely, seemingly without rhyme or reason, but if even one spore attached itself to the animal, death was swift.

"That was when the scientists decided they needed human subjects, but there was clearly going to be a high mortality rate, at least in the beginning. This had to be top secret. Bad enough the public find out The Lords aren't immortal, but finding out we're killing people to fix them? The team took people no one would miss. Convicts, orphans, runaways, bums. They were trying to save your father, My Lord."

49

Sebastian's appalled look seemed genuine, and it certainly matched my own. It was no wonder Doctor Frank had wanted to speak to Lord Sebastian alone.

"Excuse me," I said without knowing I was speaking, "are you saying they were kidnapping people and doing experiments on them?" Knowing I would have easily qualified for their program really hit home.

Sebastian put his hand on my shoulder and gave a light, reassuring squeeze. "He did," he said, staring at the doctor. "And now he's going to tell us the rest."

As we received more details about the experiments, I felt my knees weaken and my stomach churn. At the beginning, it was about quantity. They needed to discover what traits led to what results, which meant they needed a lot of people. As their studies went, they varied up the sample groups. People were chosen for eye color, hair color, skin color, or any array of genetic factors. Since the laboratory had unfettered access to virtually every electronic database in the Territories, finding the right subjects was a cinch.

Stretched over the decades, thousands of people had been taken into the lab and exposed to the synthetic spores or even been given transfusions of Lord Nathaniel's blood. None of them ever left. When necessary, the disappearances were staged to indicate the victim had run away. Sometimes they'd implicate someone else. Doctor Frank made sure to clarify they only framed career criminals. I felt my heart drop.

While the doctor claimed limited success at certain stages of the program, he admitted that anyone with whom the spores had bonded died shortly after exposure.

"Hold on, didn't you say the spores would sometimes just bypass someone entirely?" I asked, my head floating from all the revelations.

"That was the case with about half of the subjects. We did continue to study them," he studiously replied.

"To get information on why the spores didn't bond? To see if there were delayed effects?" Sebastian asked.

"Yes to both," the doctor replied. "The research helped in a number of ways."

"But those individuals still died?"

"I'm afraid so, My Lord."

"From the spores?" I asked accusingly.

The doctor gave a panicked look at Sebastian, whose eyes widened with anger. I thought he was going to take a swing, but he walked toward a bank of machines instead. Samson and I just stared at each other, neither of us knowing exactly how to react to the news that the government was the most proficient serial killer in the Territories.

To his credit, Lord Sebastian's first reaction was to make sure the program was mothballed, Samson nodding along like a dog being teased with a ball. The doctor went into crisis mode, trying desperately to calm Sebastian down.

"We have better samples than we've ever had before," he said quickly. "When your father's body began to break down, the spores that broke away were completely different from the earlier samples. They had evolved or possibly reverted as they ate his human side. If we clone these spores, well, that coupled with where our research already is should lead us to the cure."

"With my father gone, Doctor," Sebastian asked, "what value is there to continuing the program?"

"Well ..." the doctor began.

"The rest of The Lords are still dying," Sebastian soberly cut him off. He was weighing his options, which made me extremely uncomfortable. Samson whispered something, and Sebastian nodded in agreement.

"Continue your work, Doctor Frank," Lord Sebastian said with authority, "but there will be no trials until you truly believe there will be no fatalities, and any new subjects will be volunteers warned of the risks. You say there are no records of the program's origins. Make sure that that's true. And I ask that you remind everyone involved with Regenesis, past and present, to keep their mouths shut."

"For the program's public launch," Samson excitedly jumped in, "we'll start a PR campaign to help you recruit, and I'll expect in-person meetings twice weekly to discuss results. You can come to me, though."

The doctor breathed a sigh of relief as we finally entered the Regenesis lab, where he had originally planned to do his full presentation. The equipment in the room was somehow even more impressive than what we'd seen when we walked in the front door. This wasn't just a job for Doctor Frank; it was a passion project, one he intended to keep running no matter what, or who, it hurt.

Sebastian gave me a reassuring nod, but his decision concerned me. Even if no one else died, the fatality-free Regenesis had been paid for with the lives of thousands, and their killers had just gotten their funding approved as a result of their confession.

Chapter 8

So, the program went from being the villainous plot from a pulp novel to a shiny public-relations outreach overnight. Posters pasted on walls across the city screamed out for volunteers to help fill the ranks of a new Public Enhancement Program. The idea of PEP was that citizens could take part in trials for the government, with the potential to obtain powers like those of The Lords. The fine print was the stuff of nightmares, but I imagine 99.9 percent of the people skipped right past it.

The press touted it as a chance to empower the people of the Territories and bring about a new era of innovation and pride. A new Lord, a new attitude. Knowing the origins of the program, it all just made me nauseous.

Record numbers turned out, finally dying down after about a week. Many were turned away for not fitting the genetic profile Doctor Frank had developed. Others made it through, hoping to find glory, praying not to die.

It felt like a lot of them saw this as a path to personal fulfillment. There were no wars left for humans to fight, no achievements yet unachieved. Here was a chance to start over and become one of the gods.

I was present when Sebastian was assured that the tests had been made more humane and that the death statistics were an exaggeration on the part of the lab's legal team. I didn't buy it from Frank. He wasn't the type to let truth get in the way of progress.

I was glad to be leaving, having finally filed the last chapter of the last volume of Lord Nathaniel's life. I hadn't added anything about Regenesis. I wasn't ready to.

When I mentioned my departure to Lord Sebastian, he asked me to stay until a new biographer could be found. I agreed without really knowing why I was doing so.

Unfortunately, my job included watching Doctor Frank emotionlessly choose candidates for test batches, sorting people into groups based on how fat or thin they were, their gender or hair color, poking and prodding in different places without even looking up from his clipboard. I supposed dehumanizing the subjects was how a person might choose to get through something as horrific as this.

In the few early sessions I was privy to, just about every third batch of participants exposed to the spores ended with a death. Doctor Frank would call for the living to exit to the exam rooms, motion for the body to be swept out one side of the room and wait for the room to be sanitized for the next group, which he greeted as clinically as possible.

Sebastian quickly realized he didn't want me to document everything that was happening. This clearly wasn't going to be a bright spot in the program's story. While it was clear that Dr. Frank had meant what he'd said about improving the process, the mortality rate was still noticeable.

Soon after I was barred from the lab, the program's first triumph was announced. The spores had successfully bonded with Monica Salinas, an average eighteen-year-old girl from the suburbs of Dallas. Her vital signs were good, and she had already slipped into the coma during which the spores would hopefully integrate fully with her body.

The oddity of cheering for the fact that a teenager fell into a coma was not lost on me.

The day after Monica woke from her hibernation, I was granted an interview with her. She was nice, but a little flighty and sheltered. Most of my questions were answered in one or two words before she began remarking on someone or something that had caught her ever-shifting eye. She wasn't stupid, but it took some digging to figure that out.

Sebastian had seemed more distant since the relaunch of Regenesis, so most of what I learned about policy came from piecing together bits of gossip. It was clear the new Lord felt he needed to place his personal stamp on our country. The program was the first step, and now he and his entourage had begun to plan the future of the Territories.

Two days after our interview, Monica suddenly caught fire. And she was just fine. She didn't get the range of powers of The Lords or their children, but she could create and channel flame. It seemed to energize Sebastian, and in a rare one-on-one, he spoke with great enthusiasm about the development and the fact that it was just the start of giving power back to the people.

The obstacle Doctor Frank had been slamming against was the randomness of the results. Trying to stabilize this and vary that just led to outcomes that could have been drawn from a hat. With Monica, they had a real, seemingly permanent bonding to examine. They could finally see what made a success instead of what made a failure.

Sebastian assured me that the deaths were now a thing of the past and that the lab felt it was close to a cure for what had killed Lord Nathaniel. "This," he said with a look of seriousness, "is what's going to set the tone for my entire reign. You see, Simone?"

He had already been celebrating and was a bit loose, so I just agreed with him politely, apologized for taking up so much of his time, and saw myself out. I wasn't sure where things were going, but I still didn't feel like cheering for Regenesis.

Soon, of course, we began hearing of more successes, although most of the details remained a mystery, the PR machine still churning on Monica's miraculous transformation. I don't know if it was simply that she was the first success or part of a playbook, but the focus never shifted during the introductory phase. She was the face of a program that promised power to ordinary people. She got pretty popular pretty fast.

Sebastian gave a speech once the press blitz started to die down. He was different from the Sebastian who seemed to sulk in his plane seat. He was more focused, more confident. He promised that the time of gods was over, and that it was time to give the people a taste of real power. Citizens who successfully completed the Regenesis program and to whom the spores attached would serve a three-year tour of duty in America's military, paying back the government's investment with domestic service.

The end of the speech, however, took everyone by surprise, judging by the audible gasp, and it caused me to momentarily choke on a sip of water. On territory-wide television, Sebastian announced that Monica Salinas was to be the first queen of America.

It made sense as a PR stunt: marry the common girl to the young Lord. What better way to connect two worlds? If the marketing machine really wanted the idea of the throne sharing its power to take hold, how better to express it than through marriage? That Sebastian went along with the whole thing speaks to his belief in the bigger strategy, whatever that was.

I knew they had barely met or spoken. This marriage, whether Monica realized it or not, was transactional. I thought back to the first queen of The Lords, long since forgotten alongside all the faceless women who birthed heirs. I wondered if Monica, given her power, could actually live to see her child.

Now that she'd been coached for the spotlight, I was given greater access to the soon-to-be queen. She was reserved and had learned to dodge a question skillfully, tangling her long, dark hair around her finger and then releasing it, over and over again. It was infuriating. I tried to remember that she had just been thrust into this world. She was ecstatic about marrying Sebastian, although that seemed to have more to do with the rise in station it promised than actual love.

As I said, she wasn't the only one who had come through the treatments successfully, and we were told regularly that these other individuals were all being thoroughly monitored and trained in the use of their powers. Except for Monica, whose training was put on hold to allow for personal appearances. While it seemed a little shortsighted, she was about to be royalty. I imagined that got her out of the military obligation.

Chapter 9

The wedding was rushed, the government seeking to keep America so preoccupied in the whirlwind of events that certain questions might not be asked. Press releases to other countries touted it as the grandest event of the year, but on the ground, planners were fighting the clock.

I had attempted to keep tabs on both the progress of Regenesis and legislative affairs, but it had been requested that I record every detail of the wedding preparations. I no longer saw bride or groom, but I can still tell you exactly how many eggs were in the many cakes: 532.

I admit to feeling a slight flicker of relief when my invitation arrived. Having felt out of the loop, I wasn't sure it was coming. The whole affair would be recorded by TV stations around the world, so it wouldn't be too difficult to write up later, even without a biographer. I was to be seated very near the front on the groom's side; my vanity swelled a bit over my prominence. Right in front, where everyone could see me. Stan would have fainted.

When I woke on the morning of the wedding, the sun hit my eyes like a warning, telling me to go back to bed. The brightness began to sink in as I lay there, though, and then panic set in. My alarm had failed to go off, which meant I was already running late for the ceremony. Lord Sebastian had opted not to grant me entry to the wedding day preparations, preferring to keep them private, so if I could get to the ceremony quickly, I thought, my tardiness might go unnoticed, assuming that, like all weddings, this one was thrown off schedule somehow.

Luckily, I had laid out my new dress and shoes the night before. I was ready in record time, but it was soon clear that this wedding was the exception that proved the rule. The public park that had been chosen for the event had a parking lot on either side. The middle section, where the wedding was, had transformed into a dazzling array of tasteful décor, grand topiaries, and row upon row of white seats. Already filled seats.

The parking lot I was making my way through was on the opposite side of the grounds from my spot, leading me instead to the bride's side of the audience. The bride and groom were kissing, presumably after saying *I do.*

I began to silently curse myself. If I was going to be here, I needed to stay in Lord Sebastian's good graces. I had now missed his wedding. I decided it was best if I found a spot toward the back, hoping I could pretend to have at least seen the ceremony from afar.

Moving in the direction of the crowd, I heard the start of the post-nuptial fireworks and looked upward before remembering that it was still light out. My head swung back down, and I gazed across the park. In the opposite lot, cars flew through the air, a truck landing loudly on a screaming crowd of people at the very back of the groom's side. Another explosion went off, shaking the earth and sending a ringing sensation through my bones. More cars flew. The devastation was getting closer.

I'm not sure why exactly, but I began to run toward the ceremony. I made it a few steps before a wave of people hit me, knocking me backward even as I heard a third explosion go off, louder than the ones before. I struggled to get back up, but panicked feet kicked at my sides, and I eventually had to give up and shield my head with my hands, rolled up in a ball like a pill bug, knowing I was about to be trampled to death.

I felt a surge of panic inside of me and heard myself yelling for help. I couldn't breathe. When I opened my eyes, I saw flashes of light, of legs, of people. I could hear screams, but they were mostly drowned out by an intense ringing.

The fourth explosion went off, and it felt like it had done so directly beneath me. The ground lurched, throwing the crowd around me in all directions. My body felt uneven, shaky, but I knew that I had to take the opportunity to get up before they did. I managed it, aching, finally getting a look at what had happened while I was down.

The ceremony was a warzone. Wedding guests had been blown in every direction, parts of them strewn across chairs and floral arrangements. Blood had saturated the ground, giving it a dark, unnatural hue. The couple themselves were on stage, Sebastian shielding his bride with his body and Monica almost catatonic.

Looking at where I had been scheduled to sit, I saw pieces of a car, pools of blood, and scattered body parts. I felt sick, and then I felt dizzy, the dozens of forceful kicks finally taking their toll. The noise was deafening, not in its intensity, but in its circumference. No matter which direction I faced, all I could hear was panic, fear, and sorrow. I remember thinking that I should have just gone back to bed. *Always listen to the sun*, someone said somewhere.

"Simone?" A voice cut through the barrage of sound. It was a familiar voice, nice. Even as my head began to swim, I wondered who that voice belonged to, and then everything went black.

When I woke, I was in the royal wing of the hospital, catching a nurse by surprise. She told me I had suffered a concussion, broken ribs, and had plenty of bruises and cuts. Luckily, she also had pain medication for me, because in the few minutes I'd been awake, I started to feel every injury she'd just described.

After pointing vigorously at the mid-death face on the far end of the pain chart, the haze of the meds came on quickly, dulling my senses and pushing my injuries far away. I asked her to put on the news before she left, and she clicked the TV on.

"You try not to worry about all of that, darlin,'" she said on her way out the door. "Just be thankful you got out alive and focus on healin.'"

Now I was even more curious as to what had happened. The station had clearly settled into what was going to be a long stretch of news about the bombing. I saw film of the attack taken by the official videographers, who had stationary cameras strategically planted throughout the venue. It was even more devastating than I realized. I had seen cars flying, but along with what I'd seen, dozens more had been sent airborne, killing well-wishers on all sides of the ceremony. When they began showing guests torn apart and vaulted through the air, I turned away.

Sebastian and his bride were alive and well, seeming to have foiled the attacker's plans. In fact, a lot of footage showed Sebastian helping first responders. He was being applauded as a strong leader in trying times. It seemed times were becoming trying even faster than Lord Nathaniel predicted.

Although facts were still coming in, gossip from government sources pointed to the Russians. I had trouble picturing Lord Viktor, the Iron Bear, the gentle giant, ordering an attack on the wedding of Lord Nathaniel's son. And even if he had the desire, he would have made the attack himself as a point of pride. It didn't add up.

As information kept coming in, though, it appeared more and more damning. The forensics team had determined that the explosive was a matrushka bomb, an insidious device, used mostly by Russian terrorist groups, that functions like a self-opening nesting doll. Inside the first explosive is a second explosive, which is propelled forward by the original detonation. Inside the second explosive is a third explosive, and so on and so forth, each explosive smaller in size but more devastating in power than the previous one.

The final death toll was also released. In total, 364 people had been killed and over 500 were injured. This included a lot of government officials and prominent citizens. The entire territory was afraid. This sort of violence was a thing of the past, a horror of history.

When Sebastian appeared on TV to announce that not only was the bomb Russian in origin, but that he had also received verification it had been sent by the Bears to look like a civilian terrorist attack (which were extremely rare but not unheard of), people flipped out. Even though the Bear and Nathaniel had become fast friends, legend still held Viktor up as the epitome of power and rage. And with Nathaniel gone, what was there to hold all that anger in check?

I was only in the hospital for a few days, but by the time I had hobbled my way back to the palace, every bit of me still bandaged and in pain, Lord Sebastian's entourage had fully closed ranks around our leader. He was all but inaccessible to me except at official events, where he was quickly ushered away when I made any inquiries.

I did attempt to tail my way into a council meeting soon after my return, trying to look like part of the crowd heading into the room. One foot out the door, and I still couldn't handle not knowing what was happening. This was a pivotal moment for the new Lord, and even if I wouldn't be chronicling his life forever, I was still around until Sebastian let me go.

When a guard stopped me, Jason Samson waved him away, giving me a little wink. I wasn't sure if he was flirting with me or just making sure I noticed the favor, but I was confused regardless.

At the table, the court's longest-serving advisers counseled renewing alliances with other countries that might assist in retaliation efforts, but the young guns, led by Samson, favored a more unilateral approach. Their solution was so unexpected that I thought for a moment it might be a joke. To my dismay, and the dismay of many of the most senior advisers, it wasn't.

It was something unheard of in modern times: sending in the civilian military as a sign that the people of America were taking a stand. The Regenesis successes would be on hand along with a camera crew to make sure the whole world saw it. It was time the people caught in the crossfire had their chance at exacting justice, they reasoned.

"And how do you expect them to survive the royal family?" one of the counselors growled.

Samson claimed to have sources who could verify that Lord Viktor's body was in the final stages of decay. Having seen what it did to Nathaniel, I shuddered, remembering the kindness the old Bear had shown me on my visit.

"His children will be tied up in Moscow with their father. If we can quietly take this village," he said as he marked a spot on a map that had appeared on the video screen, "then we can claim a symbolic victory."

I felt an awkward hush go through the room as many people averted their gaze from Lord Sebastian. Jefferson, one of Nathaniel's most trusted advisers, was the first to respond, his confusion clear. "And then what? Do we just plant our flag and wait for the Bear's children to come reclaim their land? What is the purpose?"

Samson gave a silent half laugh, his head cocked condescendingly. "That first wave is just for show. It's a sign that the people of America aren't going to be collateral damage in a war between gods. We do it while we know we have the element of surprise. The Regenesis freaks—apologies, my Lord—come in with the press, and then the British royal family flies in and takes over the assault. Short, sweet, and we control the message: The reign of Lord Sebastian is all about the little guy, the common man. Bam!"

"I'm sorry," Jefferson shot back, "are you suggesting there will also be bombing?"

"No," Samson said, his face a little red, "I just mean, you know, it's so easy to make this work, it's going to be, like *bam!*" He made the mistake of half-heartedly making an explosion gesture with his hands.

I was finding it hard to keep my mouth shut, but although Jefferson had been cowed for the moment by Samson's idiocy, Matthew Travis spoke up. "I'm sorry, but I fail to see the reward of shipping our emergency-services force and a handful of untrained lab rats into a situation in which they will be ridiculously overpowered. If the Brits are willing to help us, why would we not start there? Or, and forgive me, my Lord, but wouldn't it be keeping with protocol for you to make a personal visit and resolve the situation?"

"Resolve the situation?" Samson shot back. "They killed hundreds of people. The resolution isn't going to come from a visit. We are the only people in the world who have cracked the superpower code. We need to make sure they know what that means. That we're ready to take them on."

"And then have the Brits actually do that," Travis said flatly, "since we're not actually ready to take them on."

"Well, sure. Did you have another idea? We have to get our country up and running again. The people need to see Lord Sebastian here, safe and watching over them. Our *lab rats*," Samson air-quoted, "need to become household names, but yes, we have to make sure Russia is dealt with too. That's like four birds with two stones."

"I'm sorry," an adviser jumped in, "it is the Lord's duty to his people to address these issues directly with other rulers. It's one of the key resolution points in Lord Nathaniel's own nonaggression pact with the other Lords."

"I'd remind you," Samson said in his teaching voice, "that *our* Lord is not one of *The* Lords, nor is he Lord Nathaniel. In fact, he has serious issues with portions of the nonaggression pact but was respectful enough not to bring them up during his noble father's reign."

Maybe that's why he was always sulking? I thought to myself.

"Fine," another broke in, partly to save his friend, "why risk the citizens our Lord so publicly stands for in an effort that's just for show?"

"We're in new territory here. Sebastian has no heir, and if anything should happen to him, America is up for grabs. The people are worried enough about his well-being without sending him to war. But," Samson seethed, "regardless of who's cleaning up this mess, the Russians need to know—the world needs to know—that we were first on the ground."

"Let's say you're right about the Bear's condition. What if you're wrong about the whereabouts of his children?" Travis said, clearly trying to steer around the roadblock.

"They will be at their father's side," Lord Sebastian said, his entrance into the conversation startling us all. "I can assure you of that."

"Forgive me, my Lord," Travis responded deferentially, "but at the speed they travel, once word gets to them, they'll be on our people in a literal heartbeat. And they could wipe out our army just as quickly."

"Lord Sebastian and I have discussed this thoroughly," Samson answered, Sebastian sitting back in his seat, once again an observer of the proceedings. "We've devised a number of different ways to prevent royal intervention. We'll be jamming all radio signals out of the area as soon as the siege begins, timing it so that Moscow won't notice the break in communications until after the village is secured. Along with that, aerial drones will be flown into Russia, causing airspace alarms to trigger in a way targeted to divide local response. There will be other diversionary tactics initiated as well.

Travis had murder in his eyes, but he reclined in his seat. This wasn't a debate, it was becoming clear, but just an introduction to a plan already in progress.

"My Lord," Travis addressed Sebastian directly, "I beg of you, don't put your citizens in harm's way for the sake of appearance, particularly given our recent tragedies."

65

Sebastian cleared his throat. "This is how they will heal. Regenesis is a success. The common man can move up the evolutionary ladder once again. They need to see these symbols of hope fire the return blow. I swear to you, Matthew, we have done everything in our power to ensure the safety of this mission. I have so much faith that I've asked my wife to personally lead the Regenesis team."

I heard a few gasps, and Travis just sank into his seat, giving up entirely in the face of madness. I thought of Monica, completely untrained and immature, and I felt a rumble in my gut.

"We're going to call them The Guardians," Samson told us. "We've already got action figures, video games, a cartoon, you-name-it in the works. We're making sure America knows who its true heroes are."

"Of course," he continued, "our military forces will have already gained control of the village by the time The Guardians arrive. Then we'll get the press set up to record the victory and get everybody out in a jiff."

I didn't share the confidence of Samson or Sebastian, but I also hadn't seen the other successes of the program. While there might have been posters at the ready, the public had yet to get a glimpse of anyone aside from Monica. Maybe there was some real power waiting in the wings.

"And to make sure we get all the vivid details," Samson said, his puckish eyes and devil's smile aimed at me, "two cameramen and the royal biographer will accompany The Guardians."

I could feel the blood leave my face as I looked toward Sebastian, who turned away when my eyes hit his. Nathaniel's last words came back to me, and I began to weigh my options, tuning out the rest of the room, lost in a swirl of confusion and terror.

Chapter 10

I left the meeting in a daze and got back home on autopilot. Panic gripped me, and paranoia set in. Not only had Sebastian cut off almost all my access to him after asking me to stay on long enough, apparently, to be sent to war, but my seat at his wedding was left a bloody pit of carnage. I knew that last part was probably just a tragic coincidence, but I was willing to accept it as part of a larger plot.

I pulled out a suitcase and began to pack my things, still a relatively simple chore. I was so used to being poor that I hoarded money, so living light was second nature. As I finished getting everything together, someone knocked on the door. Cursing the bad timing, I stowed the bag under my bed and went to greet my visitor.

That Sebastian was on the other side of the door was truly a surprise. The royal wasn't a regular in the staff dorms. He looked me in the eye and asked politely if he could come in.

I was momentarily ashamed of the size of my efficiency apartment. I could easily afford a larger unit, but having lived in a broom closet before, it felt wasteful. I gave him the kitchen chair and sat in my desk chair, its bad leg wobbling awkwardly under my weight.

"I know you don't want to go," he said to me, his eyes linking to mine again, "but I need you to go. This should be recorded, warts and all. Future generations can decide whether it was right or wrong. I also, well, I hoped you'd keep an eye on Monica."

He sounded sincere, but it still felt like madness.

"Why do this at all, though?" I asked, trying to remember who was sitting in my kitchen/dining/living/bedroom. "I understand the concerns over your safety, but shouldn't you still live up to the terms of the pact? Won't this just put you at odds with the other six territories? That doesn't sound like it's going to make us safer."

He sat back for a moment, taking in the long string of thoughts.

"I think I need to do what's right here," he replied. "I think the other territories will overlook some aspects of this, given my unique circumstance, but the people—our people—gaining confidence that they can be part of the fight? That they can make a difference? That's what's going to make this a true success."

"But shouldn't you at least talk to the Russians before you do this?"

"They'll just return the courtesy with lies. Soon, this world will be led by my generation," he said in a determined voice, "and we have to make sure America is seen as strong. And we're only as strong as our people."

"Why send Monica, though?" I asked, trying to keep my voice calmer than I felt. "Why not just keep her here and out of harm's way? If the people are concerned about your safety, surely the queen should also be protected."

"Simone, you've seen how the PR team sold the program. She's the figurehead. They didn't expect any of this to happen, but they haven't built up anyone else. If she's not the one out there leading the team, there's nothing linking The Guardians' name to Regenesis."

"That's marketing!" I blurted out, struggling to maintain sanity in the face of his rationale. "She's your wife! You're our ruler! You're supposed to do what's best for your people."

"I understand your frustration," Sebastian said, maintaining his composure in the face of my familiarity, "but, you've been part of this government long enough to know public opinion is the best defense we have. We have to solidify the territory if we're to survive."

"And if the decoys don't work? If we come face to face with Anna and the Terrors?"

"You haven't met our full team yet, but I think you'll feel more comfortable once you have. There are some impressive individuals going on this trip. Also, you've met Anna. Did she seem terribly dangerous to you?"

"It was a short chat," I replied grimly. "I wouldn't call her friendly."

"That's fair," he snickered. "You have my guarantee that you will return here, to your home and your life, unharmed."

"Why the concern about the queen then?" I pressed.

"Please use your usual discretion," he said candidly, "but Monica's had troubles since the wedding, PTSD issues. Her entire family was crushed in front of us by a station wagon. Her personal nurse will be going with you, but I would just feel better knowing you were keeping a watch too."

I nodded. It was understandable that Monica would be having issues after the attack. The fact that he was sending her into a war zone made me want to jump up and down and yell at him. There was no merit to debate, though. Minds were made up. Plans were in motion.

He thanked me and left the room. I pulled my bag out from under the bed and tried to go over everything one last time. I was about to go into a war zone with a group of amateur superheroes, led by someone whose PTSD nurse has to accompany her everywhere she goes. I sighed and pulled my toothbrush and other must-haves from the bag, pushing it back under the bed afterward. I was as packed for Russia as I was packed for running away.

My curiosity over the rest of these Guardians had gotten the best of me, and I did feel better after Sebastian's visit, mostly just because he felt he had to explain himself. Where could I run that I wouldn't be found anyway? And where else did I have to go?

Chapter 11

The palace, which had been part of my everyday life, became an inhospitable place. Uncertainty had settled in its halls. Now that I was part of the ground team, though, I was granted more extensive access to the lab and my new teammates, so I decided to avoid the palace and get to know the people with whom I would soon invade Russia.

Keeping my mind focused on the story around me helped make that whole scenario seem less real, and it had the side benefit of making sure I was informed. This, I thought, might be the most helpful thing for me once we landed on the shores of the Russian Territories. Taking human soldiers into the territory of another member of The Lords was risking disaster, but landing a ship of untrained superhumans and low-level journalists to bask in the post-victory glow was courting it.

Even worse was that I would be one of only four people there with neither training nor powers. If knowledge of the people around me was going to be a weapon, I would need to forge it myself. After practically begging Doctor Frank, I received one-on-one interviews with each member of the Guardians, as well as observer status at some of their training sessions.

There were thirteen Guardians. Each of them had been given a clever nickname by the PR people. So far, these codenames were the only information revealed, with promotional messages promising more soon. The people loved it. Of course, they didn't know that plans were already underway to send their unseen idols to Russia.

It probably wouldn't have mattered. Americans were afraid but also angry. We had been attacked physically and symbolically, and as often happens, fiery rhetoric overtook common sense. The resulting swell of patriotic frenzy made it clear that people were ready for any solution, so long as our attackers paid.

Having resigned myself to the situation, I got everything ready for my first day of interviews and training observations. I was given some statistics on the program beforehand, which just had the same information already released to the press.

The number of volunteers who had ultimately been selected for Regenesis was, statistically speaking, very small. While they unsurprisingly didn't go into mortality rates, the number of bondings was low, and most survivors of the process seemed unchanged. Of those who showed genetic enhancements, according to the sheet, only the thirteen who were now The Guardians survived the onset of their powers.

I pressed Doctor Frank further about those who died after the bonding process, and he related to me tales of two men exploding and one woman melting to the bone. I quickly reined in my inquisitiveness, already knowing my sleep would be uneasy.

When my first interviewee came through the door, I felt a little relief. I had spoken with many volunteers in line during the initial selection, and I remembered this guy well.

Kevin Smalls had been stuck with the codename Atmos. He could have cared less what they wanted to name him, and from his personality, I gathered that was how he felt about most things. A tall, lithe surfer in his early twenties, Kevin's short, shaggy, blond hair and California-dude attitude almost completely masked his Midwestern upbringing. He seemed genuinely carefree.

Kevin had entered the program because he didn't know what else to do. Interested in everything but enthralled by little, he was constantly searching for something. The costume they had given him was not that thing. Its sky-blue color gently screamed *Easter*, and it fit like a tablecloth, belted and cinched to create something resembling a shape.

A sharp V opened his sleeveless top to the beltline, with the "pants" hanging from the thick black belt in a cascade that ballooned out to the ends, which were tucked into a pair of standard-issue army boots. This was all topped off with old-fashioned aviator goggles.

Kevin looked mortified with it on, a justifiable reaction. Luckily, his powers more than made up for the outfit. He could control the wind.

He could pull up strong gusts, create small funnel clouds, and had even learned to ride the currents, allowing him to surf the sky as easily as he did water. Hearing about his abilities was encouraging; watching him train was less so.

It wasn't Kevin's fault, mind you. Things were happening so quickly that there was no way for The Guardians to fully understand their powers before we shipped out. Regardless of potential, inexperience was our Achilles' heel.

While trying to knock over a cardboard box on a table without disturbing any of the carefully placed objects near it, Kevin blew the entire table to sawdust, also destroying the reinforced protective wall at the back of the lab, recently placed there after he destroyed the original wall.

His targeting was as questionable as his control, and during one test, his own winds spun him 180 degrees and sent three lab technicians flying into a concrete wall. It was like he was trying to adjust to the kick of a gun, so far unsuccessfully.

The worries Kevin raised were only heightened by Madeline Brown, a petite woman of twenty-four. Her short bob and cherubic face gave her the appearance of a woman two decades older, and her eyes were constantly pleading for love. In our interview, she told me that she had joined the program after her husband left her to marry her sister. This was her chance to start over, she hoped.

Codenamed Hypnos, Madeline was an enthusiastically sweet woman who was also extremely dull. It seemed almost a cruel joke that her power was to make people fall asleep, which is, in theory, an incredibly useful ability. Unfortunately, Maggie's struggles with control and targeting were even greater than Kevin's. She could knock out everyone for three hundred feet in front of her, or she could put everyone in a four-mile radius to sleep. There was really no way of knowing until it was done.

If this was meant to be an empowering victory for Maggie, the costumers had seen fit to make it an uphill battle. Her pink leotard created imperfections where none existed, and the swirling black hypnosis patterns covering it broke at weird angles, leaving misshapen blobs dotting the outfit. Her golden boots and sashlike belt wailed against the pink, blinding in their intensity.

I was depressed once Madeline left. So far, I hadn't exactly seen the power Lord Sebastian had alluded to. I just hoped the next Guardian was better than the last.

When she walked in, I knew I knew her, but I couldn't place it. Her eyes lit up too, seemingly playing the same internal memory game. And then it clicked.

"Lucille?" I asked, knowing that, yes, her name was Lucille Hawkins.

"Simone?"

It was her, I realized. This was my last real friend in the orphanage before Peter came along. I had a hard time when she left, and it wasn't made any better by the fact that I never heard from her again. I wasn't entirely sure how to feel about that. It appeared I wasn't alone.

"So, this is weird," she said, scratching the back of her head.

"Yeah," I replied. "How have you been?"

"Good," she said. "I've been pretty good. You?"

"Yeah," I said, watching the conversation awkwardly crumble before my eyes. "Thanks for asking. Sorry to rush into this, but we should start the interview. We have to be at training soon."

"Of course," she said with relief. We sat down, me trying to stick to the checklist of need-to-knows before finally giving in and veering into more personal territory. As it turns out, Lucille's new family had started her in pageants and modeling soon after she was adopted. It was easy to see why.

Statuesque with flawless features, she was stunning by any standard, and that beauty had started to make a name for her in the business. She was working and traveling, her parents rooting her on the whole time. And then she went to one shoot alone at the age of fifteen and had to fend off a handsy photographer, one with the influence to end careers.

Blacklisted by sixteen, she went back to a normal teenage life. Her parents had become colder, though, like she'd done something wrong. She spent months trying to make it up to them, and when they were killed in a car accident, she couldn't help but feel responsible for that too.

As it turned out, her parents needed her modeling money to pay off massive debt, a problem inherited by Lucille. With no career to turn to and no family, she tried various classes and programs before signing up for Regenesis, hoping that success could get things turned around.

Her power to turn invisible led the PR team to dub her Stealth. She could also turn other people or objects invisible, so long as she was in contact with them. While she did her best to make her bright-red fifties-style dress and white belt and gloves modern, the promotional posters she offered a prerelease peek at traded on American wholesomeness, her half-visible beauty holding out an apple pie just begging to be eaten. At least she had easily mastered her skill.

That meant she could hide me.

We hugged when she left, promising to see each other soon, which this time I knew was the truth. The coincidence was startling, but once the shock and sudden feelings of abandonment wore off, I found myself relieved to have someone I knew going with me. It was actually pretty terrible of me, given that where we were going together was to war, but there it was.

My last interview of the day was with a girl I had spoken with at the recruitment center. Veronica George was outwardly what you might expect of an angry teenage girl: plenty of tattoos and piercings, tank top half-tucked into tight, ripped jeans, themselves tucked into old army-surplus boots. Her shaved head added some panache.

When I spoke with her, I hadn't been sure what to expect. Emotional and irrational girl or wiser, jaded woman? As it turned out, she was a little of both: forthright, intelligent, and charming with a quick wit, but she also had a hair trigger on subjects she was passionate about.

The Veronica I met now made me want to run. They had named her Arachne, a name borne out by her new look. Her hair had grown to a length that should have taken years, and while I don't know what it had looked like before, it was hard to imagine it as the shock-white mass that now fell past her face like a shroud. She was ashen, sickly, and her yellow eyes beamed from their dark sockets.

Seemingly, even the PR people wanted as little to do with her as possible. They had positioned her as a wise old sorceress, thrown a forest-green robe on her, and shot all her promos from a distance. Admittedly, it was the most successful costume I'd seen so far.

If Veronica had become creepy on the outside, her powers suggested the transformation had deeper roots. When I first watched her train, I was positioned behind a special booth, wearing boots with soles of a lab-made material. I was assured that the boots for the invasion would include the same soles, though at the time I didn't know why. I began to get nervous when a cage full of rats was brought into the room. There were dozens of them, crawling across one another in search of a way out.

The scientists cued Veronica to begin, and as I watched, tendrils shot from her fingertips. They pushed into the ground, twirling and twisting with life. Their electric blue drained every other color from the room, and Veronica's eyes glowed the same hue. One of the scientists, noticing where my attention had gone, tapped me on the shoulder and pointed to the ground.

The tendrils had shot up from below the earth near the cage, and the rats were entangled in the crawling vines, which seemed to skillfully hunt their prey. The tiny screams were barely overpowered by the electric crackling coming from Veronica, now surrounded by an aura of blue.

As the writhing energy withdrew from the cage and returned to Veronica's body, the crackling began to subside. Veronica seemed dazed, but she looked somehow healthier. One of the scientists brought in a dog with an obviously painful leg injury. I prepared for the worst as I saw the worms leave Veronica's body again and encase the dog's leg, but in a few moments, she recalled them, and the dog, as energetic as a puppy, got up and ran to its handler.

And now I was even more confused. When I asked about the shoes, the guy who guided my eyes to the rats earlier told me the soles were the only substance they'd found that blocked her powers. When I asked if they were necessary since we were on the same team, he asked if I had seen many of The Guardians train yet.

Chapter 12

Considering the insanity of the situation, I decided to try to go into my second day of interviews in a glass-half-full mood. Optimism was the name of the game, and today was when I would see the superstars.

I began with Francine Teller, a twenty-year-old accounting major whose knowledge extended to knitting and kitten rescue. I managed to veer the conversation to more applicable questions, but it was difficult to get a word out of her once we left her limited comfort zone.

In her *before* picture, her long, dark hair made her look even younger than she was, but now it was short, a spiked patch of pure white that gave her an undeniable intensity. They were calling her Frost.

She had gotten off easy on the outfit. A fitted gray jumpsuit, tailored through the waist but slackened just enough in the legs to keep the shape while blurring the definition. The goggles she wore hid her eyes completely, and I found myself almost intimidated until she removed them, her naked gaze betraying inexperience and fear.

Francine's power let her draw moisture from the air and freeze it in an instant, creating ice projectiles or shields out of thin air. It's the kind of power that's invaluable in both combat and defense.

During her first training session, she accidentally drained all of the water from one of the staff. Understandably, Francine was having trouble letting go of that mistake, and it showed. Instead of controlling her power, she was letting it control her, creating a cycle of self-doubt.

From what I was told, she had finally stopped freezing her trainers to the floor during each session, but now the projectiles she created were firing off randomly, endangering everyone in the room.

I started to temper the day's expectations. It was a rude awakening, but if I was going to hit rock bottom, might as well start there.

My next interviewee, Shondra Collins, aka Quills, was more optimistic than I was. But then again, she was used to dealing with strange people. A certified genius who became the youngest licensed psychiatrist in America at the age of twenty-three, she was different from most of the others in the program. She wasn't adrift or depressed. She was curious.

Before Regenesis, Shondra was five-foot-one, her face smeared and twisted by burns suffered as a child. Now, she was six-foot-three with unblemished skin. But beyond that miracle, another remarkable change had taken place. Her skin was covered with an almost-invisible layer of silky soft hair. When she willed it, these hairs raised and became stiff, firing off from her body in the direction she willed. Mostly. She was getting there.

The quills released a toxin that tranquilized their targets. Her agility and speed had also been increased, but somehow the confluence of all of these changes had made things more difficult instead of less. Unsure how to compensate for her swifter gait, she would reliably overestimate or underestimate when firing. She had, luckily, learned quickly how to fire only some of her projectiles instead of all, which was a problem that had caused quite a stir at her first training session.

The hairs grew back within minutes, automatically reloading her body's defenses. The costume they had put Shondra in made me cringe. I understood that her ability required a larger portion of her body to be uncovered, but the leotard was little more than a revealing purple negligee.

When I asked her about the outfit, it bothered me less. "I've spent most of my life being pitied and turned away from," she told me. "I don't condone objectification, but I'd be lying if I said I hadn't always wondered what that attention was like. I'm giving it another week, probably."

While I don't think my next subject, Pearl North, had ever cared much whether anyone thought she was pretty, what she had become made the point moot. There was no one, literally no one, who didn't think she was beautiful. Codenamed Aphrodite, she lived up to the legendary beauty of the goddess in every way. Whenever you looked at her, whoever you were, she became your ideal. In person. In pictures. On video.

No one could really decide whether she changed to suit them or their tastes changed when they saw her, but she could control anyone just by being in the same room. It actually wasn't that much of a shift for her. She already owned the world as far as she was concerned, and the rest of us could get with the program or get going.

The PR folks put her in a pink vinyl jumpsuit and called it a day, knowing everyone would think she'd look perfect no matter what she was wearing.

Her training was revealing things both good and bad. She could extend the range of her mental control while out of sight by firing a pheromone-based psychedelic gas from her body. Anyone who breathed in the gas would experience euphoria and feel a complete devotion to Pearl. She had started to get her range and targeting refined, but she had work to do.

Range, control, targeting. These continued to be common complaints, which was unsurprising given that we were testing weapons as much as we were testing people. And not new variations on old weapons, but brand-new weapons we didn't even design.

My next teammate was the one who made me the most uncomfortable. Brent Hamon was a ten-year-old boy, which means he was anxious, impatient, eager, tempestuous, and every other thing a ten-year-old boy should be. He was also a genius, enough so that Doctor Frank would sometimes ask his opinion on experiments. They obviously went with the codename Prodigy.

Unfortunately, Brent's intelligence stemmed from a series of brain tumors. He was given less than a year to live, and it's the only reason I can imagine they okayed a child for Regenesis. Of course, making a kid into a superhero is one thing, but dropping him into the middle of an actual war zone seemed like something else altogether. And things had already not been easy for Brent since arriving.

Like it had done to Veronica and Shondra, the experiment had changed the kid physically. The tumors in his brain somehow became functioning portions of his mind, unlocking abilities no human had ever unlocked. The price was steep. His head looked like a long, misshapen melon, lumps jutting up from the surface in random spots. His hair was gone, but that hardly mattered since he was rarely without his specially designed headpiece. Aside from providing protection, it helped keep his head aloft, a task made difficult by its sudden increase in mass and shift in balance.

He seemed stronger and more mature during his training sessions than I had anticipated, but the natural childlike self-centeredness and impatience remained. His powers were many. He was a telekinetic, capable of moving entire buildings with a thought if needed. He was also a telepath, which allowed him entry to the minds of everyone around him. He could read your thoughts. He could speak to you through them. And he could control both them and your actions. He frightened me.

Chapter 13

I only had one day of interviews to go and had left my optimism hat at home. I realized that my concerns all focused on my involvement in the first war of the modern era. What began as a small giggle turned into uncontrollable laughter, maniacal but cathartic. I lost myself in the absurdity of the situation, knowing there was no magic fix.

It may have been somewhat startling for my first interview of the day to find me balled up in my chair, breathing quickly as I caught my breath, tears in my eyes, and then breaking into laughter again when I saw the look on his face. I explained as best I could, once I had calmed down, but he just nodded in understanding.

"I've been having little fits for days," he said. "Sometimes it's laughing. Sometimes it's crying. Not sure I really know what to feel."

An office janitor, Jack Rice had just been looking for more respect when he signed up for the program. At thirty-one, he was sick of where he'd landed, having peaked in high school, where he'd gone all-state. Always above academics, he ended up with few options after a drunken dive off a cliff left him permanently sidelined.

His limp had disappeared, though, and now Jack was a man made of water. He was solid, but his features were carved in liquid. A waterfall for a nose, a twisting river for an ear. He was a creature of beauty.

Like Francine, Jack could focus water in the atmosphere and from other sources around him. Instead of ice, though, he was able to fire off tsunami-strength waves and start whirlpools in midair. Like a river, his body moved around obstacles, including weapons. He seemed to be taking to his powers more quickly than some of the others, a Zen-like calm emanating from him even during training sessions. I chalked this up to his past training in sports, but it was definitely helping his progress.

Jack had also killed one of his trainers by dehydration during his first session, but instead of letting the mistake drag him down, he refocused to make sure it didn't happen again. Appropriately codenamed Poseidon, Jack had amazing control of his abilities. This guy finally gave me some hope.

The PR folks wisely didn't attempt to give him a costume, and Jack was gentleman enough to add a few extra waterfalls where needed. They did, however, ask him to carry a trident, which he (and I) clearly regarded as ridiculous.

The next interview was with Sean Michaels, who had been one of the last applicants admitted to Regenesis. I chatted with him briefly when he was in line at the recruitment center, and I remembered noting the charge of energy around him, incapable of deciding if it was infectious or annoying. It was annoying.

The majority of the problem was his flirtatiousness, not threatening or even serious, but definitely not occasional. As he'd been given the codename Caterwaul, I felt I wasn't alone in my analysis of his charms. He was twenty-eight going on twelve.

Sean's laugh when I first met him had been mostly just a full-throated scream. The process had made it worse. Now he could create a highly destructive sonic blast capable of ripping through a steel building just by speaking. Outdoor training facilities were built in a remote corner of the city after his first session pulped seventeen years of paper files waiting to be digitized. He was starting to get better control, able to lessen the strength of the blasts and more finely focus them.

His outfit was a strange arrangement of stripes and patterns, argyle here, pinstripes there, neither rhyme nor reason. Sean seemed pleased with it, though. I was just happy to see him leave for the sake of both my ears and eyes.

Luckily, as soon as Justine Clark entered the room, I knew I liked her. At a youthful fifty-four, she was the oldest person on the team, but while her wise eyes hinted at her years, her attitude, a sharp mix of optimism and venom, read decades younger. Widowed right after her husband's early retirement, she decided it was time to remake herself. Her powers made that reality.

Justine's power was one of the more unbelievable I'd seen. She could alter her shape, size, and even material by willing her molecules to change. Could she change to steel? Check. Concrete? Check. Rubber? Check. Her only limitation so far was in redistribution, so if she increased size in one part of her body to, for instance, form huge fists, the tissue covering her back might become paper thin.

Her trainers were working with her on the problem, but it was a tall order, really concentrating on every single molecule of your body at once. They chose to call her Proteus, and given the nature of her powers, they tried not to give her too much costume. She was able to form some natural armor herself, with deep-blue military-issue protective gear covering any remaining vulnerable spots. For all of her photo shoots, she'd been given the pinup-girl treatment, trying to connect her age with an era that happened long before her birth. Fortunately, she had the confidence to own the look without even trying.

I had already been told that the queen would be unable to meet for an interview or training session prior to our mission, so the next person was the last one. I was still on the fence about the team's capabilities, and while I hoped there wouldn't be the need for a fight, my innate cynicism kept creeping back in. And then everything went pear-shaped.

It was Peter. He was here.

While I had been confused with Lucille, I immediately ran to Peter and hugged him, feeling tears welling in the corners of my eyes. He held a tight grip around me that loosened after a few moments. I backed away, wiping my eyes dry.

"Shall we?" he asked, motioning toward the chairs.

I nodded and sat down. "What happened? Why are you here?" I asked in a frenzy.

"I asked to be here. Finished basic training, saw a boring life waiting for a disaster to happen, and jumped at Regenesis when I had the chance. Now I'm the official military liaison. Not too bad, all things considered, huh?"

I was trying to take it all in. It seemed like too much to happen in the time since we'd parted ways, but then I looked back over my own life. Starting my job here, Stan's death, Nathaniel's death, being put on this team. Everything was happening so quickly.

"Why didn't you get in touch with me?" I asked, suddenly feeling very hurt at the slight.

"Didn't they tell you?" he responded. "I was helping with security at Lord Sebastian's wedding. I had just been brought in that morning for the event. I was the one who found you in the parking lot. I took you to the hospital."

"What?" I said. How could no one have told me? How could I have never thought to ask who saved me? Now I was angry with myself too. I hated that.

"Yeah, I had to start the program the next day, but someone from the council said they'd make sure you knew. Jeremy? Jimmy?"

"Jason Samson?"

"Sounds right. Friend of yours?"

"Something like that," I replied dryly. "Um, I guess we should start, since we only get to talk until your training session starts."

"Ask me anything," he said, flashing the smile I had longed to see, the one that made me feel like I was home.

Peter had been given the name Seismos because he could create tremors and earthquakes. He could basically control the very ground at his feet. Among all of our teammates, we had at least managed to conquer the elements.

It didn't feel like that long since we'd seen each other, but I noticed that Peter's youthful good looks had started to gently mature. His hair still swept in from the side, though, reminding me of the day he'd come to the orphanage. I wanted to run to the roof with him and never come back down.

My excitement over Peter being my last interview was only heightened by his session. He trained like his life depended on it. Peter was concise and focused, his military background giving him a leg up on the others. He could vibrate an item as small as a penny without causing anything else around it to shift, purposely moving it inches over the course of minutes, but he could also deconstruct a tank in seconds just by shaking it at the right points.

He had fared better than most of the others in the costume department, which was admittedly not a difficult task. While the red leather bodysuit they had put him in limited his mobility, it also accentuated Peter's athletic body, more toned than before thanks to military life. Black boots and a black belt pulled everything together. His goggles were state of the art, giving him the ability to zoom in and target just by squinting. I assumed his status as liaison automatically secured him better equipment, and I decided I was fine with that. The others were having enough trouble learning to handle their powers without adding new tech to the mix.

We took a walk after his training, sharing information on our teammates and indulging in some small talk. It was good, comfortable, but the number of questions fighting for answers was almost unbearable. "This all just seems like too much to be a coincidence," I said suddenly, like a crazy person. "First Lucille and now you, out of thirteen people from all over the Territories."

"Is it that surprising to see a bunch of orphans sign up?"

"But considering only thirteen people actually got powers ..."

He hushed me, putting a finger over my lips, which he knew would infuriate me. Normally it would have, but this time it didn't bother me in the least. In fact, it was a comfort. I needed someone to stop my mind from working against me, from making me feel like I was stumbling in the path of destruction.

I saw the surprise in his eyes just before I realized I was starting to cry. He put his arms around me, the park around us devoid of life. It felt good there, finally just letting my thoughts go and feeling my fear, owning it.

When I finally started to come back to reality, I realized that my sudden burst of emotions included happiness and relief that Peter was with me. I began to pull back from him, wanting to stay, but not wanting to make things too weird. I wiped my face with the back of my sleeve and apologized for making a scene.

"You can't make a scene if no one's watching," he said, motioning to the emptiness around us. As if to prove his point, he pulled me back to him and kissed me. Instinctively, I pushed away, more confused than upset.

"Whoa," Peter said. "I'm sorry. Really, Simone. I thought we were having a moment."

"We were," I said like a crazy person. "We are. I just ... we should maybe wait until later. There's a lot of little things to consider. You just got back. We're about to invade Russia."

"Small things," he replied with his trademark smirk.

"Teeny-tiny. I'm still down to hug, though."

He took me back in his arms. The rest of the evening was spent reminiscing about times past. We laughed about how we hid in cabinets while sneaking junk food out of the staff lounge. We commiserated about the living conditions and some of our co-residents. We remembered the people who came and went, the people we never even really knew. We wondered what became of them.

Peter walked me to my door before heading back to his quarters. After hugging goodnight, I shut the door and let myself soak in the warmth of the day, the joy I had found, hoping sunrise wouldn't run it through with a rusty blade, but pretty sure it would.

Chapter 14

When I reported to the lab the next day, I got wind of a mission briefing about to start. Anger over not being told about something this important clouded my thoughts as I power walked my way to the Situation Room. I got there with a little time to spare but ended up plowing through the double-door entry for some reason anyway.

The ruckus meant I was the center of attention, which was particularly exciting because I barely kept from falling flat on my face when I tried to stop. The quiet echoes of conversation lingered conspicuously in the air as heads turned to stare. I could feel my face burn with embarrassment but tried to keep from acknowledging that anything strange had happened.

"Can I help you?" a man in a crisp military uniform asked sharply.

"I heard there was a briefing. I thought, you know, since I'll be on the mission, I should attend," I replied, trying to sound as confident as possible. The man was hard to read.

"Right, you're with the press," he responded.

"Technically, I'm part of the royal staff," I said, trying to mend my ego by puffing it up. "I work directly for Lord Sebastian."

"I'll take responsibility for her, General," I heard a familiar voice break in. Peter had made his way over from the front of the room, where he had been prepping for the presentation.

"You sure about that, Seismos?" the general asked, clearly not enjoying the codenames any more than I did.

"Yes, sir," Peter said. The general just shook his head and walked back down to the front of the room.

"Take a seat," Peter said, "and it's okay if you don't just blindly run into every room like you're about to make a life-or-death announcement."

"We didn't all do basic training," I said with mock sincerity.

He shook his head and gave the hint of a grin before heading back to the front of the room.

Scanning the area, I saw Samson and some of Sebastian's other councilors sitting in a block, and scattered around the room were eleven of the Guardians, the queen apparently not attending and Peter helping with the presentation. It didn't appear that much of a bond had formed outside of training at this point, which could be an issue. I made my way to the seat beside Lucille, who smiled when I sat down.

Before we had the chance to exchange hellos, though, General Fitzgerald, the person who had almost ejected me from the meeting, began to speak, his voice bold and commanding. He made it clear very quickly that while the queen was "in charge," he would be the one calling the shots on the ground. Given that Monica hadn't shown up, there didn't seem to be much reason to voice dissent.

Fitzgerald handed the floor over to Samson. I could feel my eyes begin to roll of their own accord.

"We'll get back to the details of your part in the invasion soon," he oozed. "I want to let you know what kind of support you'll be getting here and what you have to look forward to when you get back."

He started a video presentation that announced the team and the mission with very selective training footage, photo shoot images, and news footage from the wedding bombing. Along with this digital *mood board*, he promised that TV stations were beginning to air specials detailing the softer sides of the nation's newest heroes. Interviews with elementary school teachers and childhood friends would give them life, and tragic stories of childhood loss, be it parent or puppy, could then form full characters. They would be overnight sensations just by virtue of being unavoidable.

"Know that when you return," Samson concluded, "it will be to legions of fans waiting to hear about your adventure, and some very lucrative endorsement deals, I might add." He winked in a way that appeared uncomfortable.

Samson went back to his seat as Fitzgerald returned to the floor, shaking his head at everything he'd just seen and heard. "Ladies and gentlemen," he began, "now that that incredibly vital business is out of the way, why don't we discuss the small side matter of invading Russia."

Lucille gave a quick snicker, prompting a nod of approval from Fitzgerald.

Peter clicked a button, and a holographic map blinked into existence, bathing the room with a green light. It was focused on America and the Russian Territories.

"We'll take a small submersible plane through to this area." He pointed to a coast at the northern part of the Russian mainland. The map switched to a closer overhead view before I could really get a feel for the location, and while history may have been a passion, geography had remained curiously absent from my list of interests and education.

"Now, the real soldiers have already been on their way for quite some time, keeping complete radio silence while holed up in underwater vessels that aren't half as nice or a third as fast as what y'all are gonna be riding in." I began to get a feeling Fitzgerald was not as excited about this mission as the press had led us to believe.

"All we have to do is get there without any of you folks making a sound once we hit the water. Now, we'll make good time until then, but once we hit Russian airspace, we'll need to submerge in order to avoid detection and dampen the sound of the engines, which also means we'll be at a crawl."

"You'll need to remain completely silent during this part of the trip. And when I say completely, I damn well mean completely. I'll kill any of you if you endanger the mission. You just keep that in your head at all times, and we'll be fine," Fitzgerald continued. "When we arrive, Seismos here will assist me in securing the landing site before any of you leave the vessel.

"We have not been given information for any other aspects of this invasion, and aside from one quick communiqué en route, there will be no radio contact with the initial squad. That means we're on our own until we get to the site, and that means you follow every order from me to the letter. I plan to get you there and back alive, but I can't do that if you don't listen to me.

"Since you're all so damn important, they gave us the most direct route. Like most of the world, great swaths of Russia have been changed by terraforming. Our route will take us mostly through thick forests, but don't be surprised if you run across a small desert or snowy mountain range. It all depends on how rich the landowners are. I'll take the lead while Seismos covers the rear."

"Terraforming?" Shondra interrupted, which our fearless commander clearly wasn't expecting.

"Yes," he began, as if speaking to a three-year-old, "it's a process by which land is changed using ..."

"I know what it is," she cut him off, "but it's mostly theoretical. It's not something people can do, much less something they can do on a whim. And it just ... it just doesn't work like that."

"In the wake of this mission," Fitzgerald growled in Samson's direction, "I think we've all been discovering a lot of things. For example, almost all of the territories other than America employ terraforming as a way to produce the goods they need within their own borders. It's a logging area, but you just never know for sure.

"By the time we get to the village, the advance force will have already taken control, at which time we'll enter, get filmed taking credit for what the career soldiers did," he continued, glaring at the council members, "have some nice photos taken, get super-powered reinforcement from Britain's royal family, get back in the boat, and come home. I'm thinking twenty-four hours. Thirty-six tops."

"Excuse me," I said, trying to sound as deferential as possible, "but you think we'll be back within thirty-six hours?"

"Give or take. It's really just a photo op. Keep to your writing, Ms. Smith, and we'll do just fine together."

Fitzgerald's irritation over the whole thing was strangely reassuring. Surely, he would be more worried if we were heading into real danger. Maybe this actually was just a horribly thought-out harmless PR stunt.

After explaining how we would get back to the craft to get home, which turned out to be just going back along the same path we'd already traveled, Fitzgerald ended with the showstopper, "Be back here in two hours in whatever ridiculous thing they're making you wear. We'll start launch preparations at that time. In the meantime, no one is allowed to communicate with anyone outside of the lab or leave the facility. Ms. Smith, a room in the dormitory has been set up for your use."

My eyes felt as though they'd been ripped open, but I could feel my head nodding acknowledgment. Rotating it a bit, I saw the council members gathering their things and chatting, while the rest of my team also seemed agog at the new timeline. It was maddening watching Samson leave without so much as acknowledging his precious Guardians.

After being shown to my room by Lucille, I sat on the edge of the bed, trying to focus my thoughts. For some reason, I kept thinking of Monica, though. I don't know why. Maybe it was just that she was the only one I hadn't seen, spoken with, or watched train during the lead-up to this thing, and she was supposed to be our leader, even if she was just a figurehead.

It was bothering me a bit, mostly because I couldn't help but think there had to be a reason. They had done a photo shoot with her, which I only discovered the day before when I happened upon a row of posters decorating a brick wall. She smoldered at passersby, her white sleeveless dress frayed on a diagonal, the lowest strand hovering a little above the knee. Her hair had been cut short and dyed red, orange, and blonde. It was arranged in a stylishly uneven way that suggested flames, and resting luxuriously in it was her golden tiara, seemingly trying to get noticed while pretending to hide.

She wore a golden belt of round disks slung at an angle, and armlets of the same gold held fabric wings that attached at her back, which echoed the disaster of Kevin's outfit.

There was no denying that Monica looked stunning. She was both sexy and regal, a tricky feat. Even in photographs, though, her eyes seemed lifeless and empty. I wondered how medicated she was, and then I wondered how powerful her ability to create and control flames was.

That Lord Sebastian had personally asked me to watch over her made my mission even more difficult, particularly if she was as fragile as I feared. While I had never felt any particular love from Sebastian, his father's belief in me was a debt rooted in my core, regardless of the atrocities I'd since discovered.

I pulled myself together, brushed my teeth, and took a long, hot shower, knowing it could be a bit before my next. Just as I was putting my robe on, I heard a knock. I had assumed it was Lucille coming to check in, but Peter was on the other side of the door, shoving his way into the room.

"Hey," I said as he pushed me aside and shut the door behind him. "Did you want to come in?"

"Sorry," he said. "There are short windows in each of the halls when the cameras aren't monitoring. I didn't have all day."

"And you just ran that gauntlet why?" I asked.

"Guess I just don't like people knowing everything I do," he said. "Look, I have to get back, but I wanted to apologize for not letting you know when we were shipping out."

It suddenly hit me that he would have already known. Then I slugged him in the shoulder.

"I could have gotten in a ton of trouble," he replied, "and I can't risk not being on this mission."

"First of all, I get it, it's part of your job," I said, "and second, they wouldn't pull you off the team no matter what. You're one of The Guardians."

"Can't risk it," he said, taking a look at his watch and walking back to the door. "Someone's gotta make sure you get through this alive." A soft chuckle, a sly grin, and a quick wink later, he was out the door and down the hall, a spy on a mission.

Chapter 15

I sat for a bit, trying to absorb the fact that I was being sent to war. War was something from history books and movies. It wasn't something that happened now. I reconsidered for a moment my own studies of the past, the emotions the stories had elicited. Now my unerring judgment and incorruptible will, wielded for years from behind a keyboard, were to be road-tested. I sat for a bit longer, running my eyes along a crack in the wall.

Resigned to my fate, I opened the closet, which contained a sleek black suit, as dark as night and as light as a feather. When I put it on, it felt as though I was wearing a thin sheet, but there was something substantial to it still. It came with a brief intro letter indicating it would protect against death from most major weapon types. It did, however, specify that it was not for use against bombs or tank fire, which I found a letdown.

Gathering myself together, I made my way to the meeting room a little early, wanting to make the journey by myself and hoping to chronicle entrances by the key players for my later writing—if I was around to write later, of course. The general and Peter were going over some final preparations when I arrived. They regarded me as I entered but went back to their work immediately.

Jason and a few of the council members who had been at the earlier meeting showed up to see us off, possibly just to make sure we actually left. A little after that, The Guardians began to enter the room, each wearing the uniforms that were, for the most part, unsightly and impractical. I had hoped they would just be for the posters, but it looked like the marketing agency's C-team was going all-in on the identities they'd developed.

Finally, Monica arrived looking far worse than the last time I'd seen her. She was slumped down and distant, a nurse propping her up as she stumbled in. Sebastian followed, seemingly ignorant of his wife's medical condition.

"Okay," Lucille said, mouth agape, "I see a potential issue with our leader."

It was true, but there wasn't any reason to argue, and there never had been. We had always been following a carefully executed plan, starting with that first meeting of counselors, or maybe even the first meeting with Dr. Frank. The only question now was motivation.

As the nurse successfully fought a torrent of limbs getting Monica into her seat, Sebastian strode to the front of the room and looked out at us. As he began his address, three people in scrubs entered, boxes in their hands.

"My friends," he said, "thank you for answering the call of duty. I know this must be difficult for each of you, but what you do is an important wake-up call, not just for Russia, but for the entire world. We will not let mankind be used as pawns by those who consider themselves above humanity.

"Remember that you will soon become figureheads in a movement bigger than yourselves, and that what you do on this mission will have a radical effect on the future. You may have noticed the nurses who have joined us. You'll each get a small injection behind your ear. It's entirely harmless. I've had it done myself.

"They're injecting a tiny device that will translate whatever you hear at the speed of sound. So, if you do meet a Russian, you can communicate."

"But, uh, how will they understand us?" Kevin asked.

"In the unlikely event you encounter anyone, Atmos," Sebastian said reassuringly, "you'll be fine. Their citizens were forced to get these injections years ago, so they'll all understand you."

I wondered why we were just hearing about this tech and not actively using it but decided against bringing it up. The only thing more dangerous than being out of the loop at this point was letting other people know you were worried about it.

"Now then," he said as the nurses came to each of us, a small sting at the back of the ear marking their success, "why don't we make our way to the craft. I think you'll be impressed."

I wasn't sure what had happened to Lord Sebastian since I'd last seen him, but he was acting confident to the point of arrogance. We walked out of the building, a disorganized mob, and onto the blacktop outside. Across from us, in the center of the city, was a tenement that had been abandoned as long as I could remember.

Looking at it now, it made me wonder why no one had ever torn it down, given its prime location. The *why* wasn't a question for long. A loud groan lifted into the air, accompanied by a shrill squeal, and then the roof receded from the top of the building and folded down alongside the walls, which themselves began to recede into the ground. Where the tenement had stood just moments before, there was now a jet. While the launch pad itself might not have been impressive, it was hard to deny the style of its unveiling.

The ship was a cold gray, which reminded me of winter, and seemed to run continuously with no angles or seams to disrupt its flow. The only problem being its size.

The craft was so small that it would only fit Fitzgerald, The Guardians, the two cameramen, Monica's nurse, and me, along with very limited supplies. Fitzgerald and Peter, both trained, each carried a pistol and a rifle, an assortment of ammo clipped here and there. No one else was armed aside from the knives we'd each been supplied. We had one med kit and enough rations for three days each. Fitzgerald carried a satellite phone for emergencies.

Realizing that we were starting the trip undersupplied didn't inspire a lot of confidence, but they started shooting the pictures anyway. The cameramen and I were only in a few of the shots, and the nurse didn't make her way into any of them, which wasn't a surprise. Monica managed to stabilize herself enough in her chair to make it through the photo session without much help, although the nurse intervened between shots to straighten Monica's outfit, which the queen pulled on obsessively.

Sebastian leaned over and took his queen's hand at one point in the photo session, a loving glance, both proud and worried, aimed directly at her. After about twenty more minutes of continuous flashes and new setups, the final task before we departed was complete. As the members of the council and Lord Sebastian took their leave of us, we made our way into the jet that would deliver us to Russia.

The jet, like the translators, proved to be another scientific advancement that would have seemed like magic to anyone living in America. It lifted off vertically without making any noise whatsoever, or at least none that could be heard from within the cabin, and its speed was dizzying.

The jet's silence extended to its occupants. No one was really in the right frame of mind to speak, jangled nerves leaving sentences incomplete jumbles of syllables and vowels and nothing words. By the time we dove underwater, I could barely even remember how to open my mouth.

While I was seated next to Lucille, I longed to be nearer to Peter, still the only person I really trusted in the entire crew. He, of course, was busy at the controls, which was a role I was still getting used to.

He had never been much of a joiner. It was something we had in common. But watching him now, he seemed calm, collected, purposeful. I could relate, given how my work had changed me. That didn't mean it wouldn't take me a while to get over seeing him do something someone else told him to do without a little huff.

Running through everything in my head, I tried to rationalize our impending success. Surely, I thought, the Bears would be at the side of their father in Moscow. At least I hoped so. I hated the idea of the vibrant man I spoke with dying alone.

Fitzgerald received the final coded message. This last communication was transmitted as a single beep of one tone or another, signifying success or failure. They hoped that even if it was picked up by surveillance equipment, its brevity would cause it to be overlooked.

The general looked at us sternly and gave the thumbs-up, signifying success at the target village.

Our craft struck an underwater incline close to where we would finally land. A series of soft mechanical shifts and some actual jostling of the vehicle itself made a few people gasp. I gripped my chair arms tighter, before realizing the source of the sounds. Surprising me again, the plane that had become a submarine was now climbing up along rock and sand.

We hit our landing spot shortly after, at which point Peter and Fitzgerald secured the area around the vehicle. They called us out, and I realized as I made my way down the short staircase that I was a little claustrophobic. It was good to be in the open air and on solid ground again.

Then I remembered where I was and what I was doing, and I contemplated crawling back into the ship. I focused on Peter. He might have seemed like a military big shot, but I still couldn't let him walk into danger alone. Without any other plausible option available, I selflessly dedicated myself to protecting my friend.

Chapter 16

The walk to the village was barely two miles, not that you would have known it by the complaints from our fearless queen, whose slurred half-sentences dripped with contempt. The cursing of a rock or kicking of a root she'd fallen over was always accompanied by a quick exhale of air as she turned her head up as if to ask God what she'd done to deserve this indignity.

It wasn't that I wasn't asking roughly the same question myself, but at least I was keeping quiet about it. Her nurse was attempting to keep her charge from speaking, but aside from gagging or murdering Monica, she was limited in options. The rest of us just cast big-eyed *Can you believe this?* looks toward one another.

I tried to hold back with Peter to calm my thoughts, but he was so busy keeping an eye on our surroundings that I felt more intrusive than supportive. Luckily, Lucille was in a Monica-free zone, so I moved over to her.

I realized I had been so preoccupied with Monica, I had barely even noticed our surroundings. What I was seeing didn't match up at all with where we were. It was a beautiful forest, thick and lush, composed of both expected plants and seemingly out-of-place tropical ones.

It was warm and just a touch humid. I remembered them saying it was a region made possible using terraforming. This seemed impossible, unnatural, or maybe just unearthly.

"Nervous?" Lucille whispered, glancing at me with an understanding look.

I nodded back, afraid to make too much noise, both in fear of the Russians and our own general.

"We'll be fine, Simone," her soft voice replied. "Everything's going to plan so far."

I nodded but immediately wished she hadn't said it. I knocked discreetly on a tree as we passed by, feeling as though I had to ward off Lucille's jinx but not wanting to appear crazy. Right as I thought my little compulsion had passed unnoticed, I heard two light knocks on a tree nearby, only to turn and see Peter, his head cocked to one side, that devil-grin. He had never been one for superstition. He had, however, been one for mocking my superstitions.

I was lost in my own head for the rest of the journey, sorting through questions and data, separating the wheat from the chaff. If this did work out correctly, it could be one of the most compelling chapters in the history of America, a chapter for which it would be nice to be the official chronicler. Not that I imagined I'd be allowed to tell the whole story.

When we finally approached our target—two cameramen, a general, thirteen trick-or-treaters, a nurse, and a woman in an extremely flattering spy suit wandering into a war zone, mind you—it was clear to see how the place had been taken so easily. The relevance of this village cannot be understated. If there was anything for which to applaud the place, it was for offering undeniable evidence that something could both exist and not matter.

A two-row shack of buildings surrounded by stray chickens and dogs, it almost resembled the set of an old Western movie. Its people were held prisoner in the street. They were mostly old and confused, not what one would consider a threat.

The commander of the American forces and his men remained on guard in the roadway, not eyeing the POWs at their feet, but instead scanning the skies for any sign of the true threat, the Russian royal family.

We were about forty feet away when the commander saw us. He saluted. The cameramen shuffled to the front and framed the scene as Fitzgerald began his victorious stride toward the real battlefront. He did look glorious, and in my head, I could see the news coverage of the operation, boasting triumphant shots of the country's new heroes. Maybe there was something to this after all. Maybe I was the one who just didn't get it.

And then I snapped back to attention, a sound drawing me out of my daydream. It was electric, sizzling through my skull, into my brain. It was growing in intensity, like a kettle's scream, but before I could move past basic comprehension, a solid, razor-thin sheet of red light shot down into the earth. It happened in the blink of an eye, so fast I almost didn't notice it. Then it was gone, leaving only a crisp ozone smell.

Everything was still, but I heard a sound, almost tentative, smooth. The hairs on my arm stood on end. Looking down the pathway, I saw General Fitzgerald's body slide apart, as though sliced straight down the center.

As we looked on in shock and abject terror, a second blast of energy, wider and more sustained, destroyed the town square, reducing both prisoners and soldiers alike to bone and gore. Our ground forces were slaughtered in less than a minute.

In the haze of the moment, I heard Peter yell to scatter for cover, and I dove behind a crumbling stone wall. I gripped my backpack to my chest as though it would somehow protect me.

That was when I heard the whistling. That meant the absolute worst had happened. I mean, it was pretty apparent before the whistling, but that was what made it real in my mind. I'd heard the tune before.

Anna was here.

Looking around, it seemed like everyone had found a spot for shelter, but our assailants had also stopped their attack. I peered past the corner and saw a tall woman with short hair leading a battalion of Russian troops into the devastated town square. She'd gotten a makeover, but it was definitely Lord Viktor's daughter.

As she walked toward the area where we all sheltered, she continued to whistle the same song, but the new stanzas felt darker, more malevolent. She had definitely dropped the dutiful-princess façade of our previous meeting.

Two men landed at her side, one slender and the other bulky. These were the Terrors, the twins, Piotr and Vladimir. This was truly the worst-case scenario. I looked to where I'd last seen Monica, to make sure she was okay. I got a quick glimpse of her as her nurse finished pulling her into the nearby woods. That was about as good as I could hope for.

Peter caught my eye, signaling he was going to make a move. I gave a hand gesture that clearly signaled that I didn't know what I should do with that information, which was somehow received as *move immediately*. Peter darted into the dirt road and unleashed a seismic torrent that ravaged everything in its path. From the look on his face, even he was surprised.

Glass and debris ripped through the front line of the Russian army, crushing and slicing soldiers left and right. The rear of the battalion remained unharmed thanks to the sacrifices of their comrades, but it would take them time to get through the wreckage. We had bought ourselves some time, I thought, until I looked at the Bears. They continued to stride forward unfazed, inches above the ground, not even looking back at the carnage behind them.

The army was just for show. Just like our whole mission.

Peter's face went to ash as he realized the position he was in, completely exposed and in the path of people who brushed off his most powerful attack. I signaled for him to dive for cover, but he wasn't moving. Then suddenly, I was running toward him, stopping directly in front of his stunned body.

"Lady Anna," I yelled as politely as possible, "I don't know if you remember me, but ..."

She cut me off briskly. "Oh, I remember you, Simone Smith."

I was actually surprised she remembered my name, but while her tone wasn't inviting, I hoped maybe I could at least start a dialogue.

"If you please," I started, before she shushed me with a glare that signaled death.

"Don't tell anyone, but you made me a little jealous," she said. "My father so hoped we'd be fast friends. He always wanted me to be more in touch with the people, and here comes this whip-smart, honey-sweet human girl. I spent our entire interview fantasizing about ripping out your spine. This day just gets better."

She was on me in a second, inches from my face, floating directly in front of me. Peter started to respond, but she knocked him aside, her barest gesture flinging him to the edge of the woods. He collided with a huge tree, sending a deafening crack into the air, followed by a mass of birds.

"I didn't ask for that interview," I said to her shakily, knowing that the second I turned to run was the second she lived out her fantasy.

"Oh, I know. Like I said, my father always thought I was too out of touch with the little people. Well, really just people in general. You're all so very breakable.

"I've got a group of girls who help me dress and bathe though," she said. "I suppose they're friends. I throw little tidbits of gossip their way. I'm sure I could have fit you in there if you'd shown at least a little deference."

"How much have you thought about this?" I asked rhetorically, immediately regretting my nerve-induced moxie.

She grimaced, and I noticed that the Terrors were on the move, no longer satisfied with being spectators. I squinted and turned my head, hoping death would be fast.

My eyes opened when I heard a loud noise, only to see Anna rocketed aside. Justine was on top of her, huge steel fists pummeling Anna mercilessly. Her hands suddenly shifted to giant metal meat tenderizers, and she continued her assault on the Russian princess.

Anna was on the ropes, but the Terrors were closing in. Kevin let loose with two compressed wind blasts that briefly knocked the breath out of each of them. They were already composing themselves as Madeline joined the fight, running into the field, ready to save the day.

One arm to her forehead and the other outstretched in the direction of the twins, she focused all her might on knocking the Terrors out, but instead Justine, suddenly sound asleep, dropped on top of Anna, mallet hands hitting the earth with an impotent thud.

After a second in which even Madeline seemed to be trying to figure out what had happened, Justine suddenly launched into the air. Anna stood up, her face covered in blood. She scanned our assembled forces, laughing at our incompetence.

She wasn't wrong. We had gotten lucky so far, but we hadn't used any of our fleeting victories to escape. We were too stunned by the reality of the situation. Still, Justine had done some actual damage, not that the physical punishment seemed to have slowed down Russia's cruel princess.

I heard someone yell to Madeline and realized she was still standing in the pathway, stunned by her mistake. Piotr snapped her neck before she had even turned to acknowledge her name. Everything was happening so quickly, so suddenly.

Madeline's body hit the ground just as Justine fell back to earth. Anna backhanded Justine on her way down, knocking her across the field and toward the woods from which we'd entered.

I backed off in panic, instinct overtaking everything. *Run. Hide. Go. Go. Go.*

I looked over and saw Peter, and the spell lifted. I rushed to his side and made sure he was breathing. He started to come to almost immediately, and once he saw what was happening, he was on his feet in an instant.

In the time it had taken me to get to him, Anna and the Terrors had reconvened near the wall behind which I'd originally hidden. Anna seemed to be yelling at Piotr for killing Madeline, a development I didn't have time to ponder.

Kevin, Jack, Sean, and Francine had taken up positions to try to hit the Russians with a combined blast. That's when things went south.

Francine fired her power, feeding off the nearby moisture, the largest source of which was the man of living water standing directly next to her. I heard Jack's screams before I registered what was happening, and in the end, it was over in a flash. The Bears were encased in a thick layer of ice, but Jack was gone, his trident orphaned in the dirt.

Peter and I were running back, hoping beyond reason that we could gather everyone and get out of there before our pursuers released themselves. It was difficult to even map out where everyone was, but I was suddenly so focused that no other objective existed.

I heard the crack of the ice, but still I kept running toward Francine, who had fallen to the ground, where she sat weeping with guilt. If I could get her up, I thought, she could help us carry the ones we must carry.

She held Jack's trident in her arms as though it might bring him back, at times both cradling it like a baby and gripping it with white knuckles. The shattering of her frozen prison didn't even snap her out of it, and she, Peter, and I were knocked backward by the explosion of ice as the Russians broke free. That left Kevin and Sean alone to hold the line.

The combined barrage of Sean's sonic attack and Kevin's wind blasts kept the Russians from advancing, but it didn't seem to be doing much more than that. Shondra quickly joined them, spraying her quills across all three targets, the thin projectiles, even pushed forward by the wind and sonic waves, bounced harmlessly off the Russians. Anna caught one as it flew toward her and looked at it quizzically.

Sean stopped to take a breath, at which point Anna threw the quill at him. As he passed out from its toxin, Sean let out a shrill scream that threw Piotr through a line of trees and knocked Kevin off his feet.

Anna blew a kiss at Shondra, who was flung backward by the force of the Bear's breath and slid through a stretch of dirt before slamming into a boulder. Things had quickly devolved.

Anna and Vladimir could have killed us right then. They'd still need to get the others, but we were theirs. Piotr would pull himself together soon enough. There was something else going on.

Still on the ground, Kevin fired off a field of small tornadoes, but the royals just ignored them. Then, out of nowhere, Brent flew in, held aloft by telekinesis, nearer Anna and the Terrors than I was comfortable with. It was difficult to take a ten-year-old into battle and not feel some responsibility for him.

Whatever he was doing, though, it seemed to be working. Vladimir was completely still, his body rigid in the air, and Anna's fist had begun to glow in preparation of pummeling her brother. They were both fighting the possession, Anna really sweating it out, but Brent didn't seem to be struggling at all.

Realizing Francine wasn't going to be of any help, Peter and I had finally made our way to where Kevin was standing. We had to make a game plan.

"Should we do anything to help him?" Kevin asked.

"His powers are mental. If we do anything to disrupt them, it might

107

break the spell," Peter said, hunching his shoulders.

"We need to get out of here," I said. "We should start getting anyone wounded or unconscious into the woods."

"That's a good idea, and you need to stay there with them," Peter said.

"I completely agree," I said, "once we're all there."

"You don't have any powers," he said. "You're gonna get killed."

"We are all going to get killed if we don't start working together," I said.

An incredibly hasty verbal roundup of our original eighteen included three dead, two last seen heading into the woods, two still filming, and four unconscious or injured.

We were wasting too much time, though. Brent was starting to look a little less confident.

"There's no time," Peter said. "You should both run now. I'll stay and help hold them off as long as possible. Maybe we'll get lucky, right?"

"Nah, man," Kevin said, "I'm not going and leaving you and the kid here."

"Me either," I said.

"You're not even part of this team, Simone. They're not after you," Peter said.

"Really? Has she literally told you graphic details about her fantasies of killing you?"

"Fine, fair point," Peter said. "But just start getting the wounded out, and try to stay out of the way. Be careful."

"You never say those things to *me*," Kevin said with a smile.

"I can introduce you to Vladimir," Peter responded, nodding toward the mentally imprisoned Terror. "He seems nice."

"So far, I don't think I'm digging Russian guys," Kevin said.

I rolled my eyes and started my sprint toward Shondra, hoping she hadn't suffered any sort of brain injury when she hit the rock. I was also beginning to wish I had studied field medicine. Or any medicine. I felt useless.

Anna was still fighting Brent, but neither she nor her brother had managed to break free yet. It seemed as though a chance had finally broken through. As I got to the far end of the field where Shondra lay propped against the rock, I heard a cry ring out.

"On your ten!" Peter yelled to Kevin as he shifted and took aim with his arms, but by the time he had fired, Brent was gone, taken by Piotr. Ripped away at superspeed. Anna and Vladimir immediately shook off his possession.

Luckily, Shondra was in decent shape and ready to help despite some cuts and bruises. We were both running back toward the action, hoping to wake Justine from her sleep. She had taken on Anna before, and we were running out of options.

Peter was firing vibrational blasts at Anna and Vladimir, managing to keep them from regaining their balance entirely after Brent's attack. Kevin was crossing in our direction, hitting the Bears with concentrated wind blasts to complement Peter's efforts. It wasn't doing more than buying us time, though. If Piotr came back, we were done for.

As Shondra and I neared Justine, I took a quick look around. The camera guys were still filming, just casual as could be. What had they seen before this, I wondered, that this hadn't fazed them in the least? I couldn't see Veronica, Lucille, or Pearl anywhere, though. Maybe they had followed the nurse's lead into the woods.

Anna managed to lean down and rip a clump of dirt from the ground. She threw it at Peter, who broke the clod apart with a seismic blast, but when Kevin instinctively shifted his aim to Anna to compensate for Peter, an uncovered Vladimir took Kevin down with a single punch.

Peter, distracted, received a shove from Anna. I let out a little yell when I saw him rocket by, and Anna shot another glare of death my way. I locked on, trying to hold her attention while Shondra tried to wake up Justine. That left me and the cameramen, and Anna had just acknowledged the cameramen.

"Is your country watching this?" Anna asked them.

"They'll see the footage when we get home," the older one said matter-of-factly, never even moving his eye away from the lens.

"And they'll censor it," she responded, slowly arcing around him. "I'm sure America gets all the best edits."

"You can tell me," she whispered in his ear. "I love to know how the sausage is made."

The cameraman began to stammer something, still gazing through the lens as if it was recording something happening to someone else.

"I set up a live feed on some back channels," the younger one broke in desperately, hoping this would appease her. "Folks are already watching this all over the world. They're seeing it all live."

"Good," she said, the cordial smile of a royal stretching grotesquely across her face, her eyes wide with excitement. "Because Russia is all about entertainment!"

She leaned back into the older man. "You've got to be something special to have my ear," she told him consolingly before biting down on his ear, ripping through the side of his face as though it was melted butter.

As he held his head and screamed in horror, she grabbed his camera and brought it down on his head, where it stayed stuck as its owner collapsed to the ground.

"Keep filming," she told the other cameraman, her smile disappearing and her angry-god demeanor returning. "We're just getting started, and if you've ever seen the gossip rags, you know I hate to disappoint."

The cameraman nodded in fear. Peter had recovered slightly and taken this pause to put together one last offensive with Shondra, who had given up on getting through to Justine. Just as they started, though, the sound of gunfire rang out. Peter fell to the ground, clutching his leg. I heard myself yell his name. Anna looked over at me and shook her head in pity.

Then a hail of bullets came my way. Instinctively, I dove behind a tree and tried to stay low and covered, peering around just enough to try and see the rest of my team. Anna flew forward and grabbed Peter and Kevin. She yelled for her brother to pick up some of the others and leave, but he responded by blasting her backward with charged eye beams, the same ones that must have been responsible for the death of Fitzgerald, our military forces, and the villagers.

Peter and Kevin dropped from Anna's grasp as she fell to earth. The gunfire continued, although it avoided anywhere the Bears were, which at least meant Peter and Kevin would stay safe, relatively speaking.

Anna regrouped quickly, connecting a fist to her brother's jaw, the crack audible even over the bullets. I heard a scream, but it was from a different direction than that of the quarreling siblings. I peered around to see Pearl fall into view, knocked unconscious by feedback from the punch Vladimir had taken

Even as Vladimir started to shake off her control and the punch, Anna started lifting Sean and Peter, leaving Kevin seemingly based solely on proximity. "Make sure to get her," she said to her brother, indicating Pearl, as she took off into the sky, "and make sure the others are taken care of, one way or the other."

I could see Shondra taking cover across the battlefield. We were both in secure positions from the gunfire, at least for the moment. I didn't know what we could possibly do against Vladimir, though. And then the gunfire just stopped. It was so abrupt that for a second, I wondered if I had gone deaf. I peeked around the corner. Vladimir was looking back as well, clearly puzzled by why his army would have stopped firing.

I suddenly noticed a blue glow around the army. I could almost, even from a distance, make out Veronica's little blue worms draining the life from the bodies of the Russians. There was a weird stillness as everyone stood agog, until a final burst of electricity broke through the bodies of the soldiers. Then all of them slumped in a pile to the ground.

Vladimir looked back and caught my eye, clearly both furious and afraid. No longer fearing gunfire, I walked out from behind the tree. "Haven't you gotten enough?" I said defiantly. "What is it you want, Prince Vladimir?"

I could see Lucille and Veronica appear over the shoulder of the Terror. They must have used Lucille's power to get a jump on the soldiers. Whatever their strategy, it was the only one that had gone right so far. They were heading in my direction. I knew Veronica would be overwhelmed with power. Power that could heal our friends. And I just had one little spoiled, superpowered sociopath to deal with first.

"Oh, Ms. Smith," he said, "it's not just one thing I want. I want all your little super-experiments. I want to tear them apart piece by piece until they beg for mercy, so I can laugh at them.

"Maybe I'll have my father's biographer watch, let him take notes. I would so hate to deprive future generations of such glorious pain. Pavel's not a very good writer, though, so perhaps there is something I want from you," he said, a thin smile forming.

I was trying to maintain my brave exterior, but everything inside was yelling at me to run. And then something unexpected happened. A siren rang out. Vladimir looked panicked. I wasn't sure why until Fitzgerald's satellite phone-slash-walkie talkie came to life.

"Moscow has been eliminated. Repeat, Moscow has been eliminated."

Radio silence had apparently only been in effect for the start of the mission. Vladimir looked in the direction of Moscow and then looked back at me, panicked, wondering what to do. Before I even registered what he'd decided, he picked up Pearl and Kevin, angrily crushed the phone and took off into the sky, firing a volley of beams from his eyes that charred the remaining cameraman and his equipment and wildly missed the rest of us.

I could barely register my luck as I waited for another beam to shoot from the sky and fry us. When I finally pulled in my next breath, I knew we had to get moving.

Veronica and Lucille had closed in, and Shondra finally got Justine up, but she was sluggish. As I made my way over to Francine, I saw Veronica rush to Shondra. Her worms shot into the ground again, but when they grabbed on to Justine and Shondra, both women glowed blue as the life force that had been drained from the soldiers healed them.

Shondra, who had been limping a bit, immediately seemed fine, but Justine must have really gotten whacked by Madeline. She had managed, while passing in and out of consciousness, to change her hands back into flesh and blood, so at least she was easier to keep balanced.

"Can you help her?" I asked Veronica, pointing to Francine, who had gone completely catatonic.

"I don't think so," she replied, her voice seeming to crawl toward me. "Haven't had any luck with mental health so far."

Lucille and I got Francine to her feet.

"Now what?" Lucille asked.

I looked back across the field. "We need to get moving," I said. "Something's happened in Moscow, but who knows how long that's going to keep them occupied. The queen and her nurse went into the woods, so we might as well start there. Standing in the open isn't doing us any good."

I related the story of what I'd heard as we walked into the woods, and soon everyone was speculating on what might have happened. The phrase *Moscow has been eliminated* felt fairly specific, but was it? Was Moscow a code name for Lord Viktor, or had they meant the capital city itself? What could have destroyed a city? A nuke?

"But if we were supposed to win here and have the British take over the invasion, why drop a bomb?" asked Lucille in response to my musings.

"It could have always been part of the plan," Shondra said. "For all we know, the British were never even coming. They wouldn't have told us everything, which was probably the right move, considering half of us just got captured."

It was hard not to feel misled, but she made a good point. Still, assuming they hadn't intended for Fitzgerald to die, that left us stuck with no backup evacuation plan.

"Maybe we should head back to the ship," Lucille said.

"We can check," I responded, "but they might have already found it. Plus, I can't pilot it. Anyone else?"

"Was there a radio on board?" Shondra asked.

"There must have been. Seems like something that would be standard," Lucille said.

"Let's find somewhere to regroup, and then we can figure out a plan," I said. "I'll feel better when we find the queen and her nurse too."

"If they're still alive," Lucille said.

We continued on silently, looking desperately for signs of life, either friend or foe. The start of Monica's trek was obviously rough. Bushes were trampled, large limbs were downed, and footprints seemed to start and drag. As we got further, though, their path became more elusive.

"Looks like our leader must have started to sober up," Lucille observed.

"Be kind," Veronica said. "She's troubled, but who among us isn't.

She may yet be vital to our success."

"That thing you just did back there," Lucille responded, "is incredibly creepy."

"Yes," Veronica said, showing a hint of a smile, "it is." Her playfulness sounded almost sinister, as though the energies she controlled echoed her words from within.

Chapter 17

As we walked, I began to let myself worry about Peter. At least he had been taken, not killed. Of course, after hearing what Vladimir had planned for the captured, it was possible the living might envy the dead. I quickly tried to push that thought out of my mind.

I tried instead to remember our times together on the rooftop of the orphanage, gazing into the sky, feeling like there was nowhere else I ever needed to be again. But I desperately needed to be somewhere now, and I had no idea where that was. It was maddening.

The going was slow. Justine was moving on her own, but Francine was still little more than a sack of barbells. Anyone trying to track us would have had little difficulty. We couldn't really even use Lucille's power, since walking with all six of us touching her was impractical.

I could only hope that our enemies were occupied with whatever happened in Moscow, but we couldn't count on that. "We have to start covering our tracks," I said suddenly.

Shondra looked behind us, apparently for the first time. "That's just embarrassing," she said bluntly. She volunteered to stay at the back of our group and try to cover for us as best she could, hopefully at least to the point of ambiguity. The day was moving quickly now, and as the evening chill crept in, I started to fear the worst for Monica and her nurse.

That was when the stench hit my nose. I knew it immediately, but

I'd been introduced to it only hours earlier. It was the smell of burning flesh. Lucille and I looked at each other before lowering Francine down to rest against a tree. We motioned for Veronica and Justine to stop and stay quiet as Shondra rejoined us.

"It's right ahead," she whispered.

I reached toward Lucille. "I'm thinking some invisibility is called for."

"You don't have to come with," Lucille said.

"I wouldn't want to do it on my own," I replied, taking her hand.

Suddenly, the world seemed to become liquid. Everything except for Lucille became hazy, dreamlike, like watching the world through a frosted soap bubble. This was invisibility. Lucille squeezed my hand gently, and when I looked at her, the only thing truly static, I finally felt the world around me come back into focus. It was still shifting, but my perception had stabilized.

Lucille and I started to make our way through the trees, keeping our footfalls light and watching for branches and rocks. Without Francine weighing us down, we were actually staying pretty quiet. We saw a quick puff of smoke as the wind shifted and realized we were only a few trees over from the source of the smell.

When we turned the corner, the sight was awful. Monica was pressing herself frantically back against a tree. Right in front of her were two charred corpses, the flames still snapping off their remains, licking the sky. One looked like a man and the other a woman, the pair strangely entangled, melting into one another.

"Stay calm," Lucille said. We were still invisible, and Monica began to power up her flames again, whipping her head around frantically.

"Monica," I said, "it's Simone, from the palace. You're okay. No one's going to hurt you."

Her body was still rigid, but she looked a little less panicked. "I didn't mean to," she said apologetically. "He attacked us, she started fighting him, he pulled a gun, and I just ..."

"It's okay," I said. "Nobody blames you." We didn't have a lot of time to waste on recriminations, although I felt for that poor nurse.

Monica powered down and slumped back against the tree like a rag doll. Suddenly, the world came into clear focus again, and I realized that I was visible. Lucille went to Monica quickly, checking her pulse.

"I really liked her," Monica whispered in a monotone, her dead eyes staring nowhere. Lucille was examining a pill bottle she'd found next to Monica.

"Will she be okay?" I asked.

"In about twenty-four to thirty-six hours," Lucille responded, grabbing a pack that must have belonged to the nurse and dropping the bottle into it. We got Monica to her feet and cleared the area as quickly as possible.

"Nursing school?" I asked Lucille.

"Former model."

We got back to our comrades and explained the situation as quickly as we could. Now that someone would have to help Monica, we no longer had anyone cleaning up behind us, so we found a thick patch of shrubs and brush that backed up against a large rock formation, creating a cave of rock, vines, and branches.

I hadn't realized the extent of my exhaustion until we finally sat down for a few moments. The physical and emotional stress of the day had taken their toll, and now they were fighting one another. My mind was racing, but my body was doing its best to collapse, responding to commands on a seconds-long delay.

We each had our single ration pack containing one tube of protein and vitamin paste and one tube of water. The food's sole redeeming quality was that it wasn't lethal, although it was hard to consider that a plus while ingesting it. We stayed quiet for a time, briefly joining Monica and Francine in their personal worlds of despair.

"So, how do we get out of this exactly?" Shondra said. "I mean, we *do* make it out of this, right?

"The only two people who could do anything with the ship are either dead or captured," Lucille replied.

"Then we have to get Peter back," I said, eyeing a path to the only goal I was allowing myself, the only thing staving off the weight of reality.

"Shouldn't we try to get them all back regardless?" Shondra asked.

"Discovering what's happened to the ship while we're still nearby could keep us from trekking back here needlessly later," Veronica said.

"I could go look right now," Lucille said sincerely. "I mean, I can stay invisible the entire time. If no one's there, I can check for supplies." She looked at me, exhausted but jittery.

"I don't think that's a good idea," Justine said, putting a hand on Lucille's arm. "If they're searching, they're already at the coast. Even if they aren't, we need to rest before we do anything else."

Lucille begrudgingly agreed. She needed a goal herself, but I needed her there. It was selfish, but with Peter gone, she was my link to reality, to the idea that something existed beyond the nightmare.

"So," I asked, "did it seem to anyone else like they were just waiting for us?"

"Yeah," Shondra replied. It felt obvious, but I needed to hear someone else acknowledge it. We had walked right into a trap. "I mean, they had enough time to bring in an army."

"Surely it was something we did," Justine responded, "or do you think there's a spy?" The last bit prompted a little bit of looking around the hutch. We really knew little about one another, and given the day we'd had, suspicion could destroy the last of our sanity.

"It's not one of us sitting here," Veronica creaked out, her voice like nails scraping down a chalkboard.

"How would we know?" Shondra responded.

"Don't I look trustworthy?" Veronica asked, a wry smile creeping over her face as she extended her arms, wizard robes dangling beneath them.

A few giggles started a little actual laughter, which quickly grew into an onslaught of hushes as we tried to quiet ourselves. She was right. Our only chance was to trust one another until given reason not to. We had to keep moving forward, knowing that doubt was always going to be part of our journey.

But there was so much of it to be had. Doubt. Were we the decoy mission? Were we at war with Russia? Could America even survive a full-on war with Russia? Were my teammates as innocent as they appeared? Would I ever make it back to my small apartment and my small life? Was I sent here to die? Was Peter already dead?

I felt the weight of it in my head as my brain tried to work out all the possible scenarios, knowing it was a fool's errand, but compelled to keep going. It was as exhausting as the day had been. I morbidly thought about how nice it would have been for Madeline to survive so she could (potentially, maybe) put me to sleep. Then I spent time feeling guilty for thinking that and sad about Madeline. All the while, the others drifted to sleep, one by one.

It took a long time, but I finally accepted the fact that I was asking questions I couldn't possibly know the answers to. I could feel my mind shutting down, done with me, trying to salvage what little rest it could.

Chapter 18

When the sun hit my eyes, I felt a little bit more hopeful. Making it through the night without being discovered meant we still had a chance to find a way out of this predicament. I stayed still for a bit, trying to figure out how we could handle things, but I sat up when I heard others whispering.

I joined the hushed conversation that included Lucille, Veronica, and Shondra. Justine was seeing to Monica, who was both grief-stricken and beginning to come down off her meds, and Francine, who was barely able to contain the guilt she was feeling over Jack's death.

The others had been discussing a strategy to get back to the beach using a map of the Russian Territories Veronica kept in her robe pocket, thinking (correctly) that it could be useful. I felt slightly embarrassed that I hadn't thought of it myself. Without powers, I needed to pull my own weight somehow.

They had mapped out where we probably were. If they were right, we were only a few miles from our initial landing site. A shortcut through the woods could get us there quickly.

"So, we *are* going back to the ship?" I yawned, scratching my head, wishing for a shower. And some coffee. And a ride home.

"We're so close," Shondra explained. "If there's anything in it we can use, if they haven't discovered it, it seems like it's better to check now than later."

"There is signaling equipment, which should be easier to figure out than actual flight. It makes sense to check, but I'm sure they've found it already," I reasoned.

"Maybe. I mean, it's just a big metal submarine-plane-crawling robot we left on the beach. Totally easy to miss," Lucille responded, "unless you know where to look, of course."

"I'm in," I told her, "but everyone else should stay hidden here."

"Maybe the dead weight will come around while we're gone," Lucille responded.

It was honest, if not sensitive. We spent a little time getting what few supplies we had left prepped. Luckily, everyone had conserved as much water as possible, but we'd need to find a new source soon. What made it most frustrating was that Francine's powers could easily fix that problem were she not terrified of using them.

We shared a few hasty goodbyes and well wishes before Lucille grabbed my hand, and the world went wavy again. She started to pull me, leading me off into the woods. I followed, getting my bearings. It was still an odd experience, seeing the world like this. Traces of color, shimmers of light, like you're ever-so-slightly out of sync with reality.

We were making good time, staying silent for the most part, ever vigilant for signs of life around us. It was so quiet, it startled me when Lucille spoke up. "I wanted to tell you earlier," she said, "that I was sorry I didn't keep in touch. I meant to, but everything happened so fast. My parents had my whole life mapped out. It's not an excuse. I'm just sorry."

"It's okay," I responded honestly. "We were kids."

"I just wanted you to know that, because, well, you know."

Because we're probably going to die? I thought. Maybe not on this particular journey, but soon. I had to admit that Lucille's lack of communication had been a source of pain when I was young, and maybe some of it had carried over. It was good to hear the words. It made me feel less alone.

"I'm sorry your life didn't turn out the way it should have," I said.

"They weren't mean to me or anything like that," she explained. "They just thought I could solve their problems. It was a lot."

"Yeah," I replied inadequately. "Well, things between you and me are fine as far as I'm concerned."

"Thanks," she said softly.

The rest of the trip was silent, the two of us making good time. As we neared the beach, we began to hear sounds of people and machines. Once we had cleared the tree line and gotten a view of our destination, our defeat was confirmed.

The ship was swarming with scientists, and a military perimeter had been set up around our modest vessel. *Veronica might be able to deal with this if we want the ship back*, I thought, remembering her last-minute save at the village. Then Piotr emerged from the ship, yelling a furious order back to one of the scientists aboard.

If the Bears were here, we absolutely couldn't be. We had been lucky to survive one encounter with them. Fortunately, a discussion wasn't necessary. Lucille tugged at my hand and gave a nod indicating we should turn around. On our way back, the quiet was deafening. I kept turning my head, expecting to see Piotr closing on us, but our caution proved adequate, and after a journey that felt much longer than its predecessor, we made it back to camp.

Our teammates had remained undiscovered, and Francine had even pulled herself together enough to at least make ice, so water could be checked off our needs list. Monica, sadly, was still terrified of using her powers, so filling a container was a waiting game.

"At least we know," Justine said after we gave our account of the scene.

"Then our best option is finding the others," I said.

"Brent, in particular, was quite effective against the Bears," Veronica added.

"Well," I said, "they obviously want them alive. But for how long?"

"Would they have taken them back to Moscow?" Shondra asked. "The first ones they took, I mean."

"I don't know. At the speed they travel, they might have been able to make it back there in time," I observed, reflecting on the extent of their abilities versus the timing of the notification about Moscow, "but they seemed like they were enjoying themselves. I doubt their father let them play with prisoners under his roof."

"We're talking about The Bear," Lucille said. "Wasn't torture, like, his thing?"

"Maybe," I ceded, "but if he was being genuine when I met him, I don't think it's something he would have any part of, at least not anymore."

"Safer to take them somewhere else then," Shondra said, reasoning it out. "So, somewhere between here and Moscow. They'd want something remote so they wouldn't be disturbed, but they'd need a facility large and advanced enough to accommodate their dissection and analysis needs."

"Excuse me?" Lucille said sweetly while eyeing Shondra up and down.

"I've worked with a lot of sociopaths, psychopaths, and profilers," she replied. I had almost forgotten that she was an expert on abnormal behavior. "If Daddy really doesn't let them have this sort of fun at home, they'd have found a place away from his prying eyes. The pleasure they were having, the rush that was driving them, you don't stop that just because someone tells you to."

"Okay, how do we find them?" Justine asked, holding her head as though the possibilities were causing physical pain.

"*Do* we find them?" was Lucille's sincere follow-up.

"Is there anything else for us to do?" I said rhetorically. "I mean, we don't have a way out of Russia. We don't have a way to contact anyone.

If we're going to keep moving, we need to have a goal." And I wasn't about to leave Peter behind.

"Were we really thinking about leaving them anyway?" Shondra asked, taken aback by the suggestion.

"If the Bears have them," Justine responded, "do we really have a shot at getting them back?"

"Not if we wait," Shondra said, "but right now, the Russians are checking the beach and probably the village. We're between them. If we move toward this spot here," she said, indicating a small area a good distance from where we were on the map, "we should avoid the patrols as they sweep inward. It's also the only place I can see that provides the right environment for their needs."

Within the area was a decommissioned military base according to the key on the army-issued map. It was probably a couple of days away, maybe more given Monica and Francine.

"I don't think *they* should come," Lucille said, gesturing toward our damaged teammates.

Seeing where this was going, I took the lead. "Splitting up may be the best idea right now. It's not great, but we need to be strategic."

"Fine," Justine replied, irritated with the whole thing. "I'll stay with them. We'll need to move on, though. At least find thicker woods and better cover. There's a village not too far. With any luck, we'll find somewhere safe to lay low."

"I shall also journey with the queen," Veronica added matter-of-factly.

"I'm going with you this time," Shondra said as she pointed in Lucille's direction.

Lucille gave a little grin. "Well, I do have two hands."

I began to question whether Veronica or Justine wouldn't be better assets in the field than Shondra, but then I looked around. Justine had physically recovered, but caring for Monica and Francine was taking its toll. I didn't think she'd let herself be separated from them anyway. She meant to make sure they made it out alive.

When it came to Veronica, it was obvious she really was the best chance to hold off any enemies, particularly large groups of them. She had made her choice clear, though, and I held out hope we wouldn't meet opposition in the numbers we had before.

Veronica used her worms to kill a few rabbits. It obviously troubled her, but since we had to eat, she was willing. Shondra knew a bit about plants and managed to find some edible items growing nearby, putting clippings from a few medicinal plants in her bag. Justine got Monica coherent enough to cook the rabbits without the need for a full fire, which might have alerted nearby soldiers.

After finishing our farewell meal and packing up whatever water and food we could, Shondra and I took Lucille's hands and headed off through the forest. The hand-in-hand bit was getting to be a little much.

"Oh wow," Shondra said softly as invisibility washed over her for the first time.

It was strange how quickly I was getting used to Lucille's powers, but hearing Shondra's surprise made me appreciate it anew. I imagined we were ghosts, peering into the mortal world through a thin veil. Not really there at all.

Chapter 19

Things started off well, the strangeness of our formation seeming less weird as we went. It wasn't until we were about an hour out from our hiding place that Lucille stopped dead, pulling Shondra and me back to her position.

"What about fallout?" she asked. "I mean if we did nuke Moscow."

"There might be some," I said, "but we're nowhere near Moscow."

She nodded at that, resigned, and we continued forward, watching the world wave around us. I honestly hadn't considered the idea of fallout before. I mean, we didn't even know if it had been a nuke. It seemed odd to think that one of The Lords wouldn't have handled it. Who knew if a nuke could even kill one of them? And then I started thinking about Sebastian, and a man-made weapon was right up his alley. Then I was totally thinking about fallout. I felt a deep sigh escape as I started the complex process of rationalizing my way out of another rabbit hole.

The place we were headed had been officially shuttered a decade ago, according to the notes that accompanied our military map, which meant it was a gamble. Aside from Moscow, though, this facility seemed the most likely destination for Anna and her brothers.

Just from observing the royals as children, both in the media and in coverage of their trips to America, it was clear that they relished putting one over on their father, who I imagine held them to strict standards. Even in our interview, Lord Viktor was an intimidating man, and I don't know how long the calm I witnessed had been his prevailing philosophy.

His children were having fun with us on the battlefield and wouldn't have stopped until they'd enjoyed the toys they'd captured. Of course, if their father or their home had been destroyed, I couldn't imagine what would happen to their prisoners. Would they be killed in retaliatory anger or kept around for information and dissection?

Our only hope was that whatever was happening would keep the Bears busy and away from the facility. Another fight wasn't really an option, particularly given that Lucille and Shondra weren't necessarily our heavy hitters. Of course, if anyone was the dead weight in this situation, it was me.

The path to our destination was, luckily, part of the same forest system we were already hiding in, but the buzz of activity in the area was palpable. Small military units swept the woods near us a dozen times during our first day on the road. They were closer to our location than I'd hoped, and while we had invisibility on our side, I worried for those we'd sent deeper into the heart of the woods.

When a unit did get close, we would stop and stay silent. If they were far enough away, we would take time to eat some of the bitter greens and tart berries Shondra had found for us, washing them down with tiny sips of water, trying to ration as best we could.

"How do you know all of this stuff?" Lucille whispered to her while choking down some greens during one pause in our journey.

"Secluded childhood." Shondra shrugged. "I spent a lot of time learning about nature, science, technology."

"Here's to secluded childhoods," Lucille quietly cheered, holding a small berry aloft. Shondra quickly hit it out of her hand, leaving Lucille miming her displeasure.

"I told you to eat the ones I picked," Shondra said.

"I got it from the same bush. The one you showed us," Lucille hissed.

"No, you got it from the bush right next to the one I showed you. Mine taste like death. Yours cause it. Did you eat any of those?"

Lucille shook her head, throwing up her hands in surrender while trying to discreetly push a pile of freshly picked berries out of sight with her foot.

"Is it strange that none of us have talked about being rescued?" I whispered as a Russian search unit combed a distant section of the forest.

Lucille shot me a pitying glance. "Did you think they would save us?"

"Not really," I answered, "but it does seem like something we would have discussed."

"I thought about it," Shondra interjected, "but I figured you guys would shoot it down."

"You've got solid instincts, Shondra," Lucille replied.

"But the queen is part of the team," Shondra continued. "I mean, wouldn't they need to at least try to save her? For appearances if nothing else?"

"Have you seen her?" Lucille asked. "She's a junkie, A complete embarrassment."

"She's still the queen," Shondra hissed back. "She's also a scared kid who needs help more than she needs judgment."

"You're right," Lucille said. "I'm sorry. But I bet it is what the government's thinking."

"Do they even think we're still alive?" I asked. "The last footage anyone saw was from the battlefield, and that cut off before our escape. For all anyone knows, we're dead."

"True," Shondra said, her shoulders deflating.

"Oh, who knows," Lucille said, patting Shondra on the back, "maybe they are looking, or maybe they will be. We don't have any clue what's going on, so we just have to keep looking out for each other."

During a later waiting session, Lucille and I caught Shondra up on our previous relationship. Even after that lengthy tale, the soldiers were still sweeping the area. I hoped that word of Lucille's power hadn't spread to the point that they were scanning beyond the visual spectrum.

The waiting was becoming more than I could deal with, particularly since the people holding us up were probably authorized to kill us on sight. "So, what do you think really happened out there?" I asked, ready for any hypothesis to occupy my mind.

"Well, I'm sure Fitzgerald had a backup plan," Lucille said. "He seemed like that kind of guy, but that went out the window fast."

"It was just a worst-case scenario," Shondra added. "We were lucky to have gotten out of there at all."

"Whatever happened in Moscow," I reasoned, "had to have been planned before we made it to that village, which means they knew Anna and her brothers wouldn't be there."

"So, you think we were a diversion?" Lucille asked without a hint of surprise. "We were just supposed to keep the royals busy while Lord Sebastian destroyed their home?"

"Maybe?" I answered. "They did mention diversions to keep us safe, but maybe we were the diversion to keep Moscow defenseless. And with Anna and her brothers seemingly just waiting for us ..."

"They could have flown there in the blink of an eye," Shondra said.

"With a full regiment of soldiers?" Lucille reminded her.

Shondra put her hands up in submission. "That's a lot to take in," she said, eyes wide. "I mean, did they expect we could actually take on the Bears, or did they expect us to be killed?"

Roads opened in my mind. Paths formed for every possible situation, crowding so tightly in some spots that the variable causing the offshoots was microscopic. I was hungry, I was tired, and I was stressed, which always caused my worst tendencies to magnify.

"Yeah, let's table it," I said, feeling my breathing relax, giving myself permission to shut it off. The questions felt important, but the answers remained utterly unattainable.

"Do you think the queen and Francine will snap out of it?" Lucille asked, moving on from the previous topic.

Shondra nodded. "They seemed better before we split up. They just need a little time."

"I think Queenie's biggest problem right now is detox," Lucille added. "I doubt Sebastian cares whether she's alive or dead, though. Everyone knows that marriage was all PR."

"I think it was," I said, "but maybe not? He came to me, asked me to take care of her."

"Well," Lucille said, "you're doin' a bang-up job."

"We may have killed one of The Lords," Shondra sounded out as the weight of it suddenly dawned on her.

"We don't know that," I responded reassuringly.

"Can that even be done?" Lucille asked.

I thought back to Lord Nathaniel, who for all his faults had always treated me with kindness, and I shuddered as I remembered his body breaking apart, flake by flake. "Yeah," I responded, "if Lord Viktor's body was already breaking down, he probably could have been killed, even by a human weapon. But this was retaliation for an attack on America, so I don't have a clue how the politics shake out. Nothing even close to this has happened for decades."

The Lords had maintained world peace since their ascendance. The murder of one of them was bad enough, but to add in the destruction of an entire city of innocent civilians using a weapon banned since The Lords took power? That's the fallout I didn't think any of us would survive.

"It's too bad I didn't get teleportation," Lucille said. "I mean, I could just blink and send us home."

"At least you're keeping us safe," Shondra responded. "My quills literally bounced off our enemies, who then used one as a weapon. Invisibility was in my top five going into Regenesis."

"I didn't even think that far ahead," Lucille said, looking up at the sky. "I just figured *why not?*"

I had to bite my tongue. I was ashamed at my complicity in keeping the true history of Regenesis from being known, but the middle of our botched Russia invasion seemed like a bad place to unburden myself.

"Do you remember watching those late-night movies when we'd sneak into the lounge?" Lucille asked out of nowhere. "That one from the 1970s? The one with Lord Viktor?"

I did. As a student of history and something of a cinematic masochist, I had seen all of the Bear's films. During the 1970s and '80s, Viktor felt ruling wasn't enough. He was bored and young, and he had already solved his country's problems, so obviously, he reinvented himself as a big-screen action hero. And it was bad. The scripts were ham-fisted, lowbrow trash. They were meant to be propaganda films for the Russian way of life, but their comedic value was so high that they were regularly shown in America as entertainment.

"*Fist of the Bear,*" I said. "Greatest martial arts film ever made featuring no martial arts."

"I loved that one," Lucille said, her eyes alive. "Stunt guy gets tangled in his own wire and jerks around in midair like a fish. They left a full ten seconds of that in the background of the main fight sequence. Ten seconds. We timed it. That's award-worthy apathy, my friend."

"I believe we may have different awards, you and I," Shondra said.

Lucille gave her a good-natured slap on the shoulder, stopping to look around and make sure no one had heard it. "Sometimes," she said softly, "what you really need is to see other people fail spectacularly."

"They're starting to move off," I said, looking into the distance.

Finally, I thought. This had been the biggest sweep we'd seen, unfortunately too large to go around. That meant we'd lost a lot of daylight, and while I was enjoying our talks, the more we sat, the more my momentum gave way to rationale. How exactly did we expect to rescue anyone, and even if we did, how did we expect to find the rest of our team again?

Moving helped put some of the questions out of my head, since we were all hypervigilant after sitting through so many sweeps. I hoped the thoroughness meant we wouldn't see more search parties for a long time, but there was always the possibility that it meant they knew we were in the area.

"Do you really think everyone thinks we're dead?" Shondra whispered.

"Don't know about that," Lucille said, "but if that guy really did have an underground live feed, everyone will have seen the footage by now."

"They'll be devastated," Shondra said.

"Well, they'll be thrilled when we show up alive then," Lucille responded, trying to sound reassuring.

I noticed Lucille give a tight squeeze to Shondra's hand, accompanied by a kind smile. If I had to invade Russia, at least I didn't hate the people I was with.

I did keep thinking that I had failed by not being more of a guide to Lord Sebastian the way his father seemed to have hoped. It was a ridiculous thought. I mean, I was an eighteen-year-old biographer. I was never going to hold more sway than the vultures from the council, but I still felt complicit by inaction. I thought I could have said more when I still had his ear.

Or maybe I was currently suffering the effects of saying too much. The jury was still out.

133

Chapter 20

The distance passed more quickly than I had expected, and thanks to our periodic rests, the day's journey wasn't overly strenuous. After finding a safe spot, eating and drinking, we lay curled up intimately on the ground with Lucille in the center. I began to wonder how tired she was getting of people always touching her.

"Did we ever figure out what we're going to do when we reach the base?" I whispered.

"Hopefully sneak in and sneak out," Shondra replied. "It's been decommissioned for a long time, so maybe security is pretty light."

"But if the Bears use it as a playhouse," I yawned, "we need to be ready."

"Can't do much until we get a look at it," Lucille said. "No worries about sleeping. Once I turn my power on, it stays on. Just don't roll away."

I let the miles of travel weigh down on me, pushing me beyond the bounds of the dreaming into a true void. A real slumber.

I woke early, surprisingly well-rested and anxious to get to our destination. Since we had made such a surprising amount of time the day before, we were only a half-day's journey from the lab. We prepared quickly and were on our way by sunrise. Either the previous day's sweeps had covered the entire area or we had traveled past the perimeter, because we didn't see a single search party on this leg of the trip.

I was starting to get suspicious, and when our exit from the woods and onto the base proved anticlimactic, I began to worry.

The exterior, a strong concrete building that assertively placed function over form, was overgrown with vines, giving it the feel of an Aztec temple. We began our approach cautiously, trying to ascertain whether we were setting off any sensors or traps.

We became more brazen the closer we got, feeling as though our luck might hold. Hoping that the main road in wouldn't be any more treacherous than the lawn, we took the direct route through a creaky, rusted iron gate, like the idiot teens in a horror movie.

Even knowing the facility had been abandoned, I hoped to see some support staff. It would make the rescue trickier, but it would at least indicate that we might be in the right place. Instead, the eerie silence sent waves of panic through me, but still we moved forward, heading directly toward the front door.

As we neared it, a pattern began to take shape. It was a hastily scrawled American flag. The blood used to paint it had run down the door, forming small pools on the stoop. It was dry, but not very.

We all scanned the sky, fearing the appearance of the Bears. Sorting through the glistening haze in our invisible state, I saw nothing though.

"Should we go to a different door?" Lucille asked, her voice a little shaky.

"I don't think it matters," I replied. "They obviously want us here, so unless we turn around and leave, I think we're playing by their rules."

We opened the door and crowded quickly through it, gently easing it back into place in hopes that maybe, somehow, we had gone undetected.

Even though the door made it clear someone had been here recently, the air was stale. Suspiciously heavy footprints trailed through the carpet of dust, daring us to follow. The corridor passed by menacing steel doors before breaking left down a hallway, leading us to twin doors that had *Lab rat* inscribed on them in official-looking letters, lighter spaces marking the missing letters.

We decided for a repeat of our earlier entry and made it through the doors in a flash. Once we were secure in the room, our backs literally to a wall, we evaluated the scene in front of us. It had a surprising amount of natural light for a mad scientist's laboratory. The bone saws, hammers, nightmare machines, and incredible amounts of drying blood covering the main table and nearby floor were well illuminated, which really drove the reality home.

We didn't see anyone, dead or alive, though, so we continued. As we got around a corner leading further into the lab, the stench hit me. It was a nostril-searing mix of vinegar and rotting meat. Getting past it took a second, but after we'd adapted, we scanned the room for surveillance equipment. Not seeing anything obvious, we finally unclasped hands and separated to better explore the place.

As the veil of invisibility floated off, the laboratory came into sharper focus. The gore, muted under our camouflage, now asserted its horror, and I fought to keep Peter out of my head.

I started toward the corner furthest from the door. I had been drawn to it as soon as I noticed a glowing TV there, on for who knows how long. It was tuned to a news channel but had been put on mute. The image it showed was one of utter destruction.

I switched the sound back on, the sensitive controls causing it to blare back to life. I turned the volume down in a fumbling panic, wondering if I'd just gotten us killed. Looking behind me, I saw only Lucille and Shondra walking over, both of them also scanning the room.

With the volume up just enough to hear, we found ourselves sucked into the broadcast immediately, our translation chips not simply translating the words themselves, but truly crafting a fully formatted

English report.

"... the bombing of Moscow and the murder of our Great Leader," the reporter said, mid-sentence, "his children have called for the destruction of America and its ruler, Lord Sebastian, who has vowed to protect his homeland at all costs."

Suddenly, Sebastian was on screen. He was giving an animated speech, the Russian translation being broadcast unfortunately causing our translators to echo Sebastian. "The Russians have vowed to destroy us," Lord Sebastian cried out in stereo, "but we will not be cowed by their threats. They started this war, but we will finish it. We will not let them murder our citizens, kill our queen, destroy our Guardians, and threaten our entire way of life!"

I turned the sound down, suddenly not wanting to hear any more.

"Well," Lucille said, "I guess that answers the question of whether people think we're alive."

"Maybe," I replied, looking around the room, snapping back to where we were, "but this isn't the place to figure it out. Let's finish up and get out of here."

There was no argument as we returned to our examination of the lab and its adjoining rooms. I moved down a back hallway lit by emergency lights. Small examination bays and administrative offices were sectioned off.

I was checking the desks in one of the offices, hoping for some clue, when I heard a gasp. I sprinted back through the main lab and off to a side room, arriving alongside Lucille. Shondra held Brent's red headgear, the back of it completely shattered and most of it smeared with blood.

"We need to finish this up now," Lucille snapped. "They did that to a ten-year-old kid. Think what they'll do to us."

That lit a fire. Clues didn't matter anymore. We just needed to find out if our friends were here or not. If Peter was here or not. *Please let him be here.* I made my way back down the hall I had come from.

At the end of the hallway, there was a door. I assumed it was another office, but when I opened it, I discovered a stairwell. A very steep, very dark stairwell, emergency lights breaking through the shadows every few steps.

I returned to the main lab and motioned the others over. Forming a chain with Shondra in the lead and me taking up the rear, we made our way down the stairs under the cover of invisibility.

At this point, our stealth hardly mattered. It was obviously a trap, graciously pointed out to us by the long arrow drawn on the wall in blood accompanied by the words *This Way.*

"They're just trying to keep us off balance and scared," Shondra whispered, trying to calm us.

"It's totally working," Lucille hissed back. I nodded vigorously behind her, eyes wide. The emergency lights kept flickering, making them both less useful and exponentially creepier.

I kept waiting to see the end of the stairwell, and I started to wonder if this was like the government lab in America. Would we walk down this stairwell forever, only to see the destination blink away entirely? The fact that we were walking in a chain didn't exactly help our speed or my patience either. When I finally did see the flat concrete of the basement, I felt a huge relief, not thinking for the moment that we were, obviously, walking into something far worse than the stairwell.

And it was far worse. Far, far worse than I had imagined. Corpses littered the room, strewn about with no concern for dignity or modesty. The ones not covering the floors and tables appeared mid-experiment, suspended in liquid solutions, covered in cybernetic enhancements or just torn apart and put back together in different arrangements.

I imagined this was what the first decades of Regenesis were like, disposable humans used and discarded. Maybe this was, or had been, the Russian version, although it didn't look like they were having much success. Or maybe it was just a playground for the Bears.

Something moved in the middle of the room, causing me to almost knock Lucille and Shondra over, but nothing attacked. Whatever was moving was slow, wounded.

"Oh my God," Shondra said, running across the room, dropping her invisibility at the same time. Suddenly the ground began to shake, just slightly. I looked at Lucille, and we dropped the veil and ran to Shondra.

"We have to go!" I yelled as the shaking began to become more noticeable.

As I ran up beside her, about to drag her back, I saw what had caught her attention. It was Kevin. He was slumped against a column in the middle of the room, half-covered by corpses. He was delirious, feverish. Scrawled in blood above him on the column was a question: *Are you faster than you look?*

"Do you see anyone else?" I said to Lucille frantically, but she was already scanning the area intently.

"No," she said, obviously as terrified as I was. The vibrations were becoming more violent now. Whatever was about to happen wasn't going to wait much longer. "Get him up!"

Shondra and I ripped Kevin from the ground and dragged him toward the stairs. He was dead weight at the beginning, but he found some pep once the floor started to crumble underfoot. The four of us barely made it to the stairwell, which was already beginning to sway.

Adrenaline was the only thing getting us out of this alive, I knew. One misstep and we were dead. As we rounded the edge of the stairwell door, it ripped from its frame, creating a twisting cone of stone, wood, and corpses. I almost didn't hear it over the din, but in that split second, a howl, almost birdlike, cried out from inside the cyclone. I started moving even faster.

We were at full speed down the hall now, having figured out how to balance Kevin successfully. Behind us, the floor was falling away at an alarming rate, walls exploding into showers of splintered wood and twisted metal. We were almost to the front door, though. Lucille was there, holding it open, motioning for us to hurry.

As soon as we stepped outside, we took off across the pathway at top speed, only stopping once we realized the shaking had ceased. The facility was still crumbling apart, but the tremors were over. We took a moment to catch our breath, not even caring about our visibility.

Kevin was barely cognizant, and before we had a chance to speak to him, the shaking started again. It felt as though it was directly under us. Shondra and I dragged Kevin toward the edge of the forest, opposite the way we'd come, the direction of our approach already sinking into the ground.

We were making great time, at least, the shaking propelling us forward. Then I saw Shondra fly backward. Kevin fell to the ground without her support, taking me with him. Lucille was running back to help, but when I turned around, I wasn't sure what anyone could do.

At the center of the whirlpool of dirt and debris, massive tentacles extended. One of these pale, sickly appendages had hold of Shondra's ankle and was dragging her back toward the ever-expanding pit.

Another tentacle, taller and thicker than the previous ones, crashed through the pool of debris, pelting us with dirt and rocks. It slammed down on top of what was left of the building, dragging the whole thing into the ground. Everything was starting to sink now. Over the din, I could barely make out Shondra's screams. I started to run toward her, but Lucille pulled me back.

"You'll just get caught yourself!" she yelled. I knew she was right, but we had to do something. One of the tentacles crashed down next to us, nearly knocking me off my feet. The nightmare was worse close up. Instead of suction cups, it was covered in tiny human hands, like those of an infant. They reached and clutched at the air, their chubby fingers clawing in desperation, waiting to hold fast anything they could catch.

Kevin managed to prop himself up on one knee and took aim directly at Shondra. As he motioned, one burst of wind popped up behind Shondra, pushing her forward, even as another slammed against the tentacle, knocking it back and causing the little hands to loosen their grips. Shondra scrambled to us, and we managed to get Kevin up, using her running start as an aid.

When we had run as far as we could, I took a look back. Everything was gone now, even the tentacles slowly writhing their way back from whence they came. The other path was unreachable. Whatever our reunion plans after this rescue mission, the script had just changed.

Chapter 21

"So, what exactly was that?" Lucille asked, finally pulling herself together enough to speak. We had all been still, hoping that we were out of immediate danger. So far, there had been no signs of the creature or other threats.

"My guess?" I said. "Probably a participant in the Russian version of the experiment you three willingly volunteered for."

"But why not just kill us? Why leave Kevin alive at all?" Lucille continued. "What does all of this get them?"

"I think we just passed another level in whatever game they're playing," Shondra said, clearly sharing some of my suspicions. "Kevin was probably an obstacle meant to get one or more of us killed, but they're not done yet."

"As long as we can keep outrunning everything, I suppose," Lucille sighed.

"We have to make camp," I said, nodding toward Kevin and trying not to register my own exhaustion.

Shondra agreed. "We can try to set up somewhere comfortable," she said, "but we're going to need to figure out what to do for warmth and food. If we're laying low, fire's probably a bad idea."

I hadn't even noticed that the air was chillier in this part of the woods than where we'd come from. Was that by design? It made me wonder how the others were faring. Hopefully, Monica and Francine had pulled themselves together.

"We'll just have to find whatever cover we can and huddle up," I said. "We're going to need to pile on anyway if we want to stay invisible."

Hearing a stream nearby, we found a remote area in which to stop. Shondra filled a few small canteens from our original kits, which luckily contained filtration units. Meanwhile, Lucille and I got Kevin settled in. He seemed more bruised than broken, and given his loose association with consciousness, I assumed he'd been drugged. Shondra didn't think his injuries were life-threatening, so that was one tragedy averted, at least. The three of us found branches and moss, creating a makeshift hut we hoped would blend in with the surroundings.

Shondra had found something generously called food in the woods, and we ate in silence, the few attempted conversations beginning to sound like self-eulogizing rants.

"I hope we find Peter," I said, the nervousness finally spilling out, "and the others, obviously. It's just ... he's pretty much the only family I've got. And if we don't make it out of this, if there is something after this, I hope I can meet my parents."

It was a weird statement. I really hadn't thought about my parents in years. I never knew them, and I was always around kids who didn't have parents. What I saw on TV, I yearned for, but I never really wished specifically for *my* parents.

"I forget you grew up in that place," Lucille said sympathetically. "I still remember my birth parents, and even though my adoptive parents turned out to be, well, shady, they doted on me. While I was winning, at least."

Lucille looked suddenly embarrassed, hiding her face by looking toward Kevin and then checking his pulse. She had taken some basic first-aid classes while figuring out her path. It was when she applied for student loans that she found out about the massive debt that had been racked up in her name.

We did eventually find ourselves with no way around talking about what to do, now that we didn't have a path back. It was the sort of question I both loved and loathed, the sort that begged me to map all of the different possible paths and outcomes. In my fatigued, freaked-out state, though, I wasn't in control, and I was beginning to think nothing was our decision anyway.

"Going the long way around to try to find the others will take forever, and surely they've widened the search by now," Lucille said.

"And if we are being shepherded in this direction," Shondra added, "then they're probably prepared to make sure we stay on course."

I didn't like the cat-and-mouse game we had been forced into. Knowing that they could be watching us and listening to us right now, using their enhanced senses to keep tabs on our location and hear our lowest whispers, made my skin crawl. But these were people who could kill us without ever showing themselves, so the game meant we stayed alive. If we stopped playing, our value plummeted.

Or there was no game at all, and we were just falling victim to our own paranoia. Knowing a little about Sebastian's past with the Terrors, the idea that they were playing with us seemed in character. And even if I thought otherwise, I definitely wasn't ready to call their bluff.

"We have to find some sort of loophole, some way to use the confines of their game to gain an advantage," I said, feeling like I should add something.

"Which means the advantage has to come from whatever is along the pathway. The woods, villages, farms," Lucille sighed, exhaustion sinking in.

"Or the convoys," I said, an idea forming. "Maybe information about where the sweeps are? Or where they're keeping prisoners? We could sneak in."

"*We*, you say?" responded Lucille.

"Did you see the guy using the big briefcase during the long army sweep?" asked Shondra.

"I believe you when you say that happened," Lucille replied.

"It had to be some sort of communications device," Shondra said. "We can get information, or maybe even let home know we're alive?"

"Supposing we could get one, they'd be able to trace it, right?" I asked.

"Eventually," Shondra replied, "but even if we can't get a message out in time, maybe it can at least help us help ourselves."

"Would we be able to get into it, though?" I asked. It would have to be locked and coded in some way. Obviously, the tech we were using at home was nothing compared to what I had seen since that first day at the lab.

"I think we can," Shondra replied. "I hung out with the IT guys while they broke into some fairly brilliant, although horribly disturbed, people's computers. There may not be official advanced tech in America, but there's a robust black market for it. I haven't seen everything, but I'm not going in blind."

It sometimes amazed me to realize how sheltered I'd been.

"How do we actually manage it, though?" Lucille asked. "I mean, we have to assume one of them is watching us right now, listening to us."

"They can't always be tuned in," Shondra said. "I mean, with everything going on? Surely, they're laying out a path and checking in."

"Even if they aren't, assuming otherwise is only going to lead to madness," I said. "Unfortunately, now's when we're in one place and boring."

"Which means it's the best time to head out without them knowing," Lucille sighed. "Of course."

Shondra had a better chance than I did of defending Kevin, and I wasn't about to let Lucille make the trek on her own. After we made sure Kevin was comfortable and Shondra had everything she needed,

Lucille and I clasped hands and, invisible to the eye, carefully made our way out of the shelter.

For a long time, we were silent, waiting until we had gone far enough to be out of range of anyone who might have been watching the tent. Lucille hit that point earlier than I was comfortable with.

"So, what?" she said, the silence of night momentarily adopting her voice. "We're just gonna go steal some communications box off of the same military patrol we've been avoiding?"

"Yes," I said, hoping to keep the number of hushed syllables to a minimum.

"Can we at least stop and make a plan now?"

"Let's go a little bit farther, and then absolutely," I said.

Lucille started to say something out of frustration, but she quickly gave up and continued walking in silence. We had gone for a long while without running into any signs of life when I finally felt we were probably okay to take a break.

"How about here?" I said, disrupting the quiet.

"Oh, thank God," Lucille sighed. "I'm too full of opinions to stay quiet that long."

We made our way into the middle of a circle of high, rough bushes covered overhead by majestic trees. Out of sight, we let go of one another's hand, both of us immediately rubbing the tension out. It wasn't the worst way to travel, but there was room for improvement.

"So, how exactly are we getting this case?" she asked me.

I started to speak and stopped, realizing that I hadn't gotten quite that far myself. I had spent most of the trip worrying about being heard or spotted. I thought about Peter and what was happening to him. I tried to imagine how we'd ever make it back to the others and how we'd ever manage to get out of Russia. I did not, however, think about how we would accomplish what we were on our way to accomplish.

"I think," I finally said, "that you'll have to sneak into the camp, ideally while the soldiers are sleeping or out on patrol."

"Oh," she said, her voice dripping with sarcasm, "is that all? Just wander into a base camp, grab an important piece of equipment, and hope they don't notice when it just suddenly disappears? No sweat."

"I didn't say it was a *good* idea," I sympathized. "If you can think of another option, I'm open."

She thought for a little while, almost speaking up a few times before stopping, finally giving in. "Well, it's too dark to keep going tonight," she said. "We'll literally just stumble into a camp if we keep moving."

She was right. The moon had been obscured by a long stretch of clouds, throwing the path ahead into deep shadow.

"Let's make camp here," I said. "If this whole thing seems like a worse idea in the morning, we can just head back."

"Sure," she responded. She looked hurt, distant. I couldn't help but wonder if I was asking too much of her. At the same time, there wasn't anyone else who had a chance of making this happen. We had to find a way to get a step ahead of Anna and her brothers. We'd be dead if we didn't. And probably even if we did.

Chapter 22

In my dreams, the creature screamed from its pit, crashing through the surface, yearning to be free. This time, though, I was the one in its tentacles. Dozens of tiny hands ripped at my clothing, tearing through flesh, drawing blood. They were holding me captive as the tentacle moved closer to the widening pit, carrying me to whatever was making that terrible sound. It was so loud that I thought my head would explode. I wished my head would explode. It carried up from inside the planet, a soundtrack to my death. I could feel myself being lowered. Almost there.

I woke with a start, being shaken by Lucille. "Finally!" she said. I was still trying to remind myself of where I was as she continued. "I don't remember you being such a heavy sleeper."

"Sorry, I don't usually do that."

"It would have been fine, but you were screaming bloody murder," she explained. "I can keep us invisible, but I can't absorb sound."

"Sorry," I said, realizing how much the situation had rattled her. "Really, I was just having a nightmare. It was … intense. I didn't know I was screaming."

"It's okay," she said softly. "I'm just worried about today."

"We don't have to do this," I said.

"Thanks," she said shyly. "It's nice to hear you say that, actually, but we do. There's not a better option. Trust me, I spent a lot of the night trying to come up with one."

After eating and drinking from our minimal supplies, Lucille and I hit the road, arm in arm once again.

"What if we don't find a briefcase today?" Lucille asked.

"Head back to camp or make camp ourselves until we can," I reasoned.

"If they are watching us, they're going to notice our absence eventually. Even the Terrors aren't going to be fooled by Shondra calling our names into the air every once in a while."

She was right. If there was a game, we only had so long to make a move without tipping our hand.

"We just make today work then," I replied, resolute. The odds of them watching us constantly still seemed unlikely. They had already won that game just by planting the idea in our heads. Since there was no way to know, we would always be on guard and paranoid. Embracing that philosophy at least freed up my mind to cope with the seemingly infinite number of other issues we faced.

We fell into silence, looking for any sign of a military camp. We needed some sliver of hope, and the briefcase was all we had. Surely, it could save us. It had to. Of course, I had no idea how, but I was a believer.

Lucille and I decided earlier in the day that we would do a recon of the area around whatever camp we first came to and drop me off at the safest place with a view while she went in for the equipment. That was the part that made me nervous. Lucille had proven herself more than capable, but I didn't like the idea of her going in alone. There's a reason most thieves don't hold hands while they're working, though.

After walking for forever, we found exactly what we'd been looking for. It felt like a mirage. I wanted to run straight in and grab the briefcase. It was so close, but while nothing big was currently happening, the camp was still full of soldiers.

We did a wide circle, making sure we knew where guards were stationed and finding a safe spot for me, a rock formation near where we started. It was completely invisible from the sides and close enough to larger rocks to block the back, while an overhang blocked the view from the top. The sides were still wide enough to ensure an easy escape if necessary. It felt readymade for a sniper, which made me wish, uncharacteristically, that I had a gun.

Lucille let go of my hand as I slid behind the rocks. I watched her fingers as they disappeared, the world suddenly coming into sharp focus, the sun burning in the sky, brighter than I remembered. I saw a few impressions in the dirt and grass when I looked closely, but then she was gone, invisible even to me.

The camp was really too active. We had gotten so impatient that we'd ruled against waiting for nightfall, and since a patrol had just returned, we knew no one would be leaving for a while. Soldiers were in and out of different mobile base tents, creating a living obstacle course for Lucille, but I knew she would navigate it carefully, with a sense of purpose. The case was near the middle of camp, sitting outside of a larger tent, probably that of a field commander.

I was trying to time her movement in my head, figuring out where she would be when. Was that puff of dirt a footfall? Was that pile of leaves disturbed by her gait? Was it the wind? It felt as though days passed in the span of seconds. I was helpless.

Lucille hadn't made a mistake that I'd seen, meaning nothing seemed amiss. Everything was pointing to our success. I became optimistic. I let myself feel hopeful.

And then Anna landed.

I froze. I was too far away to hear anything, but nothing unusual seemed to be going on. Some military higher-up came out of the tent and greeted Anna. There was no yelling or gesturing, which seemed like a good sign. Anna was nodding here and there. Lucille hadn't been noticed. If she could stay still and quiet, this would be just another crazy war story to tell people later. *I never thought I'd have war stories.*

Then something changed. Anna turned quickly, grabbing the soldier she had been speaking with by the neck, snapping it instantly, and throwing his body toward a patch of woods near the briefcase. There was a noise of impact loud enough that I could hear, and the soldier's body hit something unseen as if it had slammed into a solid mass before arcing toward the ground, where it lay unmoving, suspended in the air. I felt a lump in my throat, and my heart began to sink.

Anna suddenly turned to the soldiers, who had all gathered to see what the commotion was about. One of them stepped forward, as if to speak, but Anna crushed his neck like she was squeezing a tube of toothpaste. Then she turned her wrath on the others. It was quick and savage, like her father with the reporters in the history vids. When she was done, there was only one man left alive. She gestured for him to gather everything up and, presumably, return to base.

Anna crossed the road and reached down, picking up something invisible near the woods. She shook the corpse off it and slung it over her shoulder before launching into the sky.

The surviving soldier, clearly out of his mind with fear, immediately got into his truck and took off, wanting to put as much distance between the carnage and himself as possible. Everything had been left. The briefcase was still there, but it was too easy.

A little voice in my head kept yelling, telling me *It's a trap. She's just waiting.* At least a half hour went by, and I began to wonder how long it would take for other soldiers to check in at this base. The longer I waited, the worse my odds.

I slipped from my hiding spot and ran down the path into the base, not daring to look skyward. The short path felt miles long, and when I did get to camp, I had to quickly make my way through the gore Anna had left behind, leaping and hopping over arms, legs, torsos, and

151

unidentifiable bits.

I grabbed the briefcase and what seemed to be a full backpack of supplies untouched by the devastation around it. I figured it couldn't hurt. Then I did a U-turn so quickly I almost lost my footing, slipping in the muddy pathway created by the river of blood. Regaining my balance, I treaded carefully through the base and then sprinted into the woods, finally stopping once I'd gotten out of sight of the road altogether. I found a secluded spot and sat down, out of breath and wondering how I was going to navigate the road without being invisible. It was all I could do to not think about what was happening to Lucille. Or Peter.

Both of them were prisoners of war, and I was somehow trucking on without a power to my name. Were they gone because I'd been weighing them down? I didn't think so, but I'd never really know.

I started my way back through a more treacherous, thicker patch of the forest, checking branches before every footfall. It was apparent after the first hour that sweeps had increased in the area, presumably because they had captured Lucille. Luckily, I had picked up a few new tricks on this trip that, when paired with the uncanny ability to hide I had honed at the orphanage, helped me successfully evade four patrol units on the first day's travel. The worst encounter was when I came around a tall rock formation only to find myself in the middle of a small military camp. The men were getting their meals, their backs turned to me, so I slipped out of there and took a two-mile-long detour.

It was a lot easier locating a hiding place for one, though, and that was a blessing when it came time to sleep. Around nightfall, I found a large bush that backed up against a rock wall. Its vines were huge and its leaves thick, but under the layers, a few small stalks held it all up from within an empty space. I sat down and finally took a moment to relax in my secret place.

After putting down the briefcase and slipping off the backpack, I felt their weight more fully. I finally found the wherewithal to open the bag, which yielded more than I could have hoped.

There were ration packs, hydration kits, and even some basic medical supplies. I clasped it tight to my breast and started to cry. Everything had been going so wrong, and this one stroke of luck practically broke me. I ate and drank, trying not to be greedy, even though every bite was a second during which I wasn't thinking about Peter and Lucille.

I finally managed to fall asleep after what felt like hours of competing internal debates. My dreams were calm, at least. I was on the rooftop at the orphanage. Peter was there. It was like it had been before I had seen so much death so close up.

Hey, he said to me, his voice echoing gently through the air. He was leaning up against the corner near the alley, his portable CD player softly playing a big band album. The only things he had left from his parents were the player and the CDs. Most of them sounded alike to me, but he described every song as though he was an expert, full of both information and awe. And I listened, enraptured, knowing that waking meant not hearing his voice or seeing his face. Waking meant going back to war.

Which is, of course, when I woke up. I felt rested at least and, after doing a quick check outside of the bush, determined that there wasn't anyone in the area. I still took more time than I should have to get moving.

I hid when necessary. I didn't know if I should thank the terraformers or not, but the area was overgrown with thick tangles of bushes and brush, making it easy to find spots in which to tuck away. By the time I made it back to camp, I actually felt a brief swell of pride, quickly devoured by the onset of relief and fatigue.

I waited until it got dark enough to hide in the shadows before slipping back inside. If someone was watching us, they had to know

Lucille had been captured, but that didn't mean they knew I had been with her or had the briefcase. The soldiers along the way, I assumed, were to make sure she had no accomplices, because I hadn't seen any patrols in the last miles leading to camp.

My eagerness to find a shortcut through this game had been waning thanks to fear. If this was a game and we got to the end of the level, we were going to have to fight the boss. The prize was also the punishment. But I still hoped Lucille's sacrifice wouldn't be in vain.

When Shondra saw me alone, she began to cry. I held her as she wept, noticing the modifications she had made to the shelter. It was very homey. Once she got over the initial shock, I told her what had happened. Kevin just lay beside us, sedated by one of Shondra's herbal concoctions, his head on a pillow of leaves. I envied him.

The case was there, but it would wait until morning.

Chapter 23

By morning, Kevin was in much better condition, alert and fully aware. Shondra had already started trying to unlock the case, so I told Kevin everything that had happened as we ate our meager breakfast, supplementing a portion of the rations I'd found with bitter greens and berries. After I finished and he'd absorbed it all, it was his turn.

"I was kinda half-awake on the way there, just in and out of consciousness. By the time we were at the lab and they were strapping me down, though, my adrenaline just kicked in," he told me. "That little guy ... man, it's really messed up bringing a kid into this."

I nodded my agreement as he continued. "Anyway, he was laid out on a table. His helmet was off, that crazy head just on its side in a pool of blood. He was breathing. I could see that, but they'd worked him over."

"And then?" I asked, used to prompting conversation from my promising career as a biographer.

"Then," he said, looking a little embarrassed, "I panicked. Like, I don't know what happened, but I totally flipped out. I just started screaming, pulling against the chains. I kept thinking they were gonna do the same thing to me! One of them, the big one, punched me in the stomach, and his brother yelled for me to keep quiet. Hardest damn punch I've ever felt. It was just stars for a few minutes while I caught my breath. And ..." He paused.

"Yeah?" I asked.

"I must have passed out, but when I opened my eyes again, I could see Peter, but I only knew it was him because of his outfit. His face was so swollen and bruised, he barely looked like a person. And they were still beating him. I tried to use my powers, but I could barely lift my head, much less summon wind. I yelled for them to stop, and one of those lunatics was next to me in a second, telling me to shut up and wait my turn. I saw him pull his fist back, and then I was in and out of consciousness. The next thing I really remember was you guys showing up. Which, you know, thanks."

"Any idea at all where they might have taken the others?" I asked. "Did anybody say anything about another location?"

"Not that I heard. It was real crazy. Mainly flashes of things."

For all we knew, the three of us were all that was left of our landing party now. So far, we had managed to trade one captive for another. The mission's success was definitely in question.

"Why did they leave me there, though? I mean, why did they even let me live?" Kevin asked.

"Bait," Shondra said over her shoulder, "but I don't know why alive and why not one of the others." She looked up from the case, which had just clicked open, the heavy lid raising mechanically. Shondra was already typing on the keyboard before I realized there was one.

"Just from what I've seen at home," I said, "maybe for experimentation."

"What kind?" Kevin asked.

"Well, you've got powers they don't. Maybe they want to add some abilities? Become more powerful than even The Lords?"

"That makes them having Pearl and Brent scary," Shondra said. "They can control people's thoughts and actions. So, if they can study them and isolate and replicate whatever caused those specific powers to develop?"

"They could gain those powers themselves," I said.

"Theoretically. But this is just educated speculation."

Shondra motioned us over to the case, wanting to fill us in on her progress. A closer look at this thing made it clear again exactly how far behind American technology was, or at least what civilians had. Shondra, however, seemed to be having no issues adapting to the system in front of her, adding to her already impressive list of proficiencies.

"So, on the plus side, this gives us secure and unblocked network access. Unfortunately, everything is still routed and monitored from a central hub. I can get around some of the screening technologies using a temporary closed communication line, but when someone notices that, they'll be able to track this case in minutes, if not seconds."

"How long until they notice?" I asked.

"No idea. Assuming it doesn't trigger some kind of alarm, it just depends on when someone happens to check. I set my own alarm to let us know, so no reason to waste time."

"What was your field again?" Kevin asked.

"Abnormal psychology, but I might have had a little crush on one of the IT guys," she said, pushing her thumb and forefinger close in front of her face. "Just a little one."

She worked for what seemed like hours. Kevin napped, seemingly as content as could be. I envied him. I tried to rest, but I had spent so much time running that sitting still had become torturous. I thought endlessly about how I had failed Lucille, just the way I had failed Peter. I felt dangerous, useless, and reckless.

"Anything?" I finally asked, having to get out of my head, if just for a second.

"I think I found a resistance cell that's in a town not far from here. It's not much to go on, but it may be our best bet." A beeping began to sound from the briefcase. Shondra rushed toward us, practically scooping Kevin up. I grabbed our packs and followed as quickly as possible. She stopped behind a nearby stone. Just as I got next to her, an explosion rocked the area so powerfully that it made my teeth hurt.

"That doesn't seem good," I said.

"We should move," Shondra replied.

Kevin had snapped to by this point and was keeping pace. Shondra filled us in on the rest of her findings as we hurried out of the area and toward the town we hoped would hold our salvation. Her news made that a more urgent conclusion than ever.

"From what I can tell, the world believes we're dead," she said, "but the Russians know we're alive. And I don't just mean the royals, I mean everyone. And we're very valuable."

"So, our anonymity is shot," I said.

"Well," she replied, "technically not yours. I haven't seen any photographs of you at all and only a few mentions in listings of our team."

"Great," I replied, weirdly offended, "so I guess I'm the official off-the-grid face of our trio."

Shondra gave me a pitying but grateful smile. "At least it's only a short hike away," she said, "and it's a small place, so it should be easier to spot trouble."

"Or harder to blend in," I replied. "Any idea who I should be looking for?"

"Not much to go on," she said. "But their front is an alley bar off Third Street."

"But if they have this information," I said, "why don't the Bears just break it up?"

"They could use it to their advantage, plant information," Kevin said. He must have registered the surprise on my face, because he followed that with, "I watch a lot of movies. Plus, once you got rid of all your enemies, you'd get pretty bored, man."

Shondra explained that the group I would need to make contact with, Red Steel, had made one successful attack on the Kremlin itself. More impressively, they had planned the attack so that no civilian workers were present in the building at the time. That had been their only demonstration of power so far though, and once it was old news, information on the group became harder to obtain.

"Maybe they stopped bothering when Lord Viktor got sick," Kevin said. "I mean, isn't he the one they've got a problem with? I get that it's the whole monarchy thing that's the problem, but who do they protest if they don't know who's in charge?"

A sudden crunch of leaves broke our spell of safety. It was clearly boots, but the woods were playing havoc with our senses. With no idea where our pursuers were, we slowly kept moving toward our destination.

Suddenly, a heavy layer of fog rolled over the ground, rising from the surface to above our heads. In front of us, a path cleared, and I realized Kevin was giving us cover. It was an ability I hadn't seen before, but I wasn't about to argue with its usefulness. The soldiers were close now. We were walking straight into them, and the fog was the only thing keeping us alive.

I could hear voices to each side of me as we crept through the brush, trying not to give away our positions in the fog. Soldiers called to one another, giving coordinates and complaining about the lack of visibility. It felt like forever, but eventually the voices faded to echoes.

Kevin brought the fog down further as we began to feel more at ease, but no one spoke for the rest of the journey, every creak of a branch or snap of a twig causing me to flinch. We were on the wrong side of the hunter-or-hunted paradigm, and I could feel it in the air around me, palpable, terrifying. As we got closer to the town, a few small houses began to pop up in the forest we had used as cover. At one, we took our chances and pulled some semi-damp clothes from a drying line.

At least I had a coat with a hood now. It wasn't perfect, but I felt less obvious. Kevin and Shondra finally had real clothes on, even if they weren't perfect fits. It was still too risky for either of them to enter the town with me. Their faces had been plastered all over the Russian internet apparently. Mine, luckily, had not.

While making connections with known terrorist organizations hadn't been on my to-do list when I started working for the government, I was excited to have an attainable goal ahead.

Chapter 24

The town itself turned out to be barely larger than the village we had helped decimate when we first arrived. There were a few shops and a timber mill, which I assumed was the reason the place existed, but aside from that, there wasn't much town to cover.

It was sleepy. Unremarkable. Shabbily dressed women towed screaming tots along the streets. Invariably, they seemed to be balancing a load of groceries almost comical in height while fighting their fussy offspring. The men, presumably, were either at work in the timber mill or some other profession. This town did not seem to have bucked outdated societal roles, although no one living here, regardless of gender, seemed to be winning.

I made my way to the bar. Shondra was right that it was in an alley. I hadn't expected the door to be a large dumpster, but after a bit, I figured it out. After pushing the dumpster aside, stepping inside and returning the dumpster to its proper place, I was surprised to find myself the center of attention.

There were only three or four people, all of whom had glasses of vodka, and a bartender who looked as though he had built the place with his bare hands.

"Can I help you?" he said dryly.

"I was just hoping to get a drink," I replied, giving a smile that must have looked as forced as it felt.

"This isn't a place where women drink alone," he said dismissively.

"Well, can't I drink with them?" I asked, indicating the two guys sitting at the bar.

"*I* wouldn't even drink with them," he said, causing a stir of laughter from the men in the room. "You're in a dangerous place, particularly considering..."

"Considering what?" I dared him. Regret. Immediate regret.

"Considering that accent tells me your country just blew up our capital!" he yelled, slamming his hands down on the polished wood bar, a loud boom filling the space.

"Are you responsible for everything your leaders do?" I asked.

He didn't have a quick response, so I took the opening to close the gap to the bar, taking a seat on a stool. He just shook his head angrily and poured me a glass of vodka, which he set in front of me with as much menace as possible.

I suddenly had an even better understanding of good versus bad liquor. Compared to what I had had when drinking with Lord Viktor, this had a taste somewhere between the worst imaginable death and whatever death is actually more horrible than that.

I sat with my drink for a bit, not wanting to even have another sip, my insides burning. I listened to the conversations around me. Or tried to listen, at least. All chatter had essentially stopped when I entered the bar, which at least gave me some hope that I had come to the right place.

The bartender was nearby, trying to look as far away from my direction as possible, and with just a few other patrons in booths across from the bar, my only option was the guy on the stool beside me. He'd kept his back to me since the altercation with the bartender, but I figured maybe he was drunk enough to pull into a conversation.

"I don't think he likes me," I told him, indicating the bartender.

He gave a little chuckle, his shoulders moving up and down. A sign of life.

"Been a crazy day all around, though," I continued.

"Is that so?" he said, shocking me for an instant by responding.

"Yeah," I said, having thought getting this far would be more difficult. "You doing okay?"

"Doing much better now, my friend," he said as he turned his stool and patted me on the shoulder. Then, in one fluid motion, the hand patting my shoulder ripped me from the stool, the man's other palm slammed into my chest, forcing me to the ground. Even as I registered the pain in my back and my shoulder, the drunk swung around and planted his knee on my throat. The other patrons were on their feet.

"You really shouldn't have come out this way. We're a little angry with Americans right now, as you might have gathered by the greeting," the man said from above, his outline just visible against the dim overhead lights.

"I had nothing to do with that," I managed to choke out.

"Hardly matters, does it?"

"I just need . . ." The pressure of his knee hit my throat more forcefully, my words catching.

"You Americans are so selfish. Always *I need*. Well, what we need is revenge."

Panic was starting to grip me as I fought to catch a breath. I took a closer look at my assailant as my vision started to adjust to the lighting.

"There it is," he said to me. "Now you recall."

I was still struggling, but I knew this man.

"We didn't spend long together, you and I. You stuck to the side of your Lord Nathaniel while I kept watch over the children of the Bear. There was that one evening though, with Anna."

And then it all clicked. This was the caretaker for the Russian royal family. Their bodyguard. This man, I remembered, was cool and self-possessed, the sort of person you knew to fear on instinct. Mine had apparently failed.

I barely had time to notice the butt of the rifle flying toward my head before the blackness washed over me completely.

Chapter 25

When I woke, my head pounding, I realized that I was tied to a chair at the back of the bar. A quick, panicked struggle proved fruitless except as entertainment for the men, who were still enjoying their vodka.

"Who are you working for?" my assailant asked, his silky voice tinged with venom. I couldn't remember his name, which was driving me crazy.

"I'm not working for anyone," I responded, trying to keep calm while still sounding convincing. It was soon apparent that I'd miscalculated, as the fist of a nearby crony smashed against my stomach, his other hand holding the chair steady. Spots formed as I heard him ask the question again.

"You work for the Bear. You know who I am. I don't understand what more you want to know," I managed to spit out, hoping that didn't warrant another strike.

No fist came, so I took a few breaths to pull myself together.

"I want to know who you're loyal to, Miss Smith," my interrogator said, "but let's not take all day. And I'll know if you're lying. I don't recommend lying."

He seemed to actually want the truth instead of *his* truth, but I knew convincing someone which is which was tricky. Eventually, I decided to forget the protocols and niceties and just spilled my guts. His reaction was calm.

"So, you've been set up and left to die by your government," he said.

"I don't have any proof," I responded. "It's just a theory."

"That wasn't a question," he replied. "You've clearly been set up and left to die by your government. I've planned a lot of these scenarios myself."

He motioned to his men, who quickly cut me loose of my bonds. I rubbed my wrists, happy to feel the blood flow through them again. He took my arm and pulled me up from the chair, guiding me into a storage room.

As he reached behind a shelf and turned his wrist, I heard a click from the wall. The shelving popped forward, and he pulled it open, gesturing for me to continue through the secret door. He closed it behind us and led me across a landing and down a set of stairs. At the base of the stairs was a bank of computers and electronic equipment, along with a number of desks, paper files, and weapons.

"I'm Aleksei Kuznetsov," he said, clearly realizing that I couldn't remember that part, "and you, my dear, are in real trouble. But not from me. No. Your whole party is being hunted. There's no safe place for you in the country, except maybe here."

"But the Bears ..." I started.

"I'm no longer affiliated with the royal family," he said. "Let's call it an early retirement. I discovered some things that made my continued employment difficult."

I didn't seem to be in immediate danger, so I began to let my guard down a little. "What kind of things?" I asked.

"The sorts of things that make people call you a conspiracy nut."

"About The Lords?"

"About a number of things. Some sure to surprise even a royal biographer, which we'll get to if things go smoothly. For now, you need us a lot more than we need you."

"Well, I'm not going to give up much until I know I can trust you,"

I said defiantly. Somewhere along the way, I had decided to play it tough, apparently. Now I had to actually make it work. "How do I know you're not really still with the Bears? I saw your connection with Anna."

He looked down, and I noticed his fist tighten ever so slightly. I had hit a nerve.

"The children," he said, raising his head just enough to see mine, "they were everything to me. I had been their protector since they were born. I was there to make sure they reached maturity, to make sure the Bear did not suffer as your Lord Nathaniel did. But their powers kept growing and growing, and I became little more than a pet to them. Dedicated, beloved, but never more than the house mongrel."

"Are they more powerful than their father?" I asked. It had long been speculated, but I'd never dared ask Lord Nathaniel, much less Lord Viktor.

"If they aren't already, they will be," he replied, the color draining from his face. He was somewhere else. "More powerful and more cruel. Infinitely crueler." He snapped to, pulling himself together.

"How many of you are there?" he asked me.

"You've seen the newscasts," I said. "Isn't everyone on there?"

"Some of you must have died or been captured. Who else is still with you?"

"I'm here with two people," I answered, deciding I had to place some trust in Aleksei to get anywhere. "They're in the woods just south of town. I'd actually like to get them if there's a safe place for us to shelter for the night."

He seemed to consider it for a little bit. He made his way to a terminal at his desk and typed a message out.

"They should be here shortly," he said, seemingly pleased with himself. "We will work together, your team and mine. It's sort of fitting, given the history of Nathaniel and the Bear, no?"

"I suppose so," I said, a little unsure of how far to agree with him just yet.

He grabbed a couple of dusty glasses from a shelf and opened a small freezer disguised as a filing cabinet, from which he pulled some vodka. Thankfully, I could tell by the label that this wasn't the stuff from upstairs, which I was fairly certain had destroyed multiple organs on its way through my body.

As he poured and served, he explained himself. "Lord Viktor hated Lord Nathaniel from the moment they met. Not only was it during the Cold War ... You know about the Cold War?"

I nodded. It was a fair question, since so much pre-Lords history had essentially been forgotten by the majority of the public. In my case, he was in my wheelhouse.

"Good. I thought you might. Well, not only was this during the Cold War, already setting them up as adversaries, but then Nathaniel was chosen as leader of the overall crash site team, which didn't help calm Viktor's anger. I'm sure you know of the battles that ensued, and then their truce."

"Their friendship," I offered, not sure if his word choice was deliberate.

"It turned into something like that, yes. At first, it was out of necessity. Something had to be done to make sure the world was safe, and Nathaniel was the only one willing to offer a solution."

"The noninterference pact," I said.

He seemed shaken for a second, as though he had been living in these stories and was suddenly ripped out of them. He rubbed his eye. "Of course," he said. "Can't have much of a world if its rulers destroy it, can we?"

We toasted to our united forces, this vodka living up to expectations. After having survived the swill upstairs, though, anything was bound to taste better. I was wondering how far I should push my new alliance-mate for information when he started offering some up himself.

"Have you heard the latest from your homeland?" he asked me.

"I saw a few minutes of a Russian news broadcast a few days ago, but no, I haven't heard anything else."

"The Russian broadcast will not have given the full truth, of course," Aleksei replied matter-of-factly. "Currently, your country is in disarray. Half of the people are thrilled that Moscow was wiped off the map. The other half are protesting the slaughter of innocent civilians."

"And how is Sebastian dealing with that?"

"Oh, Simone," he said, stopping suddenly. "It is okay if I call you Simone, yes?" I nodded my approval, and he continued. "I do hope you'll call me Aleksei."

I got the feeling his drunk act upstairs may not have involved a lot of acting, but the longer he went on, the more information I got without having to give up anything I knew. It was my only real currency, so I intended to be as stingy as I could be without appearing rude.

"Well, your young Lord Sebastian, who really was such a sweet child, wasn't he? Such a kind boy. Even after the death of his poor brother. That one though. That was a boy who was born to rule. You could just see it. But Anna preferred Sebastian even as a small child. Timid, shy Sebastian. Infuriated her father no end. Of course, once Sebastian was the only one left, he couldn't really argue with her any longer."

He was pouring himself another. I let him do the same for me, hoping I could stay aboard his train of thought.

"I'm sorry, Simone," he started again, "it's been a long day at the bar, and with things as bleak as they've seemed since Moscow, my mind tends to wander a little. What were we ...?"

"The response from Lord Sebastian," I said helpfully.

"Ah, thank you. Well, your Lord Sebastian let it be known that he is not his father. He's commanded civilian soldiers and police to round up protestors. The information we're getting from the underground, which is scattered at best, is that people are being detained indefinitely."

"Any word about us?" I asked, referring to The Guardians. I was afraid to hear too much more about the situation at home given my inability to do anything about it.

"Only that you died to help deliver the payload to Moscow. Your teammates are being lauded as national heroes in the media. You and the rest of the technical crew have been relegated to footnotes in some minor newspapers."

But they had tied us into the plan to bomb the capital, which put us in an even worse position than I'd imagined. I wasn't sure how that would affect our chances of getting out of Russia, much less finding asylum elsewhere.

"Is there anywhere we can run to?" I asked Aleksei, suddenly feeling a swell of desperation build. I took another sip of the vodka, but it tasted bitter now, thicker, harder to swallow.

"Well," he said, "it's difficult to know for sure. I traveled almost everywhere with the Bears, and I'd say Nigeria and China are your best bets for not being handed back over. I imagine most of The Lords know the truth about what happened, but that doesn't mean they'll act accordingly."

"What about Britain?" They were supposedly America's strongest allies, and given the state of affairs between Russia and Lord Sebastian right now, I assumed that might benefit us.

He gave a little chuckle. "Feckless. They always followed whatever Nathaniel or the Old Bear had to say. There's a robust rebellion there, though, a lot of good people fighting the fight, but I'm afraid getting you to them would just multiply the danger for everyone. Giving you to the British royals is pointless. They'll just turn you over to Sebastian, or worse, Anna."

"Should we not want to be handed over to Sebastian?"

"He definitely won't want you to talk about what actually happened here. The setup, the slaughter, abandoning you. It doesn't make for good TV, as they say. You're more valuable as martyrs than as survivors."

I feared he might be right. "How do you know Anna will be in charge?" I asked, thinking of her brothers.

"She's been in charge for years. Her father used his powers a lot at the beginning, and there were some, um, events that may have caused him to deteriorate more rapidly, even though he stopped using his abilities almost entirely in his later years. The last time you saw him was probably the last time he was healthy enough to stand."

"Okay, Aleksei," I said, feeling defeated and a little light-headed, "how do we get out of here?"

"We might be able to get you to the Chinese border."

"To or over?"

"Getting across will fall to you."

It wasn't really good enough, but there weren't a lot of other people lining up to help us out. I quickly scanned the map on the wall, reminding myself of how far we'd need to travel. It was a long way to the Chinese Territories. Their pre-Lords border had extended into a fragment of what was once the Soviet Union, but the fact that China used to be even further away was small comfort.

Aleksei's phone gave a beep. After checking it quickly, he rose from his seat. "Shall we?" he asked, gesturing out of the room.

I followed him back upstairs. Kevin and Shondra were already there, sitting at a table with steaming cups of coffee. They looked relaxed. At this point, we were all resigned to rolling with it. There was some relief in their eyes at seeing me alive, though, as I'm sure that was the last part of the equation to make whatever story Red Steel had given them add up.

"So, this is all that's left of your party?" Aleksei asked, eyeing us a little suspiciously.

"I never said that," I responded, sitting down next to Shondra. "I told you I had two people with me."

There was a moment of tension in the room, no one sure how this was going to go over. The relief when Aleksei let out a hearty laugh was palpable.

"Very well," he chuckled. "Who else is still out there, and where are they?"

Kevin was about to start speaking, but I shot him a glare. Now wasn't the time to find out if he knew when to keep his cards close.

"We have some friends we left behind near our landing site," I answered.

"Some?" Aleksei countered.

"Yes, that's right," I replied.

Shondra pulled our map out of her bag and laid it out on the table. "They should be right about here. I'm sure if they moved, they left some sort of sign."

"Absolutely not," Aleksei declared. "That area is completely militarized. All roads in and out, including roads that aren't even technically roads, are monitored. You were lucky to have made it this far."

He had a point. Without Lucille, we never could have gotten as far as we did. We had seen a lot of patrols, particularly nearest the destroyed village where we began this debacle, and that was just while they were setting up the checkpoints. Now that they had established the perimeter, getting through would be next to impossible.

"We can't just leave them there," pleaded Shondra.

One of Aleksei's lieutenants, Dimitry, looked over the map. He was young, but his gaunt shagginess made him appear ancient.

"I have some friends in a village near there. We can contact them, see if they can help," he said to Aleksei.

Aleksei nodded. "Use your own equipment, though. Better the communication come directly from you. No reason to remind people

Red Steel exists until we have a reason."

Dimitry started off to send the communiqué.

"Thank you," Shondra said, calm returning to her voice.

"Now, we should talk about where your other friends are," Aleksei said. "The ones they took hostage on that video."

"And you know where they are how?" Shondra asked, her renewed calm vacating the premises. I suspected the mix of exhaustion and frustration was starting to get to her. I was about to recommend some vodka.

"You're a feisty one," Aleksei replied with a grin. "Keep clear of Dimitry. You'll break his heart." Shondra rolled her eyes as he continued. "With Moscow destroyed, there's only one place with the technology necessary to conduct the experimentation they'd plan on doing."

"And where's that?" I asked.

The talk turned into a planning session, and soon, maps and diagrams covered the table, a laptop offering support. The lab we were breaking into was large, with lots of blind corners, hiding places, and nooks and crannies, none of which was good news.

Chapter 26

There was some relief that we were finally with people who were experienced in terrorism, which felt like a wrong thing to feel, but at least we weren't alone anymore, hiding in thickets and eating bitter roots. And the plan itself felt comprehensive. Dangerous, but informed.

Kevin would bring in fog, slowly enough to seem natural but thick enough to obscure vision as fully as possible. The facility was a secret, so security wouldn't be openly displayed. Guards were posted in trees adjacent to the four corners of the building, giving them full sight from the edge of the woods to the lab. More were hidden on the roof of the building, providing the same coverage from the opposite end.

Using the fog's cover, we would enter the facility, at which point Shondra would take out the guards on duty directly inside the door, Red Steel helping as needed. From that point, it would be a clear shot to the lab. Once inside, we would split up, and Kevin would bring fog up on the roof, allowing Red Steel to overtake the snipers there. Then Kevin would lower the fog just enough for Aleksei's sharpshooters to take out the ones at the tree line.

After that, it seemed like a simple task for all nine of us to take out the interior lab guards and any scientists. Red Steel may have been small, but they sounded effective. The fear, of course, was that we might run into one—or all—of the royal family. If that happened, all bets were off.

The location was about a forty-five-minute drive. The direction we were headed, Aleksei assured me, would only have one or two checkpoints. To be safe, the nine of us took three separate cars on three separate routes. Kevin, Shondra, and I each went in a different car, hoping that the guards would be less likely to notice one infamous face than two.

It was difficult to part ways again after briefly having found safe haven, but things were moving fast, and the longer we stayed, the less likely the odds of our getting out of Russia alive.

Aleksei and I rode with another of Red Steel's lieutenants, Rooster. He had been a prisoner of the Bears at some point, and he owed his life to Aleksei. He really, really liked to tell the story of how it happened, and Aleksei had to almost shout to stop him when he began talking about it for a fourth time. Rooster was loyal, though; that much was clear.

Aleksei filled me in on some of the Russian royal family's past. While the children were kept strictly under wraps and out of the public eye directly after their births, the whole country, it seemed, had shared in the blossoming of their powers as they grew. Television specials and whole publishing lines were developed to celebrate their lives year by year. The country knew exactly how powerful its future rulers were, and if they happened to forget for a minute, a new reminder was just a birthday away.

Even more surprising was the unsettling truth of where the American Territories sat on the food chain. While we had always been told that we were the world's shining beacon, the Old Bear himself even playing it up when visiting, the reality that we were seen as a toothless relic was sobering. Lord Nathaniel was well respected among The Lords, but he had made a choice to let humanity continue at the pace it would have had the spacecraft never crashed to Earth.

It was a noble concept to let the humans chart their own path, but it ignored our sudden isolation from the world around us. It ignored the ideas that grew from other places. And the rest of the world, it seemed, had taken full advantage of the new wonders found aboard the ship. Apparently, Americans were seen as Earth's enduring cavepeople.

When we arrived at the first checkpoint, everything went smoothly. The false documents Aleksei had prepared for us seemed to pass inspection without raising any eyebrows. I began to breathe a little easier. And then the soldier asked to inspect the trunk.

I was with experts, but knowing the amount of ammunition hidden in that trunk made me sweat. I heard it close a few minutes later, and in the rearview mirror, I saw the soldier signal his comrade. I felt a single bead drip over my brow. I began to shake a little. My anxiety must have been showing, because I felt Aleksei's hand on my arm, his tight grip telling me to pull it together.

We were waved through shortly afterward, but the stakes felt more real now. We were no longer hiding from the Russian government; we were attacking it. Of course, they already thought I was responsible for the nuking of Moscow and the death of their leader, so really this was a lateral move for me.

An inevitable silence overtook us for part of the trip, even Rooster quieting down. The line at the first checkpoint had set us behind on timing, and nerves were beginning to get the best of everyone. For me, that meant dwelling on things. In this case, I started to wonder again what might be happening to Peter. I tried to think of our mundane daily rituals, but the memories slipped away as I reached for them.

I wondered what it would be like to die. I wondered what it would be like to live knowing he had died. My stomach dropped. I felt panic coming on, tugging at the back of my brain.

"How likely do you think it is this lab is going to have one of the Bears at it?" I asked, breaking the silence, needing to focus.

"Fifty-fifty," Aleksei replied. "It's doubtful we'll run into more than one, though."

"And when we get out of there," I began, "is there a way to let the Chinese Territories know we're coming, that we're seeking asylum?"

"No," he said simply. "Getting information out of Russia is almost as hard as getting people out these days."

We couldn't be too far away from the facility at this point. We made it through one more checkpoint with no fuss, which made me calm down a little bit. Rooster, who had taken a quick nap on the way, was awake and ready to get to work. He seemed like a man who really enjoyed his job, which made him a truly delightful political dissident.

It was a stark contrast to Aleksei, who I think had enjoyed protecting children as much as he'd ever enjoyed anything. There was a gleam in his eye, a more nostalgic tone in his voice, when he talked about the royals in their youth. There was a special bond there, parental, caring, powerful.

As we got closer to the facility, Aleksei pulled us off road and into the woods.

"This area shouldn't see much activity. With any luck, the others will be here soon. Get the car concealed."

We covered the car with brush and snow. It was surprisingly convincing by the end of things, and just as we finished, the second car pulled up. Kevin got out of the rear, while Dimitry and a tall, skinny kid named Maxim swung out of the front.

The second car was disguised quickly thanks in part to Kevin's abilities. After that, it was a waiting game for the third car.

"Is there any way to contact them?" I asked for the tenth time.

"No," Aleksei replied as though it had become automatic, which it had.

"Something's wrong," Kevin said.

"Yes, something is wrong," Aleksei agreed. "The question now is what sort of wrong. Were they detained at a checkpoint? Were they found by one of the royal family?"

"Was there a mole inside Red Steel?" I added to the list.

Aleksei looked at me, perturbed, but then he nodded. "Yes, that is a possibility," he conceded. "But why not take all of us then? Why just one car?"

"We're not going to find answers here," Kevin broke in, the tension clearly getting to him. "Are we still doing this or not?"

"With a third fewer troops and half our superpowers," I added.

Aleksei shook his head. "You Americans love stating the obvious. This may well be our only chance to free your friends."

"So, we do it," I said, knowing there wasn't really a choice.

"We do," Aleksei replied. "Once we've secured the ground floor, you, Rooster and I will accompany Kevin to the roof to take out the snipers stationed there, and then Kevin will lift the fog in specific sections while Rooster and I shoot the outer guards. Maxim and Dimitry should be able to hold the lower level until we've finished that."

"And then?" I asked.

"Then we take the lab and escape with your friends."

It sounded easy when he explained it, which at least felt nice.

"While Rooster rigs the place to explode," Aleksei finished.

"Back here?" I asked, deciding not to think too hard about that last part.

"If it's clear, we meet back here if we're separated," Aleksei said. "Our original plan should still be effective. It will just be a little more difficult."

We continued on foot until we were just within view of the lab. Aleksei knew the sightlines better than anyone but the snipers themselves, letting us get very close without drawing attention.

"I started working security when the children were very young," Aleksei said, the lines on his face verifying the words. "I helped set up almost every security arrangement in use for maximum effect with minimal manpower."

From the layout he had mapped out for us, it seemed he was good at his job. As we neared the tree line, Aleksei held an arm up. The fog rose quickly but not unnaturally. We waited briefly, giving the rolling white mist time to form a thick cloud.

"Open the tunnel." Aleksei whispered.

Chapter 27

Kevin flexed his hand, and a tunnel opened in the middle of the fog, which closed in around us as we moved, covering us from all sides. It was so thick that jutting just the tips of my fingers into it rendered them completely invisible.

"Shouldn't there be some sort of alarm out? This can't seem natural," I said as softly as possible.

"I made the fog near the sniper positions less thick," Kevin whispered back. "To them, it should seem more natural than what's directly around us. As long as we get through quickly, we should be good."

As we approached the door, everyone seemed hesitant. Even Aleksei hovered above the doorknob, as if he was having to force his hand onto it. When he did open it, however, we found nothing. Just an eerie darkness and a chilling stillness that felt out of place given the buildup.

Aleksei took a ball out of his bag, and I heard a click as it lit up and hovered next to him. Quickly, it split off into separate balls of light that hovered near each of us, focusing their illumination wherever we looked. I turned to Kevin, who mouthed some words of amazement to me.

"Be quiet, stay close, and stay aware. Dimitry and Rooster, cover our backs. Maxim, you stay with me and keep an eye ahead." Aleksei pulled his backpack around and reached in, producing two pistols. "You know how to use these, yes?"

I shook my head no, as Kevin waved off the offer.

"Well, you're the one who should need it the least," Aleksei shrugged at Kevin as he handed me one of the guns and put the other back in his bag. "Just point it at the bad guys and pull the trigger. Conserve your bullets for the right shot, and if the Terrors are here, save one for yourself."

I ended up staying behind with Maxim as the others went to the roof to handle the snipers. We hid in a doorway, our floating flashlights still hovering nearby but turned off using a two-blink sequence. I would have marveled more at the technology had I not been petrified.

What felt like a lifetime passed before Kevin and Aleksei returned with their crew, but even I recognized it hadn't been long enough.

"There was no one there," Kevin said, giving me a stare of terror. "No one."

"Things have undoubtedly changed since the Moscow bombing," Aleksei reasoned. "Perhaps this facility was shuttered. Regardless, I think we should continue without so much light."

The sinking feeling I'd had since our ride over dove deeper as I nodded in agreement. We walked forward, the darkness enveloping everything except Aleksei's one little individual lantern-lit circle, a terrifying North Star.

We passed multiple doors on the way to the main lab, but Aleksei clearly knew where we were heading. The frosted double doors that emerged from the shadows in front of us seemed impossibly tall, made more foreboding by the darkness behind them. The emptiness emanated from within.

It was all wrong. Where was everyone? I wanted to turn and run, and a quick look at Kevin told me he was feeling the same thing. But we were here for a reason. If Peter might still be alive, if Lucille might still be alive, Shondra, all the others, we had to see it through.

Aleksei pushed a button on the wall, causing the doors to mechanically swing inward. Even the hushed swoosh of the doors opening made me jump in the silence around us. Beyond the door, there was only more darkness, punctuated by small lights—red, white, and green—some flashing, some still.

We continued in formation, unsure what to expect. My eyes continued to adjust to the darkness, and then the overhead lights switched on. Momentarily blinded, I panicked. Was this it?

"There we go," said Dimitry, standing beside a light switch.

Aleksei punched him in the stomach. My vision began to come back, and it was clear that the lab was devoid of life, save Lucille and Peter, both of whom were in cylindrical chambers on a nearby wall, life-sign readouts running along the metal panels beside each of them. I started toward them, but Aleksei reached out to hold me back.

"Not out of the woods yet. You feel it?" he asked.

I gave a small nod, not entirely wanting to acknowledge the sensation. Something was very off. The lab should have had at least a few guards. I mean, there were war criminals being held here. The emptiness of the entire building during our rescue attempt definitely wasn't coincidence.

Aleksei looked at Dimitry, who was still recovering from the gut punch. He signaled him to be silent and then used his arms to aim Rooster to the left side of the lab and Maxim to the right. The remaining four of us stayed on the stairs, waiting anxiously.

The two returned from their sweep unharmed, and the rest of us made our way down the steps. I immediately headed for Peter's prison, examining the mechanics while simultaneously realizing I had no idea what I was looking at. He didn't appear too badly damaged, and if anything, the tube looked like it was helping him, healing him. I was just happy to see him alive.

Aleksei approached the chamber and examined the same controls I had been blindly looking over. "Probably tamper proof," he said, "but we don't have any choice but to try. Which one is more valuable to us?"

The question took me aback. "I don't really know," I said. "I mean, I hadn't really thought about it."

"Okay then. Well, this is clearly a trap. With any luck, these tubes won't explode when we try to open them, and your friends can help us whenever the bad things begin. Ladies first?"

We moved to Lucille's tube. The mechanics appeared identical to those of Peter's chamber, and Aleksei quickly went to work opening the control panel and sorting through the wires. I briefly wondered how they had made her visible again, but looking at their tech, it wasn't a stretch to imagine.

"Isn't there just a release button?" Kevin asked, clearly hoping for an easier solution.

"If you have the right code. Or the right fingerprint. Or the right DNA. Or the right eyeball," was Aleksei's reply.

"I could just trash the machine with my powers."

"And potentially kill them both," I responded. He gave a guilty shrug.

Aleksei continued sorting through the wires, his eyes never leaving the thin, multicolored strands. "Stand back."

Everyone retreated a few steps, the tension creating a whole new, entirely unwelcome level of stress for me. Aleksei took a knife from his bag and unsheathed it. He nudged it to the side of a small white wire and cut through it in one swipe.

Looking through half-closed eyes, I saw the chamber lights go down and the door open. Lucille fell out of the tube, Aleksei catching her before she could hit the floor. Kevin ran over immediately.

"Is she all right?" I asked, scared, impatient.

Kevin felt for a pulse, giving me the thumbs-up quickly. She was just starting to wake as I practically dragged Aleksei back to Peter's machine.

"So, the same should work for him, right?" I asked quickly.

"Theoretically," he answered as he moved toward the tube. "Again, we're in the middle of a trap."

He opened the control panel and found a familiar configuration of wires. Aleksei's knife butted up against the same white wire he had cut on Lucille's prison, but he paused. His face scrunched up, the look of a man struggling with a question.

"What is it?" I asked softly.

"I could have gotten lucky over there. If they wired them differently on purpose, this might kill all of us."

"There's no real way to know though, right?"

He nodded and gave a resigned grunt before proceeding to cut the wire. The blade slipped through it in a quick motion, and then the tube shut down and opened.

Aleksei caught Peter as he fell toward the floor. "Well, there's no doubt now," he said to Dimitry, who nodded his agreement. "We've just cut power to two stasis tubes. No alarm, no backup power to the tubes, nothing."

I was on my knees, and Aleksei gently lowered Peter onto my lap before getting up to discuss our situation with the rest of Red Steel. Peter's eyes started to flutter open. He seemed groggy, but he was alive.

"What happened?" he said weakly.

"No time to explain now," said Kevin, who had helped Lucille stagger over.

"You need to pull yourselves together and be ready to fight," I said, knowing there wasn't time for a full reunion.

"What?" Peter inquired. He was pulling himself up with help from Kevin and me, adrenaline bringing him back to reality quickly. The same was clearly happening with Lucille, whose eyes were getting wider by the second.

"We're rescuing you, but we're not out of the woods yet," Kevin told Peter as he helped him onto his feet.

Peter seemed to register this, and as he got a closer, more awake look at the lab, he seemed acutely aware of the danger in front of us.

"We should get out of here," I said, desperate to be done with this mission.

"I haven't even had a chance to set the bombs," Dimitry said, the disappointment clear in his voice.

"Again," I said, a little irritated, "we should just get out of here."

"That depends," Aleksei said.

"On?" Peter asked as he held his head, which was clearly killing him.

"Whether they are hoping to murder us outside or inside."

"Do you think you can use your powers?" I asked Lucille, who also looked to be nursing a mean headache.

"Maybe?" she said uncertainly.

"Which means?" Aleksei asked impatiently.

"I should be able to keep anyone touching me invisible. But ..."

"It's a slow configuration for eight people," Aleksei finished. I couldn't disagree.

"Will the fog help us again?" I asked.

"I'm not convinced it helped us the first time, given how easy this has all been," Aleksei responded. "But we have little other choice. The two with powers should stay in contact with your invisible friend. The rest of us stay in the open. Perhaps we can still retain some element of surprise."

I doubted it as much as Aleksei, but staying still felt like suicide. I could hear myself breathing as we moved out into the hall, Aleksei, Dimitry, Maxim, Rooster, and I heading up the charge, with our three invisible comrades hanging back just slightly. We came toward the front door.

"Kevin?" I said to the air behind me.

185

"Already done," a disembodied voice replied.

I held my breath as Dimitry opened the door. The tunnel was there again, just as it had been before, and for a few moments, I started to think that maybe I was letting my paranoia get the best of me. We started through, the path ahead of us clearing as the path behind us filled back in. I felt a little more hope creep in.

The fog continued to open in front of us, and I knew just from the timing that we must be midway through the clearing at this point. And then the fog rolled back just a little more, revealing the Terrors standing dead center. Piotr bolted forward at a speed that rendered him little more than a flash of blue. Before I could even respond to the events, Maxim's head flew from his body and landed at my feet. When I looked up from the horror, Piotr was back where he began, wiping his bloody fingers with a handkerchief.

"So, this is Red Steel," Vladimir said. "I guess we finally know what old Uncle Aleksei's been up to, at least."

"You boys are better than this," Aleksei began before being cut off.

"Oh, but we're not," Vladimir responded, "and you already know that. Just like you know we can tell how many of you there are whether you're visible or not, just by counting heartbeats."

"Why aren't we already dead?" Rooster asked them. "No reason to have kept any of us alive at this point."

"Good point," Vladimir said, snapping his fingers sharply. Piotr seemed to blur very briefly. I heard a crack, and then Rooster's lifeless body fell to the ground beside me. My pulse was racing, but I was desperately trying to keep it together.

"Anyone else curious?" Vladimir asked.

Silence. And then the ground shook and opened up directly under the Terrors, catching them off guard and dropping them into the earth. *Peter*, I thought.

"Run!" Aleksei yelled, and the six of us took off as quickly as we could,

Kevin's tunnel clearing a new path around the hole before closing behind us. It was only seconds before we heard Vladimir again.

"Do you really think a little dirt's gonna do it?" he screamed into the fog. His voice seemed to come from all around, and my heart skipped a few beats as I ran. Aleksei was only steps ahead of me, and Dimitry was right next to me. I could only hope the others were still behind us.

As we neared the tree line, Dimitry disappeared entirely. One second there, and the next second gone. Until we got to the tree line itself, when his lifeless body dropped from the sky directly beside my path.

"Don't stop!" Aleksei yelled. Through the fog, just barely within sight, I saw the Terrors pacing us, one on each side of the tunnel. They knew they had the upper hand. We were panicked, and in their eyes, they'd already won.

A sudden blast from Peter sent Piotr flying from view. Even as that sunk in, a compressed blast of air threw Vladimir out of sight in the opposite direction. They were potentially miles away now, providing enough time to escape.

Chapter 28

Knowing we couldn't go back to the cars since we had clearly been compromised, we headed west, a direction that would be unexpected and provided shelter along difficult terrain. Stopping at a well-covered streambed where the water and wildlife would make it more difficult for the Bears to hear us, we took a moment to regroup.

Peter, Kevin, and Lucille sat under an ancient shade tree, trying to make sense of the day's events. I joined them, leaving the sole remaining member of Red Steel in silence by the water.

"Did either of you see Shondra, Sean, Pearl, or Brent?" I asked as I sat down.

"Last I saw of Brent was right after I got nabbed," Peter said. "That thin Terror had done a real number on him."

"Yeah, we found his headpiece," I said.

"They went after me right after the kid," he replied. "Everything after that is just blank."

"You learn anything?" I asked Lucille, the day bearing down on me with a startling weight.

"Last thing I remember was being in the camp, trying to steal the case," she responded.

I looked back at Aleksei, dreading having to ask him for more help after all he'd lost. Leaving the others to their discussion, I sat down next to the grizzled Russian, who looked fragile now, regret audible in his very breath.

"I'm sorry," I said, knowing it wasn't enough.

"As am I," he said, not even moving his head. "I think I can get you and your friends to safety, but it will take some work now that my men are gone."

"I understand. Do you have any idea where the other people they took might be?"

He looked up finally, too tired to be angry or even annoyed. "No. The little Bears like their secrets, which always meant hiding things from me. They're better at it than any spy."

"What do we do then?"

"I take you toward safety. I promised to help you get on the road. I'm ready to fulfill that."

I started to say something, but his gaze had moved again to the distance, and I thought better of breaking his trance. Back at the tree, the others were discussing the trek to the Chinese border, Kevin having filled them in on the plan. They seemed far more confident in its success than I felt.

"What about the others?" Lucille asked.

"I think that's going to depend on us," I answered. "There's no more Red Steel. We're getting seen off more to make sure we leave than as assistance at this point."

"Well, we can't leave them behind," Peter said, his military training kicking in. I hadn't even had time to register my relief at his safety, and we were already talking strategy.

"Look, I don't like it either," Lucille responded, "but we need to think seriously about our odds."

"We've got two separate groups we need to find," Kevin said. "How do we decide which is more important?"

"We think we know where the queen and her group are," Peter said, "so that's where we should start."

"That sounds like the right move," I said. He took my hand and squeezed it, a soft smile on his face. The others had already moved on to finding food, so it didn't feel too awkward when he led me toward the river, far enough away from Aleksei to be alone.

It felt good, cathartic. The journey thus far had been chaotic and frustrating. At least everyone else had gotten to sit out a portion, but from watching poor Madeline die to seeing Dimitry's body fall from the sky, I was over it. I needed a moment with someone connected to another place, a different time.

Peter moved closer to me. "Are you doing okay?"

I sat for a few beats, wondering how to answer that question. "I'm doing better now," I said.

A calm came over me. After dinner, I sat next to a tree, curled up against Peter as the silence lulled us to sleep.

Chapter 29

When I woke, the sun was breaking through the canvas of branches. My back ached from sleeping on the ground, but at least it confirmed I was still alive. Aleksei had already started a small fire and was cooking what looked to be a rabbit. It smelled delicious, and I staggered toward it without even bothering to look around me.

"Get up early?" I asked him, my eyes still adjusting to being awake. I sat down on a rock and yawned.

"Barely slept," he responded. "Restless energy, I suppose. Wouldn't even have the fire again if it wasn't for him." He motioned to Kevin, who I suddenly realized was awake. He held a meditative position, inches above the ground, and it hit me that the smoke from the fire was caught in a localized vortex of wind as it leapt from the flames, dissipating harmlessly before it could expose our location. I felt bad for ever questioning Kevin's control.

Aleksei's face never shifted from the fire as he turned the skinned and cleaned rabbit methodically on his makeshift spit. "This won't offer much food," he let me know, "but it should at least give us the energy to move onward."

"Where?" I asked.

"If we were compromised, which is hard to discount now, going back isn't a possibility. We either move forward or we go nowhere. There's a small village a few days from here. Believe it or not, they make matches there. The whole economy is based on a match factory. I've got a friend there who drives a delivery truck. He can get you close to the border. Then, you're on your own."

"We want to go back for our friends," I told him.

"There is a chance they are still alive if Dimitry's contacts found them, it is true," he responded. "If not, they are probably captives. I can only offer so much help in getting you back there."

"What if Dimitry was the mole?" I felt bad saying the words even as they came out of my mouth.

To his credit, Aleksei didn't let any anger show, although I felt some frustration in his words. "I can assure you that Dimitry wasn't the mole. If his friends found them, then your friends are safe. Otherwise, if the Bears want you to have them, I think it's become clear you'll get them, at least temporarily, for a price. You can speak with the driver about getting you back to where you left them if that's what you decide."

"So, we move forward," I said.

"We move forward."

We sat in silence after that, and once Lucille and Peter woke, the fire was extinguished, and the five of us sat down to a breakfast that, for all we knew, was to be our last.

Kevin, Peter, and Lucille hung back as we walked, talking among themselves. I stuck with Aleksei, hoping to learn as much as I could.

"So how did you escape the royal family? They must have come looking for you."

"You know how I said no one can outwit me like those kids?" he chuckled. "Well, no one can outwit them like me."

"What are you hoping to do, though?" I shot back. "I mean, you obviously don't want to hurt them, so what's the goal?"

"I'm not sure," he said soberly. "I think I hoped to teach them a lesson at first, out of disappointment over what they'd become, out of a sense of helplessness. Now, I think I'm just angry."

He eyed me for a second, taking my measure. "You're more useful than you think you are, you know?" he said.

"Oh, how so?" I countered with a smile.

He tossed me a blue backpack. I caught it, adjusting to its surprising weight quickly.

"See," he said, "more useful by the second. Literally taking the weight off my shoulders."

I gave a quick laugh as I put on and secured the backpack.

"Simone," he said, all trace of humor gone, "you must not trust so easily. How much do you really know about your friends?"

Then he whistled a familiar tune.

A shiver ran down my spine, and suddenly Anna was in the path before us. I swiveled, looking for an escape route, only to find the Terrors blocking us in a lethal triangle.

"I am sorry, my friend," he said to me, a sincerity in his voice that was hard to accept, "they are still my responsibility."

"Oh, Aleksei," Vladimir said, his voice echoing throughout our surroundings, "you always were *so* dramatic."

"Quiet, brother," Anna said. Vladimir stopped in his tracks. If I'd ever doubted where the real power in the family was, it was now crystal clear. "Why don't we avoid the bloodshed? The three guinea pigs in the back come with me, and we send the little biographer back to her home in America."

"You already had them," I said, trying to keep my voice level. "Why take them back now?"

"Still working on your write-up?" Anna asked, tsking like a schoolteacher at the end. "It's none of your concern, you poor creature. I'm only sending you back as a favor to Aleksei. He's always had a soft spot for lost causes."

The ground suddenly shook and fell away, leaving the five of us standing on pillars amid a deep chasm. The Bears just floated above it all.

"Really?" Vladimir said. "Get a new trick."

A glance at Aleksei let me know that this was certainly not how he had hoped for things to turn out. There was shame in his eyes. Surely, his men weren't supposed to be killed, but here he was, still loyal to the psychopaths who murdered them.

A gust of wind picked Aleksei up and held him over the depths.

"If you think we're about to let you go to save him," Anna said, "you haven't learned much during your visit."

The winds picked up to hurricane strength, but only on the outskirts of our group. Lucille reached out and grabbed my arm. Peter was already holding on to her as she grabbed Kevin. I watched the Terrors, Anna, and Aleksei shimmer as the storm parting us grew more violent and our group took flight.

We were being carried through the sky on Kevin's air currents, Lucille keeping all of us invisible amid the raging winds. Looking behind us, I saw Anna and the Terrors flying through the clouds, shading their eyes against the dust and dirt pelting them.

Piotr rocketed forward like a battering ram. When he was just inches from my invisible face, he turned his head and opened his eyes, looking directly into my own, his cruel features enhanced by a murderous gleam. I held my breath tightly even as I felt Lucille grip my hand, letting me know she was there.

For the longest few seconds of my life, Piotr looked right through me. Had the winds not been so powerful, had I made a sound, our whole party would have been discovered. As he tore off to the side to continue his search, I let out a breath that seemed to drain from every pore of my body, relief washing over me even as I regained a sense of our situation.

It was a waiting game, none of us daring to speak, even once the

Bears and the storm were long behind us. We hadn't seen anything since we cleared the clouds, and for a moment, I let myself relax and feel the experience of floating on the wind currents. I tried not to be jealous of Kevin, but it was difficult. This might have been worth signing the form.

Chapter 30

We had survived so far only because of arrogance on the part of the Bears and dumb luck. They'd been toying with us, and we'd been smart enough to take the openings. What happened when they sped by faster than the eye could see and tore us all apart in a millisecond? Why hadn't they done that?

Realizing that my brain was running in circles, I broke the silence, yelling over the winds, "So, what's the plan? Also, thanks for pulling me out of there."

Kevin gave a quick smile over his shoulder. "Gotta stick together, right? Unfortunately, this was as far as we got. I'm heading back to where we started. With Lucille keeping us out of sight, we should be okay as long as we've lost the Bears."

"I'm pretty sure they'll regroup before their next attack," I said. "Aleksei went out of his way to make sure only Dimitry knew where our friends are, which means the Bears probably don't have a clue."

Aleksei had betrayed us, but he'd been trying to help us, or at least me, at the same time. I regretted not asking him more questions about the Bears. I was still trying to think if there was anything I was missing when my hand absently touched my shoulder.

I was an idiot. He gave me a backpack minutes before we were attacked. He thought he had cleared passage for me, so surely he expected me to keep its contents. I could hardly control myself, wanting to open it right there and see what was inside. Calming myself, I decided it was best if I checked its contents when I was no longer in the air and preferably when I was alone, the words Aleksei spoke right before the attack gnawing at my brain.

"He still knows what area to sweep though," Peter added, "so we should assume they've beefed up security, maybe doing door-to-door searches."

Lucille just gave out a tired sigh, a sentiment I echoed. "Well, I guess we should at least try to save the queen," she said dryly.

"We need to think about where to go after that," I said.

"We're going home," Peter said.

"We'll be killed before we even get that far. It's pretty clear they're not interested in taking us back," Lucille told him.

"You really believe that?" he asked, his patriotism bolder than I'd noticed before.

"Aleksei did," I said. "And he was right. We're more useful as martyrs, particularly since our story of what happened isn't going to jibe with theirs. From what I've heard, Sebastian has gone off the deep end."

"Think about who you've heard it from. We're soldiers," Peter said. "They'll have to take us back. We've fought for America."

"The people don't even know we're alive," I said to Peter, realizing that he'd found a new family after all. I wondered where my rebellious friend was hiding. "The thing is, everyone in Russia does. We need to get somewhere safe so we can make an informed decision, and right now, that's not necessarily home, and it's definitely not here."

"So, we're believing the word of a Russian who turned us over to our enemies," Peter said.

"No," I responded, "you're believing me, but we need to table it until we're not out in the open, invisible or not."

Peter shook his head, his jaw tight with irritation. He pitied me, and it made me feel a little smaller, which really made me mad.

"But you think somewhere else might be more receptive?" Kevin asked, defusing some of the tension.

"I just know Aleksei told me that China and Nigeria were less terrifying than our other options."

"Aleksei, who—again—just betrayed us," Peter pointed out.

"He was real weird this morning," Kevin said. "Before the rest of you were awake, he talked a lot about contingency plans, that sort of stuff."

"Which is why you brought it up with us on the trail?" Lucille said.

"Exactly," Kevin replied. "I think he was trying to warn us."

"Or he was just doing his part as a pawn in whatever the royals are playing," Peter responded.

I actually found myself missing Aleksei, another thing I thought I shouldn't share with Peter or the others. The Russian had been the only other regular human left. Now it was just me.

"So, China's probably the easiest, right?" Lucille asked. She had a serious look on her face, a tinge of sadness tainting her beauty. "Assuming we decide to move on without trying to rescue the others."

"Aleksei made it sound like it," I said. "And yes, I know that could just be him trying to guide us into a trap."

"He's right, though. From where we're at, I don't think we can make any other border without a plane," Peter said. "Trap or not, it's still the best choice."

"They're not going to let us go," I said. "Whatever the reason, they've been holding back. Think about the power you've seen The Lords demonstrate."

"So, what do we do when these brats go all in?" Lucille asked.

"Die," Peter said.

"We're still in the game," I said. "They could have captured or killed us so many times, but we're still alive, so we make sure we stay that way."

"Maybe they need us to lead them to the others?" Lucille speculated.

"If there's a chance we might expose them," Kevin asked, "should we even be trying to find them?"

"Have a better idea?" Peter offered defiantly.

Kevin shrugged it off, but I was getting a little concerned. The trip, at least as far as our group was concerned, had been pretty unified so far. Peter was throwing the balance off. It felt strange to simultaneously not want to be apart from him but also not really want him there. He was taking our problems personally.

"I don't think there's a good option," I said, trying to shut down the lingering tension. "I also can't think of anything else we can do right now. We only found the last lab because they wanted us to find it."

"And if the whole thing, even this journey, was a trap from the start?" Lucille asked.

"Then we might as well keep moving forward," I said, a little defeated. "Look, I think we're still alive because they underestimated you guys. We keep moving forward and hope they keep doing that."

Silence returned. Floating above the world, witnessing the land below through a wavy haze, the weight of our problems sank in just a little more. By the time we made it back to where we had left Monica, Francine, Justine, and Veronica, there was no sign of the women. I felt a little relieved that there was also no sign of a struggle.

I broke off from Lucille briefly to check out some cloth I saw in shrubbery. The bright orange was indeed from Monica's outfit, but it had been neatly cut. When I turned to head back to Lucille's security, I realized that my vision was still hazy, dreamlike.

"Lucille," I called, "I think I'm still invisible."

She looked at me and then closed her eyes in concentration, her face gently contorting as she seemed to move through mental channels and tubes. When she opened her eyes again, they were wide.

"You are," she said, amazed.

"How can you do that?" I asked.

The other two had let go of her now as well, but all of us remained phantoms. Lucille was projecting her invisibility without physical touch. I thought back to Regenesis, to the spores. To all the remaining mysteries.

"I don't know," she said in disbelief, examining her hands as though they somehow held the answer.

There obviously hadn't been time for any long-term study of The Guardians and their physiologies post-exposure. Maybe their powers were growing naturally. I wondered what that meant for their bodies and tried to push away thoughts of Lord Nathaniel burning away from within.

"Well, let's not look a gift horse in the mouth," Peter said, closing down the conversation. "We need to keep moving. I say we follow the path that looks most recently used."

Since no one could think of a reason to do otherwise, we headed into the woods, hoping to somehow find the others. The trip was simpler now that we no longer needed to be in physical contact with Lucille, which made getting through military units much easier.

"Looks like Aleksei must have said something," Lucille whispered right after we cleared hearing range of one convoy.

"Hopefully Dimitry's friends had long enough to get them beforehand," I replied.

"And hopefully Dimitry wasn't working for the Bears too," Peter said.

We finally came to the outskirts of another small village. I was beginning to wonder if cities existed anymore, and then felt bad when I remembered Moscow.

"Give it a shot?" Lucille asked.

"Seems like the best option," I replied, "but how do we figure out where they might be?"

"His people would have to be local," Peter said. "They'd be noticed immediately otherwise. Can't keep a secret that way."

"We have to go in," I said. "But maybe we shouldn't all go in."

"Haven't you guys gotten anything from our previous attempts to split up?" Kevin said animatedly. "Can we at least pretend like we're learning?"

"Now that my power's … different," Lucille said, a hint of unease in her voice, "we can give it a go, but remember—you're invisible, not intangible. If you bump into someone, they will bump back."

"We should stick close regardless," Peter said. "If we need to get out of there quickly, there's not going to be time to collect people."

Continuing forward quietly, we entered the village on a back road. I hung as close to Lucille as possible. If this power increase was a quick fluctuation, I wanted to be ready to grab an arm, plus I felt a little more at ease with her than with Peter right now.

It wasn't just that I was annoyed with him at the moment. Lucille had proven herself tough and smart. I felt confident with her by my side. The invisibility didn't hurt.

"What do you think we should really do?" I whispered to her as we crept down the back roads, checking alleys for any sign of hiding places or trouble.

"I don't know," she whispered back with a pained look in her eyes. "The thought of leaving them here after being a prisoner myself is disgusting, particularly with Brent. I mean, he's just a kid."

"That's been bothering me too," I acknowledged.

"At the same time," she continued, "we don't even know if they're alive. Our luck is going to run out eventually, and then no one gets out of here."

"Of course, there's the question of where we can even go," I said. "Sure, China sounds great in the abstract, but I should have done more research before we came."

"You've just gotta ride the wave."

"I think I used to be better at that," I said, "but right now, the numbness seems wrong."

"I know," she said. "I feel like I might actually benefit from being more freaked out."

"By rights, we should have all been like Francine after that initial attack," I said, thinking of her complete shutdown, "but some people ..."

"Just survive," she said, finishing my thought more positively.

"And then later have a complete and total breakdown."

She gave a quick laugh, which got a glare from Peter.

"I suppose we should be more careful," I said, mock admonishingly.

"Haven't been caught so far," she said. "Oh wait, never mind."

Peter made an irritated noise from across the alley. When I looked toward him, he was making a large X with his arms. We had almost walked directly into a checkpoint. Lucille and I had completely missed it, too caught up in our own conversation.

Surprised, we moved into a nearby alley. I started to speak as Peter and Kevin made their way toward us, but I could tell Peter was going to be saying plenty by the look on his face.

"Let's just assume we've learned our lesson," Lucille suddenly hissed.

Peter just shrugged his shoulders. I figured I should just let Lucille handle my interactions with him from now on.

"We can just go through, right?" Kevin asked.

"Not without tripping it," Peter replied. "They've got a ground scanner. Once they've planted it, it can check for entry and exit patterns along the full perimeter of the town. Even if we're invisible, it'll know we've gone in."

"I can just fly us over," Kevin said.

"It scans vertically too, checks density in a straight line that goes up pretty far. You might be able to get over it, but it's invisible, so we wouldn't know until we had already set the alarm off."

"So, what do we do?" I asked. Peter and I might not have been seeing eye to eye, but he was still the only one of us present who had any experience with this sort of technology.

"I have an idea," Peter said, "but we'll need to make our way further into the woods."

We moved back outside of town and then began walking its perimeter, following the path of where the sensor would have to be using the guard-station generator as a starting point. Luckily, Peter seemed fairly comfortable with this sort of thing.

"Here we are," he said.

I looked skyward at a huge tree, its top invisible to the eye, its massive branches jutting out over the rooftops of the village.

"If they calibrated it correctly, the beam will scan around natural objects," Peter said, "but the way they had their gear set up, I don't think they bothered. It was sloppy. I think they just marked it as a solid obstacle."

"So," Lucille said, "we're banking on the hope that they did a bad job."

"Right," Peter said, indicating a branch high up and wide enough for two people to walk along side by side. "We walk across on that, and we should be as invisible to their sensors as we are to their eyes."

No one had a better idea, and if an alarm did go off, we'd stay invisible and Kevin would whisk us off into the night. To start with, though, he helped us up onto the tree limb.

We made our way across one by one. It was heavy and sturdy, but too much motion could set off the sensors, and no one wanted to find out how much weight was too much.

Our belief in the incompetence of the opposition confirmed, we were quickly back on the ground near a few small farms set back from the village proper. For some reason, my anxiety began to increase, and looking at Lucille, I could see she was experiencing the same thing.

"It's too quiet," she whispered.

"The military will have imposed a curfew. Fewer people out on the roads, fewer people to sort through," Peter said matter-of-factly.

It was still unnerving. Even the animals in the area seemed to have obeyed the commands of the military, with nary a chirp, moo, or cluck to be heard. I had never been an outdoors person, but I would have given anything just to hear a sound of life from some corner of those farms.

We continued on in silence, afraid our voices would be magnified in the never-ending quiet surrounding us. As we got further into the village, noise returned, making me miss the silence I had so recently despised.

"Find them, or I'll tear your head off like I did your buddy's," came the unmistakable voice of Vladimir. "And then I'll figure out where your family is and pay them a visit."

"How close do you think they are?" I whispered to Peter. We had entered a section of the village that led off around curves and bends, streets and alleys breaking away at random intervals.

"Close," he said, raising a finger politely to shush me.

"Yes, my lord," a voice quivered out from very nearby.

Peter waved us down a small side street that jutted off into multiple alleys. At this point, we at least knew where we *didn't* want to go.

We kept moving slowly forward. I realized I'd been unfair to Peter. I was still thinking of him as the angry kid from the orphanage, but what I saw as arrogance was experience, skill, and education. And a little bit of arrogance.

When we got toward the end of the road, a fork that offered two more indistinct choices, Kevin made a noise to get our attention. We gathered around him quickly, but I wasn't sure what we were looking at.

He pointed to a spot directly behind an old metal trash can at the end of the alley closest to us as a gentle wind shifted it slightly, gently further into the alley. Behind it were three small arrows in three different colors. One aimed upward, one pointed further down the alley, toward a dead-end, and one pointed downward.

"I've seen that before," Peter whispered. "It was in the mission briefing, just a paragraph. Revolutionaries have been using this since the rise of The Lords. It's supposed to indicate the location of a safe house. "

"So, rooftop, sewer, or dead-end?" Lucille shrugged.

"It's not quite so literal," Peter said with a sense of urgency, "but I think in this case, you're right. I'm voting against the sewer."

"I am completely okay with that," Lucille replied.

"It's the dead end," Peter said.

"How do you know?" I asked.

"It's coded. The colors indicate which way is the safe route. I hope."

"Sure, why not?" I said, giving up understanding this before I even started to try. "So, how would we find this hidden shelter with just a color-coded arrow as our clue?"

"Only by looking like fools, I'm afraid," he said as he stepped further into the alley. We followed until we were face-to-brick with the wall at its end. Peter began to feel around the wall, trying to push his fingers between the bricks, pulling at them, pushing them. He wasn't having much luck, from what I could tell.

"Drop the invisibility," he said to Lucille. I looked around. The night sky was cloudy, and the alley dropped into near-complete darkness where we stood. The drowsy appearance of the world went away.

"We're looking for our friends," Peter said as he knocked on the bricks. "Dimitry sent us."

"Really?" Lucille asked, voicing my own thoughts about talking to strange walls.

Peter just gave her a look that clearly said *shut up*.

I thought I saw a shift in the patch of brick directly in front of us, but it was brief, like a quick flicker. Lucille's eyes widened. She had seen it too and shrugged her shoulders.

"We haven't been followed. We've stayed invisible," she said, which is fittingly when everything went wrong.

"Don't move!" we heard from behind us. "Now, put your hands above your heads."

We complied, and I heard one of our captors start walking toward us. As the footsteps got closer, the brick wall in front of us shimmered in place, replaced with a large, rounded wooden door, ancient and heavy. It flew open.

When I heard the voice yell "down," I felt Peter push me to the ground, covering my body with his own. Heat shot over us, intense, blistering. And then it was over.

Chapter 31

"It's okay. You can get up now."

I looked upward awkwardly, trying to lift my body while simultaneously seeing who our savior was. When I saw the queen of the American Territories standing above me, I was stunned.

"Are you guys okay?" Monica asked, a shocked look on her face, I assumed because of our arrival.

"Us?" Kevin stammered, looking back in surprise.

Having regained my footing, I turned to see what had become of our attackers, realizing quickly why people seemed unnerved. Nothing was left but ash. Flesh, blood, bone—all of it destroyed in a brief blast of intense heat.

"Come in before anyone sees us," she said, ushering us through the door quickly, her eyes never leaving the spot where our assailants had stood.

The door closed behind us, presumably becoming a brick wall again on the other side. On this side, it no longer appeared wooden. In fact, the entire wall was in place but was transparent. It would have felt as though we were still in the alley, were it not for the wood-paneled walls and aristocratic décor at my back.

"Took you a little bit to answer, didn't it?" Lucille said, still in shock.

"How did you do that out there?" Peter asked, a guarded tone to his voice.

"I don't know," Monica replied. "I haven't really used my powers since that first day, but *that* … I've never done anything like that."

I could tell from Peter's face that he was starting to harbor some of the same questions I had. Stronger powers seemed good, but what were the side effects of the synthetic spores? While I didn't see much point in comparing notes just yet, it was nice to see I wasn't the only one getting suspicious.

"Why are you answering the door instead of Dimitry's friends?" I asked, suddenly realizing that there wasn't much of a welcoming party.

"Four of them came to get us. Two of them are alive. They're injured. Not badly, but enough," Monica answered.

"And the other two?" Lucille asked.

"They were killed getting us back into town," Monica responded. "Ivan was shot leading the soldiers off when we got through the fence. Dimitry's sister was killed pushing me through the door. She shut it right before the guards came around the corner. They shot her so many times I lost count."

"I'm sorry," Lucille said, apologetic for making her relive the moment, realizing that she would have seen all of it through the one-way wall.

"Well," Monica said to me, "it's clear you've seen some troubles too, given who you left with and who you came back with. But you folks should wash up now. We can get caught up over dinner."

The terror of the day disappeared when I thought of a hot shower and a dinner that didn't taste of bitter roots and berries. I was so lost in thought, in fact, that I barely noticed the grandeur of the room we had just entered. Right off the entryway, the ceilings seemed to stretch three or four stories up. Perfectly polished wooden staircases spiraled skyward along the side walls, which were otherwise decorated with paintings by some of the great masters.

The room itself was a huge square, with sitting areas arranged throughout and decorated with luxurious antiques of the highest quality. I thought of the alleyway entrance, of the building outside, and my mind reeled.

"How is *this* inside of *that?*" Lucille asked, as if reading my mind.

A man with his leg bandaged and elevated on a chair near the entrance spoke up. "This used to be here," he said.

"This is Kristian," Monica informed us. "He's one of the people who saved us."

"Save, I don't know," Kristian chuckled, "but if you're going to be hunted, seems better to wait it out in style, no?"

We did a quick round of introductions, but even though being clean again was so very close, I just couldn't let go of what he had said.

"What did you mean *this used to be here?*" I asked

"Even before The Lords, Russian scientists theorized that a localized tiny sliver of time could be bubbled off, dragged along by the current but forever apart from the actual timestream. You take a physical element, like this house, and you build the loop around it; it always exists in here, regardless of what happens to it elsewhere. We're inside of a single ever-repeating nanosecond that stays attached to the world around it while remaining ever-so-slightly out of sync with it. Think of it as a time roundabout, if you like."

"And you know this how?" I asked, not meaning to sound rude. I was both amazed and confused. The technology around us felt like it veered closer to magic every time a new innovation reared its head.

"My grandfather was one of those scientists. When the Bear took over, his research suddenly leapt forward by generations." He motioned for us to sit on the sofas near where he was resting.

"Because of the spacecraft?" I asked, easing onto a loveseat, my body suddenly realizing what it had been missing.

"He would never say outright," he replied, "but I don't know what else it could have been. He told me about it before his death. You see, this place we're in now was his home, and before that, it was his parents' home. Our family prospered over the years, and my ancestors always had a hand in shaping the policies of the government.

"Unfortunately for him, my grandfather had been born with more of a social conscience than his parents. The family name gave him a certain level of autonomy, but the Bear didn't trust him. He chose to conduct much of his work in secret, right here in this house. Eventually, he managed to pull a fraction of a second of time out of sync and loop it in on itself, essentially creating a bubble in which time no longer passed in the way we had known it to. The next day, he brought our family here.

"My grandfather left soon after, telling us to stay inside unless absolutely necessary. We waited for two days before my father went outside to look for him. As he exited through the back door, it disappeared behind him. All that was left in its place were scorched ruins, but when he reached back in to where the field existed, the door reappeared. I can't imagine what he thought, but he was a man on a mission, and he wasn't about to let a disappearing door hold him back.

"He didn't return until later that evening. He had brought more supplies for us, including some newspapers and a few large sacks filled with money, food, and medication. The papers provided the rest of the story. A fire, presumably accidental, destroyed the mansion, which we were and are currently sitting in. Only the charred walls and foundation remained."

"How did he get back in?" Peter asked.

"Grandfather left a biometric scanning system. Got the right genes, you've got a door. They built over the remains eventually, but we still exist in an overlapping space outside of time."

"That's astonishing," I said. Orphanage was sounding pretty normal suddenly.

"If you'd like to get cleaned up, I'm a little long-winded, particularly now that I can't really move. Restless, I guess."

"Actually," I said, suddenly feeling like answers might be more satisfying than the shower and knowing the backpack could hold for a few moments, "I want to hear the rest." We'd gotten so few answers along the way that I was reluctant to pass up anything that might shed light on our situation.

"Well, it turns out my grandfather had insured the mansion for a fortune, leaving my father as the beneficiary."

"And then he somehow caused the fire," I said.

"So my family believes," Kristian responded. "From asking around, my father learned that my grandfather was picked up on the streets by Lord Viktor himself. My father made inquiries, but we never saw the old man again. In the roughest of times, this was our stronghold."

"Where's the rest of your family?" Lucille asked gently.

"Unfortunately, I'm all that's left. Mother and Father were gunned down in the street, probably by government officials. My sister was taken by the Terrors, who sent us videos of themselves violating and abusing her before finally leaving her corpse naked in the town square. My brother died trying to avenge her."

"I'm sorry," Lucille said.

"It was difficult," Kristian added. "All of them should have had unnaturally long lives. We age at a crawl in this space apart from time. The only reason they're dead is because they went outside, where the monsters are."

The thought of everything this man had been through was devastating. I felt bad for insisting he continue his story, and then I felt angry that his was a story anyone had to tell.

"Let's all get cleaned up so we can eat," Monica called out, clearly uncomfortable. Her recovery since last I'd seen her was remarkable.

There was a special grandeur to the home, a kind I'd never seen. Lord Nathaniel's palace was impressive, but it was cold, sterile, new. This place had history covering every square inch, just about every

211

trinket, portrait, and switch plate piquing my interest.

Mine was the last room in the hall. I thanked Monica, and then she clasped my hands very warmly. She told me how glad she was to see me. It felt genuine, and I realized that aside from her nurse and me, she hadn't really spoken with any of our group before we invaded Russia.

As she left, I couldn't help but feel for her. She had just gotten powers, just gotten married, just seen her entire family slaughtered, and just gotten shipped off to war. My head would be spinning. Again, I realized how she appeared to have risen to the occasion in a way I couldn't have imagined after her shaky start.

The bedroom was every bit as ornate as the rest of the house. Dropping onto the edge of the plump featherbed, I realized that it was the first time I'd really been alone since my solo sprint through the forest after Lucille's capture. Not really quality time. I began to feel a wave of sleep wash over me and forced myself to my feet.

I started toward the bathroom before remembering the backpack. I had already tossed it from my shoulders onto a nearby chair, not even thinking about its contents. I grabbed it quickly, suddenly starved for whatever knowledge it contained.

I undid the zipper and pulled a stack of papers and file folders out of the bag and laid them on the bed. An envelope with my name on it was on top. Opening it, I found a note from Aleksei, written in English. His confidence in my living must have been high if he dared put it in there.

Simone, the letter started, *I am sorry for my betrayal, but monstrous as they are, they are still my children. The documents in this bag are the basis of Red Steel. They contain secrets The Lords have kept from us all. Secrets that will change much of how you see the world. I hope you are able to put them to better use than I was able to.*

The first document after the letter was a copy of the message found in the spacecraft that created The Lords. This wasn't exactly news.

Every kid saw the message in school, but no one had worked out what it meant. At least that's what I thought until I turned to the next page, which featured a full translation. It was dated the day before the explosion at the crash site.

The organisms aboard this craft shall pass through generations, making them strong, superior. It is the only path forward when the stars disappear and their killer approaches.

I sat there staring at the paper for a long time. It was a lot to take in. It certainly indicated that the spores were meant to be spread across the planet as everyone theorized. From what Dr. Frank had said during his Regenesis work, it was possible that smaller doses wouldn't have ravaged the initial host. Then younger generations would gain power as the spores grew and mutated as they got passed along.

It was hard to know for sure, but it certainly sounded like the powers were to help stop something that could murder stars. It was easy to see why the shield would have stayed up, anyway. Trusting an alien note about spores about to be spread around your planet wasn't generally the soundest plan. But why had they kept the translation a secret all these years?

I was startled by a knock at the door, barely stifling a scream of surprise. I covered the papers with the bedspread and crossed to the door, where Peter waited on the other side.

"Hey," he said, a little uncomfortably.

"Hi," I said, giving my best *it's okay* smile. We had been out of sync since his rescue, but we needed to get past it. "What's up?"

"I think dinner, actually," he replied. "You ready?"

"I haven't even started getting ready," I said. "Enjoying the quiet for a change. I'll be down in a few, okay?"

"Sure," he said, eyeing me a little suspiciously. "I've never known you to miss the start of a meal."

"I'm full of surprises," I replied playfully before gently closing the door in his face. It felt good, the flirting, the normalcy of it. Looking back toward the documents, though, it all came crashing back down. Why had Lord Nathaniel lied to me about this at the end, and what else from world history class was untrue? It would have to wait. I was starving for food as much as for information.

The gilded bathroom was fit for a king, although all I cared about was the hot running water. Feeling the grime of my experiences washing off of me, I let myself relax for just a few moments under the steaming spray, pretending everything that had happened was just a dream. *I'm safe now*, I let myself think.

Chapter 32

It took me longer than I'd planned to pull myself from the shower and slip into the clothes our host had thoughtfully supplied. They were definitely not what I would have chosen, the stiff fabrics scratching every inch of skin they found. The smell from the kitchen had begun to make its way through the house, though, and the promise of actual food pushed my clothing concerns to the back of my mind.

I made my way downstairs quickly to find everyone else already present. Monica, Veronica, Justine, and Francine sat toward the head of the table with Kristian and another man I didn't know. Kevin, Peter, and Lucille flanked them, a seat for me left at the end.

"Sorry if I held you up," I said, sitting down in the chair and surveying the offerings in front of me. I couldn't identify half of it, but my stomach was no longer finicky.

"Just got here myself," Kevin assured me.

"We can do the introductions and compare notes while we eat," Monica said, sounding more composed than I had anticipated. I was still a little shocked at how level-headed she'd been since we'd arrived. Part of that could clearly be ascribed to the pills leaving her system, but the sudden confidence was undeniable.

We ate like kings. Borscht and cabbage dishes, meats and caviar, all washed down with a liberal amount of premium vodka, ever-present in Russia. It was a feast that no bad news could completely dampen, even though we all had some bad news to share.

The other man at the table was Mikael. He had been a friend of Kristian's since childhood, as had Dimitry and his sister, now both tragically gone. The four of them had been the original core of Red Steel, although ironically the group hadn't really coalesced under that name until Aleksei joined them.

The news of Aleksei's betrayal and Dimitry's death hit Mikael and Kristian hard, each of them slurring out a vow to track down and destroy the traitor. I felt a little guilty suddenly over my affection for Aleksei. The backpack was proof he planned for my safety, and its contents made clear he knew the truth had to be told. He just wasn't going to be the one brave enough to do it.

As everyone began diving in for seconds without a hint of modesty, Veronica told us what had happened to her and the others in the seeming eternity since last we'd been together. Her gravelly voice made me wish someone else had relayed the tale, but luckily there wasn't much to it.

As it turned out, the area of forest we sheltered in was somewhat out of the way. The guard who had surprised Monica and her unfortunate nurse earlier had probably strayed off course. Once they moved deeper into the woods, they didn't see anyone else, which, given the state of affairs when we left, was probably best for friend and foe alike.

Monica had started coming back to herself the day after we started for the lab, her meds wearing off even as the shock began to dissipate. Francine got a grip soon after. Aside from the tragedies on their way to this mansion, our comrades had been pretty lucky. In fact, it was starting to feel like maybe I was the curse.

"At the door," Monica said once we had finished relating how we had made our way back, "I've never felt as in control of it before."

"Same thing here," Kevin chimed in. "Used to be a mental strain to make myself fly, but now it's a snap to lift everyone."

"Process is probably finally fully integrating with our bodies," Peter said like it was obvious, still chewing as he said the words, his fork dangling off the side of his hand. "Just means we weren't quite done evolving. Also means maybe we can actually handle the Bears if we have to." He gave a look in my direction, glancing away quickly when my eyes caught his. I was right. He worried something was wrong too.

I wanted to discuss it with them, but introducing a new unsolvable problem into the mix seemed cruel. We would probably all die before whatever was going on could kill them anyway.

"I'm hoping we don't have to find out if we can take on anyone," Justine said. "Even if we could handle them, then what? Do we take over Russia? We just need to get someplace safe."

"And where is safety?" Veronica said. "In which direction do we travel?"

"Toward China," I said. "Or Nigeria. At least that's what I've heard. Of course, my sources have been majorly unreliable so far."

"No, those are both good choices," Mikael interrupted. "Probably your only choices."

"What about Britain?" Monica asked, most likely still thinking we could return home.

"I'm not sure that's a good idea," I said. "I'm not so sure America's on our side right now. It's just, we saw this news report, and there was a sound clip from Lord Sebastian, and he was really using our deaths as—how do I phrase this?"

"Skip to the end," Kevin helpfully broke in.

"America thinks we're dead, and just based on everything I've seen and heard, I don't think Lord Sebastian's in any rush to have us miraculously return."

I looked at Monica for a hint of surprise, but none came.

"You knew," I said to her, "that he didn't mean for us to come back. Didn't you?"

She blushed a bit and shifted in her seat. "I didn't know," she said, her head slanted in shame, "but I thought so. One night I went to his study with some tea. He was working late, and my mother always said it was the little things that make a marriage work. I knocked, but no one answered.

"When I entered the room, he was in the middle of talking with a few of his advisers. They stopped pretty abruptly when I put the tea down, looking at me like I was insane. Sebastian dismissed them and called me over to his desk.

"When I got there, he grabbed me by the wrist and lifted me off the floor. He was so angry at me for interrupting him. He tossed me across the room. I hit the wall thinking that was it, but when I looked up, he was still coming.

"He crouched over me like an animal. I could feel his breath on my skin, burning my nostrils. Then he just spoke to me in this normal tone, but too normal. Abnormally normal. He brushed my hair behind my ear with his finger and told me how he couldn't wait to get rid of me.

"He told me Russia would be my grave. Then he told me he hated that they would get all the fun. He told me all the things the Terrors would do to me. He said he requested tapes," she stopped. "Anyway, they've got some amazing healing machines at that government hospital. Real sci-fi kind of stuff. Looked as good as new in like twenty minutes."

I felt sick to my stomach. I hadn't seen that side of Sebastian, but I was starting to believe I'd only ever seen exactly what he wanted me to see.

"Hearing that," Lucille said, "is the only thing that makes me want to go back to America. That man needs to be put down."

Monica brought her head back up a bit, as though she had expected a different response.

"So, were we always meant to be martyrs for him? Why even bother?"

Justine asked.

"I'm with her," Lucille said. "What do they gain? Why create us just to kill us?"

"Unless they *needed* to create us," Peter said, looking in my direction.

"They needed to isolate a cure for the other Lords," I responded. "At least that's what they said at the lab. "Maybe they're worried about their own future health? Maybe they're trying to figure out how to gain new powers?"

"But they could just get rid of us once they'd finished creating us, right? Why put us in stupid outfits and make a fuss instead of studying us and killing us?" Lucille asked.

"There's a logical explanation somewhere," Peter said. "The military wouldn't do this if they didn't believe in us." He was starting to look confused and conflicted. The military training had burrowed deep.

"But we were successful in their eyes," Lucille responded. "Moscow's gone. And now we're out of their hair."

"We're not going to find any answers to any of that tonight," Justine said, saving us from ourselves. "Is there really anyplace safe? I mean, The Lords all have their pacts."

"Well, mostly," Mikael cut in. "There are still rivalries and feuds, but the power of the overall group keeps these things in check."

"Of course," I observed, "the overall group is getting smaller. It's just five now."

"Weren't they supposed to be immortal?" Justine asked.

"They were," I replied, "but they most definitely aren't."

"Are we really just going to leave?" Francine asked, making me realize this was the first time she'd contributed to our discussion. "I mean, what about the others? We're just going to leave them here?"

"If we try to get them back," I said, "I don't think any of us are going to make it out alive. So far, we've been lucky, and they've been careless."

"Simone's right," Kevin added. "I don't want to leave those guys here, but maybe we can find a way to get them out once we're not busy fighting for our own lives."

"You really think freeing them from outside the territory is going to be easier than doing it while we're here?" Peter said.

"Look," Kevin said animatedly, "I know you've got the *Leave no man behind* thing going, and I respect that, but if we don't get out of here soon, we're not getting out at all, and then no one's trying to save them."

Peter started to get up to say something, but I put a hand on his chest, guiding him back into his seat and back to calm. We exchanged a quick glance as I tried to give him whatever reassurance he was clearly craving.

"We all want to save the others," Lucille said, "but I think it's clear that the Bears are using them as bait. Every rescue mission has been a trap, and we have to break the pattern."

"And you don't think they'll expect us to try to escape?" Peter asked.

"Of course, they will," she conceded, "which is why we have to figure out the least likely routes to wherever we end up going. Hopefully it takes them a bit to find us."

"Couldn't we just stay here until this all dies down?" Francine said softly.

"That is your safest option," Mikael said. "It will be a long while before the royals give up their search, but this place has gone undetected for a long time."

"That just means they haven't really been looking for it," I said. "It's just a game to them. If you're no fun, they don't bother."

There was a moment of silence, a realization of the inevitability of our decision. We could stay put, but the longer we waited, the more we put everyone in danger. The Bears would never stop toying with us. Anyone in their way was collateral damage.

"So," Mikael's voice broke in, "we must figure out your best path to safety, but at least for tonight, let's celebrate your survival and reunion."

He broke out into some Russian song or another, his mug of vodka apparently lightening his spirits. It may have also been lightening my head, thoughts of our captured comrades haunting me.

"Ahem," Lucille said, "care to come back down to Earth?"

"Sorry, lost in thought a lot lately," I said.

"It's cute that you think that's a new thing. What's on your mind?"

"Probably the same things we're all thinking," I said.

Rejoining the conversation, I found that our hosts were pulling out all the stops, refilling glasses and offering jokes and tricks galore. I tried to get in the spirit, but I started thinking of the backpack. Now that I was full, I wanted nothing more than to sort through everything in it, Aleksei's warnings still stuck in my head.

I finally gave up appearances and excused myself, feigning exhaustion. Peter took the excuse to make his own exit by offering to walk me to my room. It was a surprisingly quiet walk, but once we were near my door, he took my hand.

"You know I won't let anything happen to you, right?" he asked me.

I searched his eyes, looking for the person who had been my family for years. I could still see him.

"Of course," I replied. "But I'm pretty sure I was the one who rescued you the other day."

He gave me a hug before leaving me at my door and returning to his room. I watched him as he made his way down the hall, never turning back, making me wonder if he knew I was still looking.

Once in my room, I locked the door and pulled back the bedspread to reveal the papers and folders. I knew I needed sleep, particularly before going through documents sure to set my paranoia aflame, but it wasn't going to happen. This was too big.

Looking at the stack, I wanted to rip into it and just ingest everything at once. I restrained myself, though, and started with the file folder directly under the translation of the alien message.

Inside were medical documents. Luckily these had clearly been meant for sharing among The Lords, so translations for all languages accompanied the pages of notes. Scanning them, I realized that they were examinations of the Russian royal family. The Iron Bear was first in order, and the outlook from his doctor was as grim as Lord Nathaniel's must have been.

Viktor was falling apart. The spores were eating away at him at a rate the file noted as *aggressive, much more so than has been seen in the other Lords.* It made sense that The Lords were trading health information, since they were the only people with their particular physiologies, but I still found myself surprised. We were so sheltered from the world in America that the idea of this transcontinental cooperation seemed unreal.

The pages that followed were examinations of his children. Their bodies, it noted, weren't rejecting the spores. They were, in fact, constantly growing stronger, but their psychology notes mentioned severe psychosis, violent outbursts, and a list of other maladies each more terrible than the last. No link was obvious, but it was clear the doctors worried it was the doing of the spores. I closed the folder, hoping to find answers further down the pile.

The next section was a collection of stapled copies of documents that appeared to be directly from Lord Viktor to the other world powers. Its contents weren't damning, but it was clear that The Lords and their families had regular meetings where they trained the children in the use of their powers and discussed strategy. There was no indication about what kind of strategy would be on the table, but if they knew something that could kill stars was on its way, the sky was the limit.

By the time I had made it through Lord Viktor's letter, my yawns had become increasingly severe. Still, I turned to the next document. It was a picture taken by a telescope. I didn't recognize any constellations, and the coordinates and notes that accompanied the image didn't help me place it. When I went to the next page, I realized it was a picture of the same stars, that same place in space. Something was off, though. The stars. Some of them weren't there anymore. The dates in the corner of the two images placed them a year apart, the earlier from five years ago.

The murderer was on its way, and instead of a planet full of powerful citizens, we had a disjointed band of psychotic despots. I looked at the picture again, trying to isolate the places where the stars had seemingly burned out. Was there a shape there? I could have sworn I saw something in the dark.

Focus on the dark.

Chapter 33

I woke to a rumbling sound, my head lifting quickly from its clearing amid the files. I was getting used to the sounds of danger, and yelling people running through the halls definitely fit the bill. I cursed myself for falling asleep while reading, but I had thought there would be more time in the morning.

I threw the documents back in the bag, as quickly as I could right before a tremor shook the house. I had just gotten the backpack over my shoulder when Peter burst through the door in a state of panic.

"Come on!" he yelled, grabbing my arm.

Luckily, I was still dressed, and quickly pulling myself out of my early morning daze, I matched Peter's footfalls. The house shook, its old beams creaking with the waves. We ran.

I wasn't sure what time it was, but no one seemed to have been up and about yet. As we got to the living room, people's outfits ranged from pajamas to fatigues. Another rumble sounded off, and the place shook more violently than before.

I looked at Kevin and Lucille, finally realizing what had found us. As our eyes met, it clicked for them too.

"We have to get out of here, right now!" I yelled.

I felt Kevin start to lift us into the air, but Mikael and his friend had stopped to gather some belongings. They were running toward us, nearly in range of Kevin's powers, the rest of us hovering above the shaking floor, waiting for them.

"Almost," Kevin growled, his face contorted in concentration and fear.

Just then, the floor gave way, collapsing underneath the two. A tentacle, large and heavy, shot out of the hole, smashing up into the high ceilings. The little hands that dotted it reached out grotesquely, grasping at the air for anything to clutch. I heard Francine scream. I had hoped not to see this thing again.

"Now!" Peter yelled. The world went liquid in front of me as Lucille turned our party invisible. Kevin began to raise us quickly toward the ceiling. The tentacle was retracting, and it looked like a clear shot through a hole in the roof. Kevin was towing us as fast as he could, trying to keep a steady wind around us to knock away stray beams and chunks of building material.

Even as we cleared the makeshift skylight, a second tentacle shot through the ceiling, flying so high into the air that it sideswiped Kevin, causing us all to start falling. Luckily, he regained his composure quickly, and we were seemingly out of trouble, until I heard a scream behind me. The tentacles had overtaken the entire structure now, destroying it in both the pocket loop and the real world from what I could tell. What had been two tentacles was now at least eight, and whatever creature was using these appendages was hauling itself out of the ground with them, the tip of a beak emerging from the pit.

Soldiers stationed at the entrance were being dragged into the pit by the tiny little hands, the tentacles bringing them directly over the gaping maw of the beak before the baby fists opened and dropped their prey. I suddenly realized where the scream had come from. Justine was in the clutches of the hands on one of the large tentacles. She was caught by her hair, arms, legs.

A seemingly endless barrage of tentacles had emerged now, dragging people, animals, and even buildings into the dark void below the village.

The tentacles and beak seemed to be from nowhere, the rest of the creature's massive body presumably still ensconced within the time loop.

I signaled to Kevin to drop me down, bringing Justine to his attention. He lowered with me, both of us diving in quickly. He fired a burst of heavy wind at the base of the tentacle that held our teammate, but it barely flinched. A sound of rage emanated from the beak, however, terrifying in its raw anger.

I felt something brush past me before seeing the tentacle reel as though hit hard. Looking back, Peter was pulling back from firing a seismic blast. Justine was still stuck, though, and she was being pulled closer to the beak. The others, finally wrapping their heads around what was happening were trying to find a way over to help us, but then Peter shot a soft blast that knocked them back upward.

"We can't help her!" he yelled. "If we keep trying, we're all going to die!"

"We can't leave her!" I screamed, angry, frustrated, terrified.

"We have to!"

I tried to move closer, unsure of what I could even do, but I was held back. Kevin reached out and took my hand. He looked me in the eye, bringing me back to reality before pulling me upward into the sky. I could already feel myself sobbing when I heard the gurgle from the creature in the ground.

It was over then. The day was barely even new, the sun just now taking to the sky, and already we had lost three friends. I thought that we were in a safe place when we got to that house, but like everything on this journey, it was an illusion, a lie.

"How was that even possible?" Lucille finally asked, breaking the silence with a question that had clearly been rolling around in her mind. "If we were outside of time, how could that happen?"

"Well," Peter theorized, "if the residence was coded so their family could enter it from the outside, it's just a matter of breaking that code to access the time loop itself, I guess. Maybe if the ground below the building was part of the loop, they just ported it in there."

"Was it our fault?" I asked, still ashamed of the thought that Justine's last sight was us abandoning her to die. "Did we lead them there?"

"Maybe," he said. "I don't think it's worth worrying about right now."

"Could someone tell me what the hell that thing was, at least?" Monica asked, clearly still terrified from the encounter.

"Not sure," I yelled to her. Kevin had figured out how to keep the noise down, but it still wasn't a quiet way to travel. "It's what we ran into when we rescued Kevin."

"Would have been great if you'd killed it then," Peter joked.

"A little busy not getting killed at the time," I responded, still too distraught to joke.

"We need to stay out of populated areas," Peter yelled to Kevin, who had flown back toward the front of the group.

Kevin nodded his understanding, flying us far enough away that even from the sky we couldn't see homes, cars, or people. We landed in a wooded area miles from the site of our most recent disaster. A river of ice-cold water roared through the land, and the tall trees provided places to rest. We were, all of us, exhausted from the physical and mental exertions of the morning. We needed to take stock before we just kept blindly running.

Given that we hadn't had time for anything before our escape, we all greedily drank from the few shared filtration canteens remaining. Thirst quenched, I flopped onto my back, trying to sort through the events of the day but finding too much running through my head for any one thought to achieve resolution.

"So, what now?" Kevin said to the air.

"Is there any chance at all that Justine is …" Francine started to ask before trailing off.

No one answered. Even grief was on an accelerated timeline now. Survival had taken over. Harboring illusions about what we were facing was no longer an option.

"At the moment," I said, "I'm tempted to just hide here for the rest of our lives." It was feeling like a real possibility for a second. It wasn't like we had anywhere to be.

I got a slight chuckle from Lucille and Kevin, but the others, Peter included, remained grim. It was hard to blame them.

"Mikael had us heading toward the Chinese border, so maybe that's what we should keep doing," Monica said.

"We don't have any supplies, though," Francine responded. She looked like she was ready to collapse again.

"We can't change that," Peter responded, "at least not right now. I think Lady Monica's right. We should keep moving forward."

The reaction to hearing Monica's title was strange. To most, it didn't have much effect, but Lucille's eyes did a quick roll even as she grabbed my upper arm in surprise. Monica looked a little embarrassed, as though she'd forgotten she even had a title.

To be honest, I had expected more infighting among the group, but everyone's inexperience seemed to have kept that problem at bay. Peter butted heads with people on occasion, but even he was too new to all of this to act overly superior.

"We should stay here tonight," I said. "We can start out tomorrow when we're fresh and ready."

"And then?" Kevin asked.

"We slink through the center of the country avoiding contact wherever possible. At the Chinese border, we fight if we have to."

The time from the beginning of the day to its end had felt like a blink. The rest of our evening involved gathering what supplies we could from around us, eating a few rabbits Veronica caught, and gnawing on bitter greens, which I knew how to expertly spot by this time.

I had taken up my seat below a large tree, seemingly as ancient as the land it grew upon, even though it might have just been a few days old, given the terraforming technology. Peter came and sat next to me. "I'm sorry," he said. "About Justine, about arguing. I'm just trying to keep us safe. To keep you safe."

"You don't have to," I said. "We're all in the same boat here." *Of course, some of us had powers.*

"I just want things to be like they were," he sighed, putting his hand on mine.

"Let's just make it out of Russia first, okay?" I said with a soft smile. "Nobody's quite themselves here."

"Or maybe they never were at home," he said. He leaned over and gave me a kiss on the forehead before walking back toward the fire.

My sleep was so deep that my dreams were completely eradicated upon waking, with the terrifying exception of the sickening gurgle I heard earlier that day. That sound stayed with me.

Chapter 34

Rolling out of my little nest, I made way to the fire. It looked like I was the last one up. Someone, I assumed Peter, had already been out to catch breakfast. There were at least sixteen eggs of varying sizes and a few birds I couldn't identify post plucking.

"How much farther is it, roughly?" Monica asked.

"A ways," Peter replied. "It was easy yesterday because we were in the air, but going through the terrain will add plenty of time."

"Who said we have to go through the terrain?" Kevin interjected.

I was just sitting down and grabbing a handful of berries. "You were exhausted after yesterday," I said to him. "It's too dangerous for you and Lucille."

"Don't bring me into this," Lucille said. "Really, I was fine."

"And I was mostly tired because yesterday sucked," Kevin added. "The flying isn't the hard part."

It wasn't, at least not to him.

"I should be able to increase our speed," Kevin continued, "and as long as Lucille can keep us invisible, I think we can stay off the radar. It'll actually let us go further off road and maybe avoid more problems."

"You'll tell us if it's too much?" Monica asked.

"Sure," Kevin replied, a tired grin on his face.

"Can't you just heal him every day?" Peter asked Veronica.

"My ability to heal comes at a price," her voice scrawled out. "At the village, I was charged up by the army. I had energy to spare." She sounded both defiant and offended, and looking past her ashen face and the scratching-nails voice, it was easy to see the woman she had been still there. It had to be bittersweet being able to heal only by first using your powers to hurt.

I hadn't considered before that her body had been changed so radically that physical nourishment no longer provided what she needed simply to survive, but it had become clear watching her morning ritual. She fed on life, meaning she would always have to drain at least a little bit from something around her. It was easy to understand why she might not want to do more than necessary. I imagined there was temptation in power like that.

Before long, the strange shimmer of Lucille's invisibility had surrounded us all once again, and I felt the wind start to swirl, lifting me off the ground. It was smooth, though, like a platform of air, eventually easing me into a horizontal position and pushing me onto a bed of gently undulating waves of air. Looking around, I could see that we were all strategically placed, Kevin looking perfectly fine under the pressure.

The first day was fairly simple. Lucille kept us invisible as long as we were within a reasonable range of her. Peter hunted food for us when we were on land, bringing back fish and rabbits. Water was as simple as Francine drawing moisture. Fire was simple with Monica along, although we limited our use. Even with Kevin dispersing the smoke, we had all chosen the path of caution since our encounter with the creature at the mansion.

Had we been traveling before the rise of The Lords, getting to what was then China would have been a much longer journey. Their science officer, An Wu, was a diligent, admirable man, more in tune with the modern era and Western democracy than many of his contemporaries. Nonetheless, when The Lords gathered around their table, suspicion of China tinted their views of the person with whom they worked. Lord Wu still managed to negotiate for part of eastern Russia and some surrounding islands. So, once we got past the mountain range that had come into clearer view throughout our first day, we would be at the border.

Kevin's abilities let us ride high-speed winds above treacherous land. Unfortunately, with so much time to think as we rode the winds, I worried more and more about the health of my comrades, both mental and physical. There was no way of knowing for sure where the growth of power would stop or what that would mean, given the synthetic nature of the spores. For all I knew, Kevin could just burn up midair, leaving the rest of us to fall to our deaths.

"Thoughts?" I heard Lucille ask in my ear. I had been so wrapped up that I hadn't realized she'd floated into position beside me.

"Yeah," I said, "but none that are going to be answered anytime soon."

"What do we do if we get there and China won't take us in?" she asked.

I honestly hadn't given it much thought, which struck me as odd as soon as she said it to me. "I don't know," I said. "We find a way to Nigeria and hope we have better luck there, I guess."

"And then what?" she asked sincerely. "Do we ever get back home? Do we build new lives? I've had more time to think these last few days than I've had since we've been here, and I'm really starting to not like it."

"Our situation?" I asked.

"Thinking," she responded with a little grin. "I've just been going on adrenaline for so long ..."

"Except when you were asleep in that tube," I interjected.

"Okay, fine, except when I was ..."

"Because I really haven't had a lot of good sleep this trip," I said, "so I don't know that I ..."

She reached across and put her hand over my mouth.

"I get it. You're funny. I should be less of an airborne pity party. But I am wondering where we go from here. Seriously." She looked less tense than when we had begun, but it was clear she was ready to move on to the real topic at hand.

I was about to start my response when Kevin pulled back alongside us swiftly. We had all learned how to move about within the current, but his control of the wind was art.

"We're coming close to the first section of the mountains," he told us. "Any thoughts on whether we should camp or keep moving?"

"Well, how are you holding up? I asked him. If he was asking the question, I assumed the strain must be getting to him, at least a little bit.

"I can keep us going," he said, "but if there's a fight ahead, I don't know how much use I'll be."

"We should camp," Lucille said. "But is the queen going to be upset if you let us decide?"

Kevin gave a little shrug, not really getting it. "Just tell her we should camp," I sighed to him, glaring at Lucille.

"What?" she snapped.

"Do you really want to be the mean girl of the group?" I said.

She started to say something but stopped herself. She put her palm against her face, her eyes mostly closed. "You're right, especially knowing what Sebastian did to her. I have no idea why calling her *queen* even sets me off"

"Well, we're about to try to escape Russia, so now's probably a bad time for whatever it is. You also may not want a living crematorium angry with you on the battlefield."

She gave a little laugh and clearly wanted to say something. I told her to go on, but she waved me off until I finally insisted.

"Are you talking about friendly fire?" She laughed.

I felt a smile cross my face, and my own stress melted a little. "I hate you."

"Oh, trust me, I completely understand," she replied.

We began to drift downward, and as he glided by, I heard Kevin call out, "Ladies and gentlemen, we're beginning our final descent." The rest of his words were lost as he continued to the front of the pack, touching down on the ground before us and turning to ensure everyone's landing was smooth.

Veronica, as she always did after these flights, immediately lay on the ground, the side of her face pressed against the dirt, the electricity of her tiny worms crackling in front of her. I had noticed that she looked weaker, more fragile the longer we stayed in the air, but after a short time back on terra firma, she was solidly creepy again.

We were in the foothills of the first mountain range, which gave us enough added cover to actually make us feel secure for the night. It occurred to me then that Lucille's power had been running virtually nonstop since we began this part of our journey, but she didn't look at all tired.

"Hey," I said to her, "I think we're safe down here. Maybe we can go visible for a change."

She responded with a look somewhere between confusion and irritation. "Why would we risk that?" she asked.

"You've been going for days."

"It's not like their powers," she said, indicating the rest of the team. "It's like a light switch. I turn it on, and it stays on. I turn it off, and it goes off."

"But it still has to be consuming some sort of fuel," I said. "I don't think now's when you want to test your limits."

She stopped for a second, thinking about the words, finally nodding in agreement.

We relayed the plan to the others, mapping out a method to ensure we remained undetected. In the end, we stayed as close to the mountains as possible, tucked away in little crannies and jagged nooks as we slept.

Chapter 35

When we woke in the morning, everyone showed signs of stiffness, except Veronica, who looked radiant, all things considered. We'd made it through another night without incident, and I felt more hopeful than I had in days, our goal closer than ever before.

My biggest fear still loomed: that Anna and the Terrors would exact their vengeance on us before we made it across the border, but we had come so far from where this had begun, I couldn't help but hope they'd given up. They still had their hostages. Maybe they'd finally tired of the chase.

It would actually be their cruelest move yet, leaving us looking over our shoulders while they forgot about us altogether.

Then I thought of their faces, their eyes, their smiles, and I realized they would never tire of the chase. The chase was what drove them. A loss was failure. It couldn't be admitted to, and it couldn't stand. Power, cruelty, and stature were all that mattered. Nothing would keep them from us, and their revenge would be vicious.

The Bears didn't consider themselves human enough to be concerned about morality, and judging by Monica's account of Lord Sebastian, they weren't alone.

"Did you catch any of that?" Peter asked, his drooped eye and slack head already correctly insinuating that I hadn't.

I snapped to and realized that a circle had formed around where I was sitting. I had inadvertently called a meeting at which I was not in attendance.

"Come on," he said, throwing his hands up melodramatically. "We're not going to be able to look out for you if you don't listen up."

"Ouch," I said. "See if I rescue you again."

"We're going to ride the winds close to the mountain face all the way to the first ridge we can pass through," Monica said. "From there, we should have an idea of whether or not there's any added security before we burst into open airspace."

I nodded my agreement. It was smart. We had no real idea what kind of sensors and monitors they would have in place to keep the area secure.

"I still think the roads are more direct," Francine said.

Monica put her hand on Francine's, and the woman stopped speaking.

It was a quiet journey, much more so than in previous days. Still, the tension that had eased away at the mountain's base returned in full force midway up. Kevin was at the head of our floating line. Monica was at his side, followed by Lucille and Francine. I was side by side with Veronica, whose presence both creeped me out and made me feel ashamed for being creeped out, an emotion that must have beamed from every pore.

"Not fond of me," she said, "are you?" That voice, like gravel in a garbage disposal, set my nerves on edge.

"I'm just stressed," I dodged, "and we don't really know each other yet."

"Remember that last part," she said with a little wink that seemed out of place on her weak, ashen face. "We will, before our parts have been played."

"What do you mean?" I asked, thoroughly tired of surprises.

"I don't know," her voice creaked above the wind, "but I will."

"What?" I asked, adding *slightly angry* to the list of emotions vying for face time. Any other day, I would have just written it off as *whatever* weirdness, but there was too much on my shoulders, and I could feel the balance tipping. "What do you mean?"

She remained calm, almost serene, even though I could feel the intensity of my glare without seeing it. "The Earth exists in all times at once. We're echoes on its surface. It knows where we begin and where we end, because for it, everything that has ever happened or ever will happen is happening at this very moment."

"And it tells you?" I said, tired of cryptic messages and questions piling atop questions.

"It tells me a little," she replied. "It forgets some of the details, but it knows when events, even small ones, are important. It feeds off our energy as much as we feed off it. We're the birds on the back of the elephant."

"And what has it told you specifically?" I asked, hoping to power through the philosophical part of the answer.

"Nothing specifically," she said, "but we're at the start of something massive, and we're still needed."

"Needed for what?" I asked, knowing what was coming.

"I don't know," she replied.

"And the others?" I asked, now feeling the tension settle into every bit of my body.

"I don't know," she said simply. "The details aren't always clear."

"Can we find out? Can we change anything if we do find out?" I asked, irritated at her calm resignation.

"Technically no," she told me. "But theoretically, yes. There's a catch, though."

"Which is?" I asked, my anger and stress decreasing as the words started to make more sense.

"Our best chance of changing things is not knowing how they're supposed to turn out to begin with."

"How will we know if we've changed anything then?" I asked.

"This is why I just try and go with it," Veronica responded.

I laughed and caught myself before the noise became too loud. She had surprised me.

I let it sink in and reacquainted myself with the sights around me, trying to picture every second of every hour of every year, millennium after millennium, stacked on top of one another, all happening at once. I tried to close off that line of thought quickly as we headed toward a break in the mountainside, perhaps our chance to cross through into the valley.

It had always existed, but once the territories were laid out, the Iron Bear himself pulverized a perfectly clear section between the two ranges, also digging tunnels into each country, tearing through the mountains in sections. I tried not to think about what kind of destabilizing effect that might have as we glided up and landed on the mountain alongside the rest of our group. Looking over the side made my stomach twist, but not because of the height for a change.

The entire middle section was essentially a military stronghold. I had thought that civilian troops had been taken off the field until I got to Russia, but now I understood why they were still in play. The weaponry they had with them and the machines ready at the gates were the stuff of science fiction. While it might not be enough to take down one of The Lords, they looked like they would at least do damage.

A pair of binoculars Peter had managed to grab during our escape days earlier gave us a clear view of the actual border, right in the middle of the clearing. It was lined with Russian vehicles and troops, barracks and station houses at each end. The Chinese side was similarly prepared. If anything went wrong, it was a prefab war zone. No assembly required.

We were well hidden in our little perch on the mountainside, but between us and the Chinese Territories stood an electric grid that stretched as far and wide as we could see. It hadn't been visible from below, but once we reached eye level, the slight gleam of one beam led to the sudden acknowledgment of the others around it. It was massive and presumably deadly. The actual checkpoint between the two territories had some cargo trucks passing through. The two coming from China into Russia were waved through easily, but the three cargo transports leaving Russia had been detained and were undergoing an incredibly thorough search, guards armed with high-tech weaponry positioned at every imaginable angle.

As a larger cargo vehicle came through from the Chinese side of the border, the gates suddenly slid into motion, nearly silent as they pulled outward and upward, expanding the actual border crossing itself to a size through which the transport could fit. Even as the metal beams pushed into it, the electric web that divided the sky moved, displaced by the incursion. Once it had achieved its width and height, the metal gate began to increase its depth, extending itself far enough to equal roughly two of the transports. After the transport had made its way into the Russian Territories, apparently passing inspection, the gateway shrank back down to its smaller form, the web of lasers following its guidance.

"Okay, so metal might disrupt the fence," Lucille said, her mind trying to come up with any idea that didn't bring us close to the gate itself. The mass of vehicles and soldiers milling about in the area below us were best avoided, I agreed.

"Or it could just be this metal, possibly a coating. Or the gate could even be the starting point of the fence," Francine pointed out. I realized how little I'd ever spoken with her and was surprised by her analytical skills.

"Even if we can disrupt the fence, though," I pitched in, "surely that would trigger an alarm, or even backup defenses, safeguards."

"We might be able to get through during that moment of confusion, though. A large enough hole and one strong gust of wind could do it." Lucille said.

"If we don't do anything that would set off sensors, we could hitch a ride with a transport going through," Kevin suggested.

Peter pulled back from his binoculars for a few seconds. "Don't think that's gonna work," he said flatly, emitting a small sigh and handing the binoculars to me.

Putting them to my eyes was startling. I felt like I was in the middle of the Russian encampment. I panned around for a few seconds, unsure of what to focus on until I felt Peter's hands cover mine, guiding me to the right spot. To the right of the gateway was a large sensor screen. When a smaller transport passed through, the screen appeared to register the contents of the transport, human and otherwise.

"The gateway's a scanner," he said, gently taking his binoculars back, his sly half-grin making an appearance.

"So, what happens if something that shouldn't go through tries to go through?" Lucille asked.

"What did you have in mind?" Monica countered.

"Well," Lucille began, clearly fighting the urge to add a snarky *Your Majesty*, "maybe we blow a bird or lizard onto the top of a transport as it goes through and see what kind of response it gets."

"It might be specific to the size of the object as well as whether or not it's organic, though," Peter chimed in. "They wouldn't want to stop for every rodent or bird that tried to go through, so what happens to them might not represent what would happen to us."

"We have to start somewhere," Lucille said, respectfully if a little anxiously.

The decision was easy enough to make, and it delayed the need to think any further past this step for a little longer, which was a welcome relief. Kevin, still invisible, floated closer to the gate and, with a precision I found stunning, lifted a small rodent, about the size of a mouse, in the wind. Lucille reached her invisibility out as far as she could to cover its flight across the military encampment, but as it neared the trucks, she hit her limits and it came back into view.

The mouse battled against the air currents. I understood its frustration, and it made me feel bad for drawing the mouse into a conflict we didn't even want to be involved in. I gave a silent thank-you as it floated up to the transport. Luckily, the creature was light enough to blow through the hole on the canvas back of the vehicle. The transport entered the gates. Within seconds, a loud buzzer sounded, and the gate interior lit up. The fence netting surrounded the transport, isolating the offensive cargo.

"There's smoke from the gate," Peter let us know. "The screen … okay, yeah, there's a note saying the unauthorized cargo was incinerated. The transport is moving on through, though."

"That's not promising," Lucille said.

"Well, it definitely doesn't look like we're getting through that easily," Peter said, handing Lucille the binoculars. "Look more closely at the laser netting. The shifts are irregular. It's a series of small drones set up to project lasers between one another, forming a full fence. America has some of this tech, but nothing this advanced. These look like they can fire lasers from anywhere on them, and working in conjunction with the other drones, they can probably get inside of and exterminate anything."

"What if they were cut off from one another?" I asked.

"Maybe, but without knowing how the gate works, I don't think I'd want to try to take on a free-floating chain of those suckers."

Peter rolled over onto his back casually, rubbing his eyes with his balled fists. "So, we're dealing with weapons that most likely move at the speed of light and a gateway that burns unwanted entrants. And I'm sure they can just collapse the passage entirely with the touch of a button, leaving us absolutely no way through."

Kevin began to say something before weighing the statement and thinking better of it. Peter was right. If the gate expanded to accommodate any size transport we'd seen so far, why would there be a limit to how far it could collapse, presumably the metal eventually just clanging against itself, leaving a net of deadly lasers?

"So, what do we do?" Monica asked, clearly as lost as I felt.

"I don't know. For all we know those little individual units can extend out of the gate and disintegrate the lot of us before we even figure out how to work it," Peter answered. "So, even if we take out the guards without alerting the Bears, there's no guarantee we'd get through anyway."

"It might not even work like that," Francine said.

"But it might," Monica replied with resignation.

"So, our options are all terrible," Lucille said to no one. "What else is new?"

"Is there another place to cross?" I asked.

"Worth checking before we try this," Peter conceded.

"It won't be any better," Veronica said. Her palms were flat against the ground, her fingers probing the dirt, a faint blue glow illuminating their tips. "The gate stretches as far as I can probe, covering the border and beyond."

With nowhere else to consider, I looked up. "How high do you think this fence goes?" I asked.

"Too far for me to lift all of you over it," Kevin responded. "I can sense the disturbance it provides in the airflow, but it goes higher than I've ever flown. I can't sense high enough to know where it ends."

"*If* it ends," Peter said.

"It has to end," I replied. "There's no way it can project that sort of power perpetually."

Kevin looked startled, surprised that the line of conversation was moving forward. "Even if I could get to the top, they have to have some sort of way to deal with air traffic at that height," he said.

"They would for aircraft," I said, "but you're not the size of an aircraft."

"Okay, but let's say the Iron Bear was going to fly into China," Kevin posited. "Wouldn't they at least have sensors to indicate his presence?"

"Yes," Peter answered as he started to get on board with this line of thought, "but they wouldn't risk ticking him off, so it would just be to let them know he'd entered. If it's just a sensor, you could bring the authorities we need to get across right to us."

"Do you think you could carry anyone else at all?" I asked.

"Maybe one safely. It's hard to know without having any idea how high up we're going," Kevin answered, sweat beginning to show on his brow.

"Please," I started, "tell me if I'm crazy, but our best shot is for Kevin to get over the fence. We can hide out here for days if we need to, but Lucille's got to go with him."

"That puts everyone at risk," Lucille shot back, angered by the idea. "My powers could help out more here. You should go with him."

"You're not wrong," I said. "But if there's an alarm, there's probably some sort of visual record they can review. If the Russians see nothing, maybe the equipment's broken. If they see people flying across, they report it to the Bears."

She was silent for a few minutes before reluctantly agreeing. No one else had a better idea, so we were at least ready to take some action. Now we just had to figure out what the rest of us would be doing while our friends drifted away.

Even as we began to consider returning to our previous camp, a whistled tune rang out, bouncing off the mountains, echoing through the cavern. The soldiers on the Chinese side, still visible through the lasers, looked around, mystified.

And then Anna and the Terrors landed right in front of the Russian side of the gate. We saw them as they descended, their focus squarely on the Chinese.

"Helped anyone get through today?" she shouted, taunting the soldier on the opposite side of the border gate. She stopped for a moment as the confusion on the ground became audible. Then she yelled, "Quiet!"

Everything stopped. There was no movement, and the air itself went still. I found myself holding my breath, terrified of giving away our location, even as Anna turned in our direction.

"Come out, come out, wherever you are," she sang to the wind, the highest note ringing against the mountainside. "Oh brothers, dear, a little help?"

She pointed directly toward the ridge on which we rested, as Vladimir picked up a large truck and hurled it at high speed directly at us. I felt the wind whip up as we were all violently torn from our perch by Kevin, the truck smashing into our safe spot even as we took off, the resulting explosion knocking us all toward the ground.

Kevin managed to regain control, and amid the chaos, brought us down behind a truck that was clear of enemy vision.

"You have to go now," Peter said.

"They'll hear the wind shift," Kevin hissed.

"No, they won't," Peter said.

Kevin seemed to understand his meaning, and he and Lucille lifted directly upward, fading from view even as the world around me came back into focus. We were visible now, vulnerable.

The ground began to shake beneath us, causing enough noise to drown out our friends' ascent. Peter kept a rocklike position, but Veronica's face twisted, glowing with crackling blue electricity. She reached her arms out to her sides, palms facing downward, as her eels shot into the ground with a ferocity I don't think even she expected.

From my hidden perch at the truck side, I could see the ground writhe with motion. Some of the guards noticed the trails of dirt speeding toward them. Some even had time to fire their weapons. It didn't matter. The eels tore up from the ground, wrapping around the soldiers, draining them of life. It was even affecting people in vehicles. Vladimir was the only Russian royalty on the ground, and he screamed in agony as his siblings looked on from the air, too afraid to expose themselves to attempt a rescue.

The Chinese soldiers were at attention, yelling across the border and beginning to execute emergency protocols. The Russians were starting to look close to death, something I had seen enough of.

"Did the Earth say their lives had to end today?" I asked Veronica as I reached out to grab her shoulder. She turned to me, the demon face reconfiguring itself by the second, like a melting pot of emotions, until it stuck in a face that, while terrifying, was at least familiar. Veronica pulled back, falling to the ground, as the men who had been in her grip seconds before also fell, unconscious but still breathing.

I could see Vladimir hit the ground, his brother racing to his side. Anna landed, kicking soldiers out of her way as she walked to where her brothers were. Vladimir got back to his feet, but he looked unstable.

"Is that the best you've got?" Anna yelled. "You know we're going to kill you. Why not make it easier on yourselves? It doesn't have to be painful. Well, actually, it does."

Our placement between the trucks had proven a good choice. We still had a few moments to figure out a counter strategy. Maybe we could get to the border and be let through by the Chinese before the Bears got us.

That idea fizzled quickly, though, when the border gate suddenly collapsed in on itself. Now, as predicted, there was just a solid wall of deadly lasers. It was hard to blame the Chinese, given the madness they were witnessing.

I heard a commotion and saw a transport vehicle fly overhead, crashing to earth somewhere beyond my sight.

"Not here," Anna snarled.

"Okay," I whispered, "ideas?"

Monica broke away from the group, out of reach before any of us could grab her and too far away to say anything to without giving away our cover. She made her way around the back of the military convoy closest to the gate. Another truck had gone airborne during this short period. They would be to us soon.

With our queen going rogue, we waited to see what would happen next, so used to rolling with the punches that we'd learned not to bother anticipating the next blow. Another truck crashed, no more than two rows over. Then I heard her, and I craned my head back around, trying to stay as covered as possible.

"Enough," Monica said, sounding confident, almost regal.

"Oh my," Anna said, her arms opened wide as she gave a little curtsey, "it's the queen! I have to admit that I didn't peg you getting past the first round of this little invasion of yours. Well done, Your Majesty."

"I request safe passage into the Chinese Territories for me and my people," Monica said, her voice shaking slightly. "There's been enough bloodshed."

"You just don't get it yet, do you?" Anna said. "Oh Queenie, there's no such thing as too much bloodshed." She snapped her fingers, and the Terrors sped off, Vladimir seeming to have largely recovered, even though the soldiers were all still unconscious.

An idea struck me. I got Peter's attention and pointed to a soldier who had dropped just around the corner, his gun poking out from behind a tire. There was another one near enough for me to grab without being seen too. I hoped they were as powerful as they looked.

The Terrors were back in a heartbeat, each one throwing a large, moving sack on the ground in front of them.

My stomach dropped as the bags were removed. Both Shondra and Sean were bruised and bloodied, but also awake and alive.

"So," Anna said, "let's talk about bloodshed. You and your friends give yourselves up right now, and maybe we can come to an arrangement."

"What kind of arrangement?" Monica asked defiantly.

"Maybe you can be our house staff," Anna said simply as Piotr cracked his knuckles. "It's so hard to find people you really enjoy killing when they get out of line."

"And the other option," Monica said, "is simply to fight this out here?" She made it sound like only an idiot would want to fight her. She was surprisingly convincing.

"No, sweetie," she said, "your other option is to die here."

Vladimir reached down and picked up Shondra, her arms in one hand and her legs in the other. She was gagged, but her eyes screamed in terror. He was going to tear her in two. It was clear as he raised her over his head.

I began to start forward with the gun, but before he could even pull his arms apart, Vladimir was engulfed in flames so hot and forceful that just the proximity blasted Anna and Piotr off their feet. Vladimir screamed briefly, his flesh twisting, before Piotr pulled him from Monica's sight and extinguished the flames.

Piotr and Anna both looked at Vladimir with astonishment. They had played with us too long, not realizing that evolution seemed to be on our side. While they were distracted, Monica swept Shondra behind a nearby truck.

The sudden motion broke the trance Anna was under. I could see where Monica had taken them, and neither of them was ready for another round with the Bears. I started to move forward again, but Peter grabbed my shoulder. I was ready to knock him away, until I realized he was pointing me to an entry point that wasn't just charging headfirst into death.

Whatever was happening to Veronica, she wasn't ready to enter the fray just yet. The power her eels brought back to her must have been more than she'd ever received, because the glow about her, the blank stare, everything, broadcast *not open for business.*

That left the three of us. Peter moved quietly closer to where Vladimir lay smoldering in the dirt, while Francine and I moved toward Anna, who was starting to collect herself.

"What have you done!" she roared, her voice shaking the mountains themselves. Piotr looked toward his barely-alive brother and gave out a scream unlike anything I've ever heard, the high whine of a pained animal mixed with the low growl of a fierce predator. Anna was on the move in an instant, ripping two trucks off the ground and tossing them into the air. It was clear we had to go now if we were going to save anybody.

Francine swung around the side of the truck we'd sidled along with a confidence I'd not expected. Her arms stretched outward, and ice instantly formed around Anna. She started to crack it off, annoyed. As Francine focused, the ice grew thicker, beginning to form in heavy layers around the princess.

Piotr lunged forward to help his sister, only to be knocked back by a powerful seismic burst, slamming him into the side of a truck, which curled around him like a blanket.

Francine continued to add ice to Anna, and while I thought she was overexerting herself, she was still going, and no one appeared to be dying of dehydration, so it was hard to tell her to stop. Peter came to my side, neither of us able to help Francine. Both the guns and Peter's powers would just destroy the integrity of the ice prison she was creating.

Veronica was on her feet and around the truck now, I noticed. She had gotten to Shondra and Monica and was heading to Sean, releasing some of her energy into our wounded teammates. Shondra was back in the fray and had picked up a gun of her own, while Monica stayed crouched behind the truck, weighing her options.

"You okay?" I asked Francine, who was clearly at her breaking point. Anna was entirely encased at this point, Francine stopped pouring on the ice, collapsing into my arms before finding a rock to kneel against.

The quiet overtook everything suddenly, and I wondered if it could possibly be this easy. Piotr hadn't pulled himself out of the truck yet, so I assumed he was unconscious, and Anna's ice prison was holding so far.

"I guess now we find out how this all looks," Peter said with his trademark grin.

He pointed back toward the gate, where a squad of Chinese soldiers stood, ready to defend the border at all costs. We gathered toward the Russian side of the gate, Monica and Shondra joining us while Veronica healed Sean.

"We're refugees from America stranded in Russia," Peter said to the soldiers on the other side of the crackling laser webbing. "We seek political asylum."

The commander moved closer to the netting. "We cannot let you in," he told Peter. "As enemies of another territory, we lack the authority."

"But these people are savages!" Peter yelled. It wasn't the best approach, but our chances weren't looking good anyway.

"Regardless," the guard said, sternly but sympathetically, "we cannot grant your request without Lord Wu's approval."

We had gotten to the finish line, only to find out we hadn't filed the appropriate paperwork.

"We'll be murdered here," I said. "Or worse. You know what these monsters are capable of."

The guard started to say something, but his eyes suddenly grew wide with terror. I heard it before I made my full turn. The ice encasing Anna was cracking. Francine was trying to pour more onto it, but she was too weak. The encasement shattered, flinging huge chunks of ice everywhere. Francine managed to erect an ice shield in front of herself in time, but Monica took a shot to the gut, knocking the wind out of her, and Shondra got one to the head, compounding her long list of ailments.

Veronica took a glancing blow to the back, pushing her across the ground like a rag doll. She was already rolling over by the time I had returned my gaze to where Anna stood or, more appropriately, where she seethed.

"You know," Anna said, shaking off the ice as though she had just stepped out of the shower, "it takes a lot to make me cold, and I really, really hate being cold." She looked toward Francine, and I flashed back to the battle at the village. How long ago had that been? Days ago? Weeks? Time was nothing anymore.

Peter made a move before I could, not that I was sure what my move would be. He shot a wave of force at Anna that knocked her off her feet. The Russian princess was already getting up when I heard the sound of metal twisting. I fired the gun at the twisted wreckage, but Piotr was already free and off at super speed before he could be hit, stopping to lend his sister a hand.

"Took you long enough," she growled at him.

"You're welcome," he responded.

As Peter prepared to generate another wave, the proximity of our teammates keeping him from really letting loose, Piotr disappeared and, in a blink, reappeared, Peter unconscious at his feet.

"So," Anna said, eyeing Sean, Francine, and me with a malevolent gaze, "I guess it's just us. Look, all we wanted was to study you. That's it. It was all for science. How cool is that? Like being an organ donor."

We clearly weren't giving her what she hoped for.

"But we're done now," she said, "and the lab rats don't get to scurry away."

I gave a sudden snort. It came out of nowhere. Just an involuntary snort at the absurdity of it all.

"Something funny over there?" she asked me. "You know, you're the one I really thought wouldn't make it this far. I mean, how many people have died for your worthless little human carcass, I wonder?"

"Fewer than have died for your selfish little whims," I responded, surprising myself in the process. She was on me in a millisecond, her hand around my throat, my feet dangling above the ground.

"You were never part of this, you little speck of dust. You were just the extra trash that needed to be disposed of." Her eyes stared directly into mine, empty of emotion, devoid of empathy.

Chapter 36

Specks of black started to blot out the world, and I suddenly knew we were meant to die today. Then I realized that I still had a gun in my hand. Why hadn't I realized it was there? Had it been there the whole time? I squeezed the trigger in rapid succession, firing toward the blur from where the arm below my chin originated.

And then I was on the ground, coughing myself back to life. The spots started to lessen just in time for me to see Anna in the distance, struggling to her feet. Sean sent sonic shockwaves toward her to keep her off balance, while Francine kept Piotr frozen to the ground.

"Enough!" I heard Anna shout. I saw her fist suddenly appear on the other side of Sean's sternum. My teammate's eyes glowed with one last recognition of surprise before he fell silent and limp. Piotr just started laughing as his sister threw Sean's corpse into Francine, knocking her down and out. It was just me now.

I took in my surroundings as quickly as possible and reached for the nearest gun, mine now drained of energy. I aimed at Piotr and pulled the trigger, squinting nervously as a wide blast of energy blew him across the canyon, knocking aside every vehicle in his path before he skidded into the side of the mountain.

I looked at the gun in shock, but quickly realized my mistake as Anna came upon me, violently shaking it from my hand. Her eyes were full of rage. "How?" she screamed. "How have you survived?

You're nothing, you know? You were never anything, not even when they let you feel like you were."

Anna's face paled, and her grip slackened. She fell backward. I looked around and saw Veronica, her worms returning to her. I was suddenly very thankful for my boot soles.

"You're not so great yourself," I said as I punched her in the jaw, hard enough to knock her out in her weakened state apparently.

Veronica was already on to healing Monica by the time I looked up to celebrate the one punch I'd thrown. Then I was suddenly slammed against the side of a jeep, a jolt of pain running across my back.

Piotr's hot, fetid breath misted my face; his eyes bored into mine before looking down and back up.

"I can make do with you," he whispered in my ear. "You'll love being my slave. Doing everything I say. When I say it."

The border gate groaned to life behind us, distracting Piotr, but right when I feared he would just whisk me away at super speed, the ground opened up at his feet and then solidified around his legs, keeping him still.

He dropped me, unsure what to do. Peter, back on his feet, was already at my side, helping me up. I spun around in time to see the gate push the laser webbing apart.

On the other side of the gate was Lord Wu, as quietly regal as in every newsreel and magazine photo I'd ever seen. He was flanked by Lucille and Kevin, which meant a plan had finally been successful.

"What do you want?" Piotr shouted defiantly while vibrating his legs free of the earth.

"I want you to keep your battles off my doorstep," said the Lord of the Chinese Territories.

"It's our battle," Piotr shot back, "and it's happening on our side."

"Your father isn't even in the ground," Lord Wu said as he passed through the gateway unharmed. Piotr looked taken aback that he should so casually stroll onto Russian soil.

"Would you like to take a shot at me as well?" he said. "I promise to provide a challenge despite my age."

Piotr stood his ground, but he seemed unsure of his next move. "Our prisoners have been recaptured," he said, reciting his diplomacy lessons. "I apologize that this disruption came to our shared border, but it's been successfully resolved."

Piotr made a low bow.

"But, Little Bear," Lord Wu said, "these people have requested asylum. I've chosen to grant it."

"We're on our side of the border!" Piotr yelled back petulantly. "They hurt my brother! They killed my father! You don't have the authority."

"Actually," he said, "if you go back through the actual agreements, you'll find that we're technically in a neutral zone. The fact that you even engaged in a battle here is enough cause to initiate a full meeting of the remaining Lords."

Piotr's eyes grew wide. "Fine," he said, "they're yours, but this agreement you had with our father, that's all done, old man. New generation's coming around."

"If they are all like you," Lord Wu replied, "I shall be glad to vanquish each and every one. Collect your sister and your brother and go home."

Anna was gone in a second, followed soon by Vladimir, and Piotr didn't return after delivering them to safety. It was done.

"Thank you," I said, turning to Lord Wu.

"You're quite welcome," he said to me kindly. He signaled his men through the gate. They quickly gathered the injured and began leading us across. "We have a hospital nearby where you and your friends will be well cared for, Miss Smith."

"You know my name?"

"Nathaniel spoke of you on a number of occasions. I've followed your journey to the best of my abilities. I only regret that I was unable to act until you reached the border."

"So, what happens to us now?" I asked him, starting to feel the battle in my very bones.

"That will be for you and your friends to decide. You're welcome to stay in my domain as long as you wish. I fear the world is on the verge of great change, so I'm afraid I can guarantee little more than your immediate safety. I'm only sorry I didn't arrive fast enough to save you all," he said.

I couldn't bring myself to look back at Sean's body. I didn't need any more reminders of the horrors we'd endured.

When I crossed through the gate with Lord Wu, I practically ran to Lucille and Kevin, throwing my arms around their necks.

"Thank you," I said.

"It looks like we were a little late," Kevin said, his eyes tearing up.

"We'd all be dead without you," I said.

"Indeed. You have very brave friends, Miss Smith. Although it would appear it's a trait you share with them."

Lord Wu bid us farewell as we climbed aboard the medical transport. He promised to host us as soon as we were given clean bills of health. We had made it out of Russia and into friendly territory. Two of our number were still hostages, but at least now that we were no longer fighting for our own lives, we could begin to focus on theirs.

Chapter 37

None of us were seriously injured, which was partially thanks to Veronica and partially just due to luck. Whatever miracle drugs they had pumped me full of had made the intense aches I felt when I first arrived disappear. Almost everyone was asleep, but my mind was still racing through the day, trying to make sense of everything we'd gone through.

I couldn't sleep. I needed to, but I could tell it wasn't happening anytime soon. I got out of bed and made my way through the quiet halls of the facility. The technology on display shouldn't have been a surprise after everything I'd seen in my travels, but I still found myself unable to believe the advancements that were apparently commonplace throughout the world.

I found a stairwell and slowly made my way to the roof. The meds were good, but that didn't mean I was at full strength. The roof door was unlocked. I honestly hadn't expected it to be, but I had to try. I needed the night air, a look at the sky. It was a treat to actually be somewhere and not feel like you were being hunted by killers. It was strange how quicky that had become my every day. It was something I was glad to be rid of.

The night was clear and brisk. Looking out from the rooftop, I felt a freedom I hadn't felt since before we left America. Maybe before I started my internship. Or maybe ever. We were somewhere safe now.

I was ready to try to make a new home.

I heard the door open behind me and turned. It was Peter, his hospital gown a match for my own.

"Thought I might find you up here," he said as he walked toward me.

"You thought right. How are you feeling?"

"Better," he responded. "Surprised a little. I honestly wasn't sure we were ever getting out of Russia."

"I'm not sure I did either. It's strange. I still feel like I should be afraid, but I'm not."

"What's there to be afraid of? You already beat the wicked witch. There's no way they'll come to China for us."

"I know," I said quietly, "but we lost so much getting here. It's a little hard to believe it's over."

"In some ways, it's just starting," he replied as he put his arms around my shoulders from behind, his head next to mine. "We need to get Pearl and Brent out. We need to figure out exactly what living here means, what we want to do about Sebastian, all of it."

"Not yet, though," I said. "I think we deserve one night without world-ending drama eating up all of our energy. It's been a while since we've had that."

"Yeah. The stars are nice."

"They are," I said, looking up into the night sky.

"I don't think I told you how impressed I was with you out there."

"You mean when you didn't have to protect me?" I asked in a tone cattier than I intended.

"I know I said that, but the thing is, I never really had to. If anything, you protected me. Hell, you protected all of us at one point or another. You never gave up or gave in. You fought for every single victory without worrying about your own safety."

"Oh, I was definitely worried," I replied. "But we all did our part. I don't think anyone has anything to be ashamed about. We got thrown into an impossible position, but we came through it. But thank you. It means a lot."

"They checked on us all, by the way. Whatever's going on with our powers, with the spores, it doesn't seem to be hurting us. At least not yet."

That was a relief. Knowing that the dramatically increasing powers of my teammates seemed to be benign in terms of their health definitely answered one of my most desperate lingering questions. "Did they have any ideas about what *is* happening?" I asked him.

"Not that they're saying. I figure we can ask Lord Wu when we get a chance to sit down with him. He seems reasonable. Hopefully that means he's honest too."

"I still can't believe he knew my name. Or that Lord Nathaniel bothered telling him about me."

"How could anyone know you and not want to tell everyone they'd ever met about you?" he said.

"Oh, I imagine there are more important topics when you rule one-seventh of the world," I replied.

"You need to have your imagination checked then."

We stayed quiet for a few moments, looking into the night sky, as we'd done so often when we were younger. It was different now, though, not just because of everything we'd been through, both apart and together, but because of everything else I knew now, about the past, about The Lords, about the spores, about the translation. All of the history I'd grown up with was sanitized. It was something I'd guessed, but in the absence of evidence, it had been an easy suspicion to push aside.

I thought about telling Peter about it all, and I knew I would eventually. But it would wait until tomorrow or the day after. It would wait until we'd had a few moments without the torture we'd endured. We didn't say much more because there simply wasn't much more to say. We'd made it through an ordeal I could never have imagined I'd experience, much less survive. And somehow, we were back on a rooftop, peering into the night again.

The familiarity of the stars made me feel like I was still at the orphanage, as though all that we'd endured had been a nightmare from which we'd finally awoken. I tried to mentally name all the constellations I knew, which wasn't as many as it should have been. We'd always been more interested in creating our own names than bothering to learn the ones other people had chosen. When you got past the Big Dipper, nothing ever looked very much like what it was called anyway.

Even as I tried to put all the new questions occupying me out of my head, I found myself looking for blank spaces where I knew stars would be. Trying to see if whatever the spacecraft had warned of was as close to Earth as I feared. I knew it was something I'd have to bring up, not just to Peter but also with Lord Wu. I was done not having answers, tired of being a pawn in other people's games.

I found the willpower to banish the thought from my head, to pull myself back into the present. To enjoy the hug of my friend. To enjoy the fact that we were still alive, that we had made our way to safety. The dawn brought change yet again, but this time, I wouldn't face it alone.

About the Author

Brad Converse lives and works in Austin, TX. He's been a college English instructor, marketing copywriter, theatrical producer, and rhinoceros distraction over the years. He received his MA in English from Stephen F. Austin State University and his MFA in Playwriting from the University of Southern California. His writing borrows from a lifelong enjoyment of comics and graphic novels as well as a keen interest in people and weird things.